Tabitha

Tragédie et Triomphe

A novel by
Dorothy K Morris

"Tabitha, Tragédie et Triomphe," by Dorothy K. Morris. ISBN 978-1-63868-035-2 (softcover).

Published 2021 by Virtualbookworm.com Publishing Inc., P.O. Box 9949, College Station, TX 77842, US. ©2021, Dorothy K.. Morris. All rights reserved. No part of this publication may be reproduced, stored in a retrieval system, or transmitted in any form or by any means, electronic, mechanical, recording or otherwise, without the prior written permission of Dorothy K. Morris.

PREVIOUS BOOKS IN THE MOCKINGBIRD HILL SERIES

FOREWORD

IN 1526 SPANISH EXPLORERS SAILED along the Atlantic coast and into the natural harbor at what would become Charles Town in 1680. There was no city of gold for the Spanish to discover, only natives who lived and thrived in the swamps along the coast. The explorers did not recognize the wealth that lay untouched in the swampy land...the land which was perfect for growing rice. That land and the men and women who tilled it would eventually bring real gold to the new colony of South Carolina.

The native tribes had, through generations, learned how to survive in the water-world that was coastal Carolina. Rivers, both wide and narrow, flowed from the foothills of the Appalachians to the coast and into the Atlantic. Swamp land bordered on creeks and inlets leading to the ocean.

With the settlement at Charles Town in 1680, others from England followed. In the early 1700's King George opened the coastal land to immigrants to thwart settlement by the Crowns of France and Spain. They came from France, Wales, Scotland, Ireland and Germany. These settlers drove out many of the native tribes, drained the swamps as best they could and planted crops. After the Yamasee War of

1715-16, the remaining natives were sold into slavery, leaving more land to European settlers. With the prevailing commercial crop being rice, slaves from the West Coast of Africa were brought in by the ship loads and plantations were established.

At the beginning of our story, slavery was legal but, encouraged by the Quakers, the day was dawning when men stopped to consider the right or wrong of it. However, men's minds do not change overnight.

CHAPTER 1

In the lovely plantation house, surrounded by tall pines draped with wisteria blossoms lived Marcus Durandeaux. He was the only son of Guillaume Durandeaux, a Frenchman who had departed Nantes, traveled to Holland, thence to Britain and finally to the thriving colony of South Carolina. Descended from aristocratic forebears in his father's native France, well-educated and ambitious for the good things this new land promised, Marcus clung to the idea that the white European male was God's ideal of humanity...His greatest creation. His father, the immigrant, had lived that premise throughout the years of Marcus' youth, and when the lad grew to young manhood, he saw no reason to believe otherwise. It was for him simply a fact. The European male ruled at the top of the food chain. Neither the premise nor the practice was destined to make for kind and gentle men.

The elder Durandeaux had settled along with others of his nationality on land in what was called the Low-Country, from Georgetown down the coast to Savannah. With the area swept clean of the original inhabitants, he was free to clear hundreds of acres. All he had to do was to purchase slaves to tame the swamp and then to plant rice, the golden crop that would make him and his descendants wealthy. When he passed away from one of the various and prevalent fevers that periodically ravaged the Low-Country, the thriving plantation came into the possession of his only child, sixteen-year-old Marcus.

While still a gangly youth, his sexual arousal by a mulatto slave girl had come as a shock. Marcus had been taught by his father that those people were not quite human in the same way as he. However, after being introduced to the delightful ways of Cassie, young Marcus concluded that his father had been totally wrong. Cassie was human enough and they enjoyed their clandestine pleasures equally. In addition to Cassie, Marcus explored the pleasures of others of their slave-women who performed at his will, without the usual prudery and timidity that he had learned to expect from young women of his class. Enjoying the pleasures of the bed, he never felt shame for indulging whenever he pleased with the women at his disposal, willing or not. They belonged to him. They were his property.

During the years after his father's death young Marcus' slaves cleared more land and extended the acres in cultivation. He bought more men and women to work those acres. In the process of buying slaves to work his land, Marcus realized that trading in slaves was another way to add wealth to his family's coffers. With a word here and there to men in the business, he involved himself in the buying and selling, and began to make periodic and extended voyages in his private ketch to his growing number of clients in towns down the Atlantic coast and throughout the Caribbean islands.

Marcus considered himself to be a good citizen. He worked hard. Although he supported his family's traditional religion, he did not consider himself devout. He gave The Word of God little credence. He saw supporting the church financially as a social and business obligation that worked for him within his community; therefore, he attended service and willingly donated his tithe. But as for prayer and asking God's guidance, he thought it best to make decisions in a pragmatic way. The question was always: which choice was the better for him.

His early marriage to the bride his father had chosen from among their community had not brought marital bliss to either of them even though he had done all he could think of to please her. The marriage brought two sons, George and then Charles. While his wife was expecting their third child Marcus hoped for a daughter to spoil. A daughter of his own was the only thing he really wanted and could not buy. Why he so desired a daughter, he never knew or asked himself. If someone had asked and if he could have been honest, he may have replied that a daughter would represent the opposite of himself and therefore, gentle and kind, which he knew himself not to be. If anyone had been bold enough to express what they determined about this, he would have said that Marcus wanted a daughter to sit at his feet and adore him the way men want a spaniel...someone to give him innocent adoration and to help him hide from himself. But no one ever was bold or brave enough to suggest that Marcus become acquainted with himself. Instead, Marcus imagined her sitting on his knee, planned her childhood, thought about whom she would marry and counted his grandchildren by that daughter; always living in his house.

When his wife died giving birth to that daughter and the baby girl died days later, Marcus suffered the first real loss he had ever felt. The death of his baby daughter caused him to become even harsher, and for the first time he relinquished his religious neutrality and cursed God. Even though he continued to give support to the church and the community, Marcus never forgave Him.

He did not mourn his wife for seldom had she given him pleasure. As he had since his youth, he continued to enjoy the pleasures of certain of the women from the quarters, with Cassie, the first to stir his blood and to pleasure him, remaining his favorite.

Slavery was an institution as old as mankind. His women were willing and therefore, he felt no guilt or shame. This became a way of life, and he continued to indulge himself throughout his years of widowhood.

Marcus' two sons, George and Charles spent their childhood barely knowing their father. Away for weeks at a time, remote and stern as he was, they rarely called for him or wondered when he would return. They turned for their needs to household slaves; to Bruneau, the butler, and to Lacey, the housekeeper, and to M'aum Sue, the cook. The boys grew up associating black people with love and kindness and wise advice. Lacey bandaged scraped knees and elbows and Bruneau made sling shots and taught the boys how to use them. M'aum Sue cooked their favorite foods and Harvey, the elderly stable man, taught them both how to ride. They ran to the quarters to play with the boys and to join them at the river's edge for crabbing, fishing, or swimming. George followed the workers as they worked in the rice fields and learned how they did their work. Charles chased butterflies and kept an assortment of bugs, leaves and dead frogs in a box in his room. They did not miss their father, and when he was at home, they felt a sense of awe at the man whom the household help called Mastah. Neither

George nor Charles was sure what that really meant until they grew older.

CHAPTER 2

Another French gentleman, Francis Battailes, owned the plantation closest to the Durandeaux holdings, a distance of at least two hours of riding or driving a carriage. Of an equal station in their community, the two families were acquainted through their issues involved in the running of their rice plantations. Francis' father, Gerard Battailes, had immigrated to the colony in the same manner as had the original Durandeaux. Once settled, he had followed the same path as Durandeaux but for one thing. Battailes had bought slaves for his fields and for his house as he needed them, but he considered them just as much human as he, and he respected them as such. Once a slave of the Battailes, that slave was never sold or traded away. The Battailes plantation was their home. Couples who married and had children were never separated. Most families were second generation. Following his father's ways, Francis Battailes continued to earn wealth from rice but not from slave trading.

Brought up in his father's old-country's ways, Francis had been wed when he was deemed a fully grown man at nineteen. His bride had been arranged between the two fathers who expected the two young people to obey. Francis not especially pleased with his father's choice, but Gerard was adamant. There were certain affiliations the fathers had agreed upon. The young man was compelled to make his vows to a woman he did not want.

His father had assured him that he would learn to love Joan but after his wedding night he liked his bride even less. Less than attractive, spoiled, a shrewish young wife, she treated their servants unkindly, something unthinkable in his household. To make matters worse, the new Madame Joan found her wifely duty to her husband to be painful and shameful; something that a lady should never be expected to endure. She insisted the deed be completed as quickly as possible and Francis went to her only because he wanted sons. He wanted sons and if a daughter came, he would love her, too. But he desired sons first and a daughter later. They would serve to blunt the edge of an unhappy marriage.

When Joan became pregnant with their first child, she took to her bed at the first sign of morning sickness and, except for certain occasions, she remained in her room throughout the months until time for the child to enter the world. The idea of anyone seeing her in her condition was abhorrent. When the months had passed and time for her delivery arrived, from her behavior the household thought that she would surely not survive the ordeal. Joan refused the doctor and insisted the midwife be summoned. The woman tried to calm her, explaining that the process would take hours, but Joan wanted it to be over immediately. When she did not get her wish her screams racked the house until all inside left, except those few who were required to tend her. Even the midwife accepted the haven of the kitchen with Rhoda, the cook, who plied her with hot coffee, peach pie, and conversation. After twenty hours of labor Joan Battailes was delivered of a healthy baby girl. Disappointed that he did not get his son, Francis named her Cecily and as was his nature, he welcomed her. A wet-nurse was brought from the quarters and the baby girl was handed over to her. The only concern for Joan was to be finished with the mess and to selfishly reclaim her life, such as it was.

Each evening the wet-nurse brought the beautiful child to her father. At first, he had held her clumsily, then with more assurance. As weeks passed, he began to feel pleasure when her tiny fingers reached up to pull at his beard and she smiled at him.

Three months after Cecily's birth Francis entered Joan's room once again. He had one purpose in mind; to get a son. He would be happy with only one, but he must have that one. His wife attempted to refuse him, but he demanded his right. When the act was completed, he prayed that this time would bring his heart's desire, for he knew he would never come to his wife again.

When Francis left her bed, Joan cried herself to sleep and prayed that she would not have to go through another pregnancy and birth. She vowed that she would rather die. She hated being married, she hated Francis, she disliked her daughter and when the wet-nurse brought her to Joan, she would have nothing to do with her. Her dismay was evident when, weeks after Francis' nighttime visit, she discovered that she carried another child.

The months passed during which Francis came to relish his hours with his baby daughter, and she became the delight of his life, much more than he had ever expected. He counted his blessings and cherished her as he awaited the birth of the child that Joan now carried.

When Joan again went into labor, within hours she was delivered of a healthy boy. The infant handed to a wet-nurse, the mother turned her head to the wall and would not speak with anyone. For days she lay in bed at times cursing and at other times sobbing as though her heart were broken. She again refused to see the new infant and it came to Francis again to parent the little one, who would be his only son.

Francis settled for his son and his daughter. He had his little family and could not bring himself to go to Joan again. Never again did he go to her bed or even wish to. He left Baby Amos to their nanny and went about his daily work with Cecily tagging along behind him or riding in front of him on the saddle.

The years passed quickly. Both children occasionally attempted to see their mother, to talk with her, to coax her to meals, but with no success. Cecily learned to leave her be, and only Amos persisted. Sometimes he was allowed in his mother's room, but conversation with her was impossible. She only wished to complain to him, and he could do nothing to remedy her situation, for she would take no reasonable advice from anyone. The two youngsters grew up in the care of their father, Trish, the housekeeper, Rhoda, the cook, and Joel, the butler. Cecily learned the ways of a home and Amos learned the way of the plantation. Trish or Rhoda became the women they went to when sad, hurt, had bruised knees, or suffered tummy aches. Those two tended their emotional bruises as well as physical. By the time they were in their teen years neither cared to make any more attempts to be close to their mother.

Not being a man of great passion, Francis was content without a wife's companionship. His children and the plantation were his life. He hired a live-in tutor and both children received a classical education. When Amos was sixteen years of age Francis sent him to the University of

Paris for his higher education. Soon thereafter, Cecily came of an age when he must consider her future. He needed to find her a husband. Perhaps she would give him a grandson or two. There were young men available from whom to choose, men of their class, but most lived either in Charles Town or on the other side of the river. Francis wanted Cecily and her children close, not so many miles away that he would be far from his grandchildren. He thought of Marcus Durandeaux, a widower with two sons; a man of great wealth who had been without a wife for years and who might be amenable to a suggestion. With Marcus' plantation no more than two hours' ride away, he considered it a good place to begin.

Francis sent a rider to ask for an appointment. The rider returned with a suggested date and time. Francis attended the appointment and after a while of conversation about farming and weather, a bit of complaining about the latest price that the Crown would pay for their rice, and church affairs, Francis judged the man acceptable. Both knew it was time to get down to the object of the visit and Marcus made the call.

"What brings you here, Francis Battailes? I know it is not a simple neighborly visit, although I have enjoyed our conversation immensely."

"I came to enquire if you are interested in a second marriage."

"Well, well, this is a surprise. I thought you needed more workers. I never expected..."

"My daughter, Cecily, is of marrying age. Do you recall her? Seeing her at church on Sundays, perhaps?"

"I may have, but..."

"Of course. You would have been involved with gentlemen's conversation and not noticing young girls."

"What, if I might ask, is your reason for choosing me?"

"You are a neighbor, close enough that I won't lose touch with Cecily. We are close for father and daughter. I would like to be allowed to visit my grandchildren. That is one reason. Second is that you are a substantial planter, well reputed in our circles and you are a widower. I assume you miss conjugal pleasures?"

"You thought deeply about this, I see, and you are straight forward. I admire that. If I agree, would this lovely young Cecily also agree? I am a few years her senior."

"She trusts me and is of a good nature. She will be a good wife."

"Another reason? Does your wife approve?"

"My wife chooses to be a recluse. I do not ask her approval. I am certain you have heard talk."

"Seems to me that you are the one who needs conjugal pleasure, Sir, if I may be so bold to say."

"It is something I have never had and therefore do not miss. I made vows and keep my word."

"When might I meet this daughter of yours?"

"At your convenience. We will be happy to accept you if you come to call."

"Does Cecily know about your visit here today?"

"She does. I would not hide this from her, and she is excited to know if you will return my visit."

"How about Saturday next? That will give the young lady time to ready herself."

"Two in the afternoon?"

"I will be there."

"You have sons, do you not?"

"Charles and George."

"And you would like more? Perhaps a daughter?"

"I would, Sir. Indeed, I would."

"Then I will take my leave. Good day, Mister Durandeaux."

"I think we can be Marcus and Francis now, don't you?"

"Surely. Good day, Marcus."

Marcus, the pragmatist, felt it best not to let his future father-in-law know that he had little reason to miss conjugal bliss. It would dampen the man's enthusiasm. Best to leave his private life secret.

Cecily received her father's declaration with her usual aplomb. She had met no young men who sparked her interest and therefore accepted that her father had done as he had to assure her future. Cecily had seen Marcus Durandeaux at Sunday services and when guests had gathered for holiday parties, funerals, or weddings. She knew he was a man of substance and only questioned the man's age.

"Father, are not his sons Amos' age? Do you not consider him too old for me?"

"No, my dear. Marcus is not too old. He is wise with experience. That he has been married means that he understands the needs of a wife. He is wealthy beyond our family, and you will have anything you wish. At least meet him and see for yourself that he is a real gentleman."

"Alright, Papa. If it will make you happy, I will meet Mister Durandeaux."

"It is a good French name, don't you think, Daughter?"

"It is. As good as Battailes, Papa."

"Prepare yourself for tea on Saturday. He will come to inspect you as well as you him. Be at your most beautiful. Wear that delphinium blue dress that I like to see you wear. It makes your eyes even more beautiful."

"I'll make sure we are prepared. Rhoda will out-do herself in her kitchen."

"Tell her to put hickory nuts in the cake?"
"Yes, Papa."

Saturday came and the household was abustle with preparations for Miss Cecily's prospect's visit. The house was cleaned from top to bottom, rugs taken out and beaten, bannisters dusted and polished even in the tiny places, chandeliers sparkled, and vases filled with flowers from the garden. The cook prepared her best tea cakes, and the most expensive tin of China tea was taken down from the high shelf to be prepared in their cherished porcelain teapot brought from France.

A downpour brought Cecily to tears, thinking that her caller may not come, but as the chime inside the hall clock sounded at two o'clock, Marcus Durandeaux drove his calese into the front drive. She ran to the front window to see him, but the hood was up to protect him from rain, and she could not get a glimpse of her beaux. Not wanting to be seen as too anxious, she ran back into the drawing room where tea was already laid out. She knew a groom stood by to take his horse and calese to the stable and the man, himself, would soon be in her presence. She sat quite like a lady, trying to still the excitement she felt. She heard the front door open and then heard Joel, the family butler, speak. She knew Joel would have gone out with an umbrella to shield their guest and there would be a moment of brushing raindrops from Marcus' coat. She heard her father join Joel and his words of welcome. She waited patiently. And then Marcus Durandeaux filled the doorway.

He was quite a bit taller than she. His shoulders wide and his torso displaying strength, he seemed a man of great substance, if not debonair. His brown hair, pulled back from a strong face, had streaks of grey. His classic French nose and piercing blue eyes under a heavy brow told her that he was no man to be trifled with. A bright blue satin waistcoat under a darker blue topcoat served to soften his countenance. She felt intimidated until his charming smile, showing a full set of strong, well-formed teeth, gave her reassurance. Cecily remembered her manners and smiled in return, whereupon her father proceeded with formal introductions.

The pleasantries completed, the three settled down for tea and conversation, which, at this first meeting, would be between her father and their guest and would not include talk of marriage. That would come later if both Cecily and Marcus agreed, and Cecily would hear little of it until agreements were made and contracts signed. She knew that this may be the only occasion during which she would be permitted to sit quietly and listen to grown men converse about subjects of which she knew little to nothing. She used the occasion to judge her suitor on the things which her father had taught her to be important in a husband. He was substantial and would provide for her quite well. He seemed healthy and vigorous. His own sons proved that he would give her children. Her father seemed to like and to approve of the man and she trusted her father above all men.

The first few bits of conversation with the young lady told Marcus all he needed to know. His experience with women was not small and he fitted her into a category immediately. More mouse than cat, she would be a perfect wife for him; however, he intended that she should be aware of the sort of man he was, with no surprises after the vows were said. That decided, he gave his attention to her father.

"Your wife is well?" asked Marcus, who recalled what Francis had told him."

"As well as can be," Francis replied, a bit defensively.

"You have a son, do you not?"

"I do.

"Is he here?"

"He is not. He is in at university in Paris finishing his studies. I was afraid he would find love there and wish to remain, but not so. I look forward to his return."

"Are you in need of new workers," he asked Francis. "Next month we expect a new ship to harbor off Sullivan's Island and after quarantine, I will be happy to select and reserve as many as you would like. The best of the lot."

Francis did not approve of talking business in front of ladies, especially not slave trading, which he considered a not so decent profession, but a necessary one. He responded a bit too quickly.

"No, Marcus. We have what we need. Thank you for thinking of me."

"If you change your mind, let me know. This shipload will be coming right from the West Coast of Africa...directly from their own rice growing region. If you intend to expand your fields, you may be in need. I admit, newcomers, right off the ship, can be difficult at first, but given the right overseer, they soon learn. Along that train of thought I must add that I am away from home quite often. Trading can require much time. Sometimes I am away for several weeks. I say this because you both should be aware."

Francis quickly changed the subject from slaves to the Rice Council in Charles Town and the two men spoke of prices and shipping. Then the conversation turned to the Colonial Assembly and the fact that they were banned from that organization because of their religious stance: neither were Anglican.

"I have a friend in Charles Town who is a member of the Assembly," declared Marcus. "Name of Jasper Perrin. If I need a favor, he is all too willing to help. If he can ever help you, just ask me. It may even be that my son, Charles, will be betrothed to his daughter, Julia, when the time is right."

"Isn't Perrin a French name? Would he be one of those who left..."

"He did. He left our religion and gave his allegiance to The Church of England, which, as you know is required to hold any public office. Soon thereafter he was admitted to the Assembly. That way he can speak for those of us who do not convert."

More than an hour had passed, and out of the corner of his eye Marcus noticed that Cecily had begun to squirm, and he knew better than to outstay his welcome on the first visit. Just enough time to be polite, but not too much to be offensive. He had said what he came to say. He rose and politely spoke to Francis.

"Francis, Cecily, it has been a delight. I wish to get back before dark and the road might be difficult. May I invite you to Durandeaux next?"

Francis knew that if he accepted the invitation for Cecily and himself, it would constitute a silent agreement that he was willing to give his daughter to be Marcus' bride. He was satisfied that he and Marcus would get along and to him that was more important in a marriage contract than anything else.

"Cecily, would you like that?" asked her father.

"I would, indeed," she replied, now totally infatuated with the distinguished gentleman who wished to have her as his bride.

Both men noted that she could not hide a blush under her coy smile. Francis, pushing to the far reaches of his mind the talk of slave trading, felt relieved that he had found a good husband for his daughter. Cecily walked on air as she contemplated being chatelaine of Durandeaux Plantation and Marcus was pleased at the thought of their wedding night. It had been a long time since he had bedded a Caucasian virgin.

Months in the planning, the wedding was the event of the season. Marcus and Cecily were joined in holy matrimony at a lavish affair to which everyone in the community were invited, and who moved heaven and earth to attend. A positively beautiful delicate, blond, and blue-eyed bride, Cecily glowed with happiness all through the ceremony and afterward when speaking with guests fitted out in their finest satins and silks and brocades; the ladies wearing diamonds and pearls on their wrists and around their necks; the gems sparkling in the sunlight.

The guests departed and Francis returned alone to Battailes. He felt satisfaction that he had done the best for Cecily without sending her to a bridegroom in Charles Town, much too far away. While Francis lounged in his comfortable chair by the fire, his spaniel at his feet, a warm brandy in his hand, inside the great Durandeaux mansion, Cecily lay in Marcus' bed, awaiting her husband.

CHAPTER 3

A shy and sensitive young wife, Cecily determined to do her utmost to settle quietly and smoothly into the routine of her new home. Bruneau and Lacey made sure that the household help accepted her without question, but their cautions were not necessary. Cecily showed herself to be gracious, kind, and fair to all, from Bruneau on down to the chambermaids. She praised M'aum Sue's cooking and asked advice of Lacey. She thanked the maid for her morning tea and did not complain when her bed covers were not distributed evenly. She conducted herself as her father and Trish had taught her. Without Marcus being aware, she soon had the household help doting on her. It was a particularly good beginning to what she hoped would be a long and happy marriage.

Keeping in mind her father's wish for grandchildren Marcus came to her every night before retiring to his own room. Within two months of their marriage, she was pregnant, and Marcus hoped again for his long-awaited daughter. However, when Cecily announced her pregnancy her husband left her alone at night. He had found that conjugal pleasure with another Caucasian woman offered him no more satisfaction than had the first, and he continued his trysts with Cassie, even to the extent of bringing her from the wash house to the mansion to be his wife's personal maid. Every soul in the house, except for Cecily and Charles, suspected the nature of this intrusion, but out of kindness, no one dared to inform their new Mistress.

When Cecily's time came, she gave birth to a son. He came as a genuine disappointment to Marcus who did his best to hide his feelings, for he knew that proud Cecily thought a son would be his first choice. She asked his permission to name the baby Joseph and he allowed it as he had only chosen a name for a girl: Tabitha.

CHAPTER 4

With the birth of his grandson, Francis' visits to the Durandeaux plantation to visit his daughter and the baby boy increased. He possessed no special talent or instinct for seeing or feeling undercurrents of discontent and noted only the outward respect and politeness that Marcus extended to his wife and baby son. Francis remained so pleased that he had chosen so well for his daughter that he missed noting early vibes when a wrinkle developed within a few months of Joseph's birth. Cassie had informed Marcus that she was carrying his child, a volatile situation which the master tried to avoid by giving Cassie to Bruneau to wed. Truth was impossible for the household not to notice and, although Cecily gave no hint to anyone that she was aware, she recognized subterfuge and suffered the first twinges of doubt.

It is the way of people like Marcus Durandeaux that they rarely, if ever, consider the feelings of others when deciding for themselves. They feel as though they are wrapped in gauze and others cannot see the real inward person, but rather the image they want to convey. They veer toward what pleases them and forever expect others to accept and adjust as they plow on to fulfill their desires. And that is how Marcus dealt with Cecily, who may have been young but was no one's fool. Outwardly she kept silent but inwardly, she knew that the first major lie had infiltrated their marriage. Her gentle heart betrayed, she began to fade into the woodwork, spending her time in the garden with her watercolors and Baby Joseph. She spoke of none of her pain and sadness to her father. It was not the way of a well brought up woman to complain.

When Bruneau became the proud father of a beautiful baby girl the lie continued; the truth obvious but ignored. Given the name, Tabitha, by Marcus, himself, no one who saw little Tabitha believed that Bruneau was her father, but no one dared to venture a word of it. Bruneau's skin was dark...a smooth ebony, while Cassie was light in color. The baby girl was lighter even than her mother. Marcus only saw that this little bundle as the only daughter he might ever have. He then instructed Cassie to take the girl to the nursery where she would be reared alongside Joseph.

For Cecily this insult was the final straw. She could remain silent no longer. When Marcus came to his room after supper; poured himself a brandy and sat comfortably in his easy chair, Cecily knocked on his door. At his command, she entered and without hesitation, spoke quietly.

"Husband, do not think for a moment that you are fooling me or anyone else. Bruneau is not that child's father. You are."

"Cecily, how could you..."

"Easily, Husband. I can say it easily. You know and I know what goes on between you and Cassie. You would have been wiser to tell me the truth in the beginning. My maid? No, Marcus. Your mistress. Now you take the baby from her body and from your seed to be brought up in our boy's nursery? Can't you think of a greater insult to me and to our boy? Have I displeased you so much? Did I not give you a son? Isn't that what men want most?"

For once, without understanding why, Marcus held his temper. He could have shouted her down, given his orders and stomped away, but there was something to what she said. And she *was* his wife. Even he saw her position and spoke gently, but his words were a sword through her heart.

"You are right, Cecily. About Cassie and me. Since we were young. And you are right that most men want sons, but I wanted a daughter. I already have sons. I very much wanted a daughter. Cassie gave me that daughter and Tabitha will have every advantage that Joseph will have. You can accept that or return to your father. The children will remain with me."

Even in gentleness he was cruel. He waited a moment for her response.

"I will accept it on one condition."

"What is that?"

"That you send Cassie away. Sell her. Take Cassie to the auction. I will be rid of her, or the entire community will know. Cassie goes. I want your answer by tomorrow."

This was a Cecily that Marcus had never seen, and he liked this one more than the original. He had until tomorrow to decide.

"Then good night. I'll give you my answer tomorrow."

The solution to Marcus' dilemma came easily. It was something he had been thinking of since his marriage to Cecily and the time had come for it to be implemented. The next morning, he assured Cecily that Cassie would no longer be on the property and then he extracted a promise from Cecily that Tabitha would be welcomed into the nursery with baby Joseph. He summoned Bruneau to his study. The butler joined him feeling dread for he felt the tension in the air among Mistress Cecily, Cassie, and Master Marcus. Marcus broached the subject with little delicacy and no sympathy for Bruneau.

"You are aware, I am certain, that my wife is not pleased with Cassie. She has demanded of me that I send her away. I have considered her request and have determined that it is the best for all of us. I will take Cassie on the ketch with me tomorrow. I am sailing to the islands on business and will dock long in enough in Charles Town to see that she will be included in the auction on Saturday. My decision is final Bruneau. You will lose Cassie but there is Tabitha who will remain here. Since you have become accustomed to having a woman in your bed, you may choose any of the other single women from the quarters who please you, or you may attend the auction with me when I return and choose for yourself. Have you anything to say?"

Bruneau ached to speak but he dared not. He wanted to ask why he had been given Cassie when the woman had never allowed him her body. Bruneau knew that he had been used to cover the master's dalliance. He must continue with the charade and allow everyone else to believe what they wished. No doubt, Madame Cecily was already aware.

"You are quiet for a long time, Bruneau? You are waring with yourself?"

"Naw, Suh. Just thinkin' I'm gonna miss Cassie. I got used to her."

"I said you can choose another."

"Yes, Suh, you did. I'll think on it."

Marcus was the master and could do as he wished...answering to no one.

"Mastah Marcus, how long you be away this time?"

"I have enough business to require at least a month. I am trying to develop more. Do not expect me home before then."

Baby Tabitha joined toddler Joseph in the nursery and, true to her word and to her loving nature, Cecily accepted the lovely girl-child as she would her own daughter. The child was innocent. Cecily was wise enough to say nothing untoward concerning the baby girl. Outwardly, the household accepted that Tabitha was no more than a companion to Joseph and kept the secret as the children grew up, but even though no one said the words aloud, whispers went into every corner of the plantation of the kindness and generosity of Mistress Cecily.

CHAPTER 5

When Marcus returned to Durandeaux after his voyage, without Cassie, and came to her bed, Cecily continued obedient, but he was not satisfied with obedience. He wanted more than obedience and soon left her be. He had his daughter and spent hours playing with her. He had the pleasure of his slave women who pleased him and kept themselves in his good graces. Marcus left Joseph to Cecily and set about shaping George and Charles in the ways of Low-Country planters. His trading contacts now extended far south to the Caribbean Islands, and he often sailed for weeks or months making contacts and contracts to expand even more. The people at Durandeaux grew accustomed to Marcus being away for extended periods of time and cheered when sight of his mast was seen coming into the inlet after a long voyage.

An early bonding developed between the two little ones, which was to continue throughout their childhood play times and into their studies with their tutor.

Cecily doted on Joseph. He and Tabitha played quietly while Cecily painted watercolors in the garden. Both children admired her paintings of flowers and trellises, birds, and vines with pretty buds, and both wished to learn how to make the lovely pictures. Joseph's quiet, studious nature and manner caused people to see in the youth a man of the church in the making. This did not displease Marcus for he had George and Charles to care for the plantation and their other businesses. He made plans to send Joseph to seminary where he would devote himself to a lifetime of service. Perhaps he would even earn a prominent position in Charles Town religious circles. For the first time Marcus the pragmatist saw Joseph as someone of value...someone he could use. As for Tabitha, Marcus was as pleased as he could be. As his only daughter, he expected that she would remain in his household, either married or not, to serve him.

Few observed closely or gave thought to the special closeness that had developed between the two youngsters as they grew out of childhood and into their youth. Joseph and Tabitha entered young adulthood as educated, cultured young people. That they were best friends no one could dispute. They complimented each other. Tabitha seemed to have a positive, calming influence when Joseph went into a dark place, which had happened more often of late. However, Lacey the housekeeper, saw something else. Instinct, experience, observance, and a shrewd woman's intuition came into play. To Lacey's sensibilities, what for years had seemed to be an ideal situation had become dangerous. She feared that no one in the family would imagine the consequences until too late. Lacey knew it was time to speak with Bruneau.

CHAPTER 6

Marcus had expanded the great house at Durandeaux from being a comfortable home to being a mansion. It was shaped as a large square, after the order of a French farmhouse, except that the courtyard in the center was not the realm of pigs, chickens and dogs that had roamed at will in his father's time. When Marcus became master, he hired a man to design a lovely garden with shrubs, flowers, bird houses and places to sit scattered about the greenery. It was here that Tabitha and Joseph spent their free time as grew up.

Tabitha knew Bruneau as her father and she respected him as such, without question. She addressed Cecily as Mistress and was duly respectful to her. Mistress Cecily was kind enough to teach her about painting. Often as they sat together with their easels and pots of paints and brushes Tabitha would see, from the corner of her eye, Cecily gazing at her with a strange look, which the young girl did not understand, but one that gave her shivers.

When she didn't have a brush in her hand, Tabitha either read books chosen for her by Cecily, or cut flowers for the house. Joseph would find a shady spot under the rose arbor and read Aquinas and other respected churchmen.

It happened one day when Joseph, a lad of seventeen years, stood by his bedroom window looking out onto the garden below. He watched Tabitha cut delphiniums and yellow roses to place in vases for the small tables scattered about the great house. On the opposite side of the garden Cecily also stood by her bedroom window, looking down as Tabitha chose just the right blossoms to decorate the house for Charles' birthday and betrothal celebration. The girl had a talent for arrangements, and it had become her daily task. Something caught Cecily's attention and she raised her eyes to look across the garden to the opposite wall to see Joseph through the window, gazing down at Tabitha, now a lovely young woman who any man would desire. As though someone had hit her, Cecily clutched her stomach, realizing at once what had occurred while they all had been as though asleep. They had assumed that silence meant peace, but their lack of awareness had not led to peace. It had led to exactly the opposite. The resulting situation, she could not and would not allow. The scandal would destroy her family, fingers would point to her and even more than that. The lie that had lain unspoken and filled the corners of the house since Tabitha's birth would be known for if she were driven to it, she would spill the truth.

A solution must be found. She could speak with Tabitha, but Marcus would be irate. Best leave it to him to deal with his son. The two must be separated, and soon, but with the coming of a celebration for Charles' engagement, it would have to wait. She would hold her tongue until after the festivities and then she would tell Marcus what she had observed and encourage him to choose a bride for Joseph and see to his betrothal. He would have to send Tabitha away just as he had sent her mother. It would not do to have her remain, no matter how much pain it would cause either Joseph, Marcus, or Tabitha, the object of both men's love; one sort father's devotion and the other of a vibrant young man.

Cecily had not been the first to notice the initial signs of a shift in behavior between the two young adults. Lacey's eyes and ears were everywhere at once in the great house and halls and little avoided her sharp mind. Tabitha helped to serve at meals, and the housekeeper noted that Joseph could not keep his glance away from her. Tabitha returned look for look, with a smile. Lacey's first inclination was to speak with Bruneau in hope that he could curb his *daughter's* enthusiasm when in the presence of Joseph. Lacey found an opportunity and cornered Bruneau in the back hallway. She knew that she would not fare well, nor would she earn praise for her observation and prescience, and she was correct.

"Bruneau, I got somethin' to say to you and you ain't gonna like it," whispered Lacey.

"I don't like much of what you say, Woman," replied Bruneau, with his usual lack of enthusiasm. "You always givin' me sh..."

"Don't you say bad words, Bruneau! God gonna strike you down. What I got to say, you got to hear and then you got to do somethin'."

"Why you whisperin'?"

"So, nobody hear me but you. That's why."

"Say it then."

"You gotta do somethin' 'bout your gal. She been in Mastah Joseph company all they life. Too close now. All grown up and ain't young'uns no more. Ain't playmates. Mastah Marcus don't see it, but when he does, he'll gonna tear into somebody and you know it."

"What happened?"

"I got to spell it out, Man? Mastah Joseph, he's gone on her. You know..."

"What do I know?"

Exasperated with the butler, Lacey spoke slowly, nodding her head from side to side and with a serious expression, her dark eyes spitting fire.

"You *know* what! Mastah Joseph and Tabitha ain't got no business feelin' that way 'bout each other! Shame Cassie gone and you ain't told Tabitha who she is. Just let her grow up thinkin'..."

"Hush up, Woman! Don't you say no more 'bout that."

"Well, then, you better *do* somethin' 'fo it too late!"

Bruneau's face got a shade darker as he grew worried. He knew that Lacey spoke the truth. Bruneau hated for Lacey to be right, but he had to admit that there was something to her warning. He had seen Tabitha and the master's son grow even closer as the years went by. He had put it in the back of his mind telling himself that they were children, and everyone approved, and no one thought anything bad. But Tabitha had grown into a beauty and the two were no longer simple playmates. They were of courting and marrying age.

"I'll talk to Tabitha tonight. Don't you worry none. And don't you go tellin' anybody else!"

"Jus' you do it and right soon," Lacey cautioned. "You best be askin' Mastah if he can find a man to marry her. You know why those two can't happen and it's more than one bein' a mastah and other a slave. Mo' lies than secrets in this house. You know and I know!"

Bruneau knew that in being given Cassie, he had simply been chosen to do the master a favor and felt that he was being used. After his talk with Lacey, either it was resentment or anger at being a slave, but whatever halted him, Bruneau did not speak to the master. Or to Tabitha.

CHAPTER 7

"Don't walk so fast, Reg. I can't walk fas' as you," Dubie called from a few yards behind his friend. "I totin' dis pig."

"You betta hurry up," called Reg in reply. "Ain't gonna be light all day. We got two mo' to ketch."

"Anyhow, wid only you and me...how we gonna tote t'ree pigs?"

"I got rope in my pocket," said as twelve-year-old Reg as he stopped and waited for ten-year-old Dubie to catch up to him.

"Dis swamp full of skeeters," declared Dubie."

"And snakes and dey gonna bite you, you don't keep up and we git dem pigs to home."

"What dey need t'ree pigs fo'?"

"Big doin's. Mastah Charles big day. Gonna be twenty-one and gonna git roped and tied, too."

"Dat old, Man! You think we gonna live to git old? What you mean git roped and tied?"

"He gonna got married," said Reg. "Dat mean he a man now. But he ain't old. Mastah George, he old."

"I gits twenty-one, I gonna leave dis place," vowed Dubie.

"You ain't goin' nowhere. You a slave jis lak me and we stuck heah till ole man Marcus sell us or we die."

"Who tole you dat?"

"My Mammy. She know ev'ything," replied Reg.

"My Pappy know mo' dan yo Mammy know," quipped Dubie. "He say we gonna up and leave some day."

"Now hesh up, Dubie. Ain't dat a pig up yonder?"

"Where?" asked the younger boy, looking in each direction. "I ain't see nothin'."

"Look where I pointin'. By dat cypress stump. See? Up yonder. He rootin'. Ain't seen us."

"I see 'im. I got dis one. You go git dat one. Sneak up on 'im."

Reg began to sneak toward the pig, his bare feet quiet on the damp swamp mulch. The pig was so busy rooting beneath the cypress stump that he did not hear the boy sneak up on him until a little dark hand grabbed him by one ear and then the other. The pig squealed in mortal fear and struggled to get free of the grip of the boy's hands and legs. Reg straddled his back, clamped his knees behind the pig's shoulders, reached into his pocket, pulled out the piece of rawhide rope and tied it around the new pig's head as Dubie's pig added his voice to the melee.

"Reg, we got two. Dey big fo' pigs and we can't take no mo' even if we ketches one. Let's take dese and see if we gotta come back tomorrey?"

Reg thought for a moment and realized that this time Dubie was right. They had their hands full with these two squealing, squirming creatures and no way could they get another before dark.

"Alright. All Mammy gonna do is fuss. Won't give me no whuppin'. We come tomorrey. Let's go back with dese."

The boys were silent on the way home through the swamp, the reluctant pigs struggling to free themselves each step, until Dubie spoke.

"Yo' Pappy gonna roast 'em outside like last time?"

"Yeah. But he got a week, he say. Gonna put de pigs in a pen and feed 'em on co'n and goobers. Make 'em fat and sweet. Gonna make dat sauce he make. Big tub."

"We gits to gnaw de ribs. Umm, dat gonna be so good."

When her maid knocked on her door Cecily was obliged to put aside her fears for Joseph while she dealt with another crisis

"Ma'am Cecily? You comin' down?" she called. "Bruneau, he say Reg and Dubie back with two pigs. He say..."

"Yes, Jolly, I'm coming. Go tell Bruneau I'll be right there."

"Yes Ma'am. I will."

Cecily threw on her shawl, descended the stairs and hurried to the kitchen where Jolly sat with Lacey, both shelling peas for supper.

"Where's Bruneau?" she asked.

"He outside by the pig pen with the boys and the pigs. He want to know if you need three or will two be enough. Said them boys couldn't bring in three but them they brung is big."

"Alright, I'll go and see."

Cecily went outside and walked toward the dominant odor, the pig pens which lay on the other side of the stable to keep the smell away from the house. Holding her shawl tightly around her shoulders and hunched over from the chilly wind, she found Bruneau and the boys.

"Mornin' Ma'am. Here are the pigs. Come and see if they big enough or do you want me to send the boys out to the swamp for another?"

Cecily held her shawl over her nose and walked closer. Two young shoats nosed in the mud of the pen seeking that last grain of corn from their feeding. She saw that they were healthy and fat and deemed that those two on the spit would be enough for the guests. Most ladies would never touch the roasted meat, anyway, preferring the delicate finger sandwiches to hunks of meat, which might cause bloat. That would never do against the tight corsets they wore. These two would easily feed the men.

"Those two will be enough. Thank you, Bruneau."

"Yes, Ma'am. I'll tell the men when to get them ready. They'll be tasty, for sure. You best go on back inside. It gettin' right chilly out here. Hope tomorrow is better."

"So do I, Bruneau. So do I," replied Cecily, with emphasis that caused him to give her a studied look.

"Miz Cecily, you got to take it easy now. Don't you go getting yourself all tired from these doin's. Tell that Tabitha to take on more. She can help you and not spend so much time doing what she likes. She nearly grown-up now."

His remark caused Cecily to hurry away in fear that others had seen what she had seen.

Cecily endured the remaining days until the birthday and betrothal festivities in a state of anxiety and guilt that she had not seen what was happening under her own nose; fear that she might be wrong; fear that she would not be able to stop it before too late if she were right. She suffered anxiety over what friends and associates would think if truth were known and fear of her husband's reaction. She lived in dread of having to tell him what she saw and what she suspected. It would upset his world and he would immediately place blame on her.

There was work to keep her busy with Lacey and Jolly through the hours of the day, but when night came, she lay in her bed unable to sleep. It didn't take long before Jolly broached the subject as she drew back the long curtains from the windows of Cecily's bedroom.

"Ma'am, you don't look so good. You feelin' bad? Can I get you some Castor Oil? Maybe you betta go back to bed?"

"No, Jolly. Just a few nights when I could not sleep enough. Thinking of the festivities, I suppose. I do so want it to come off well. Charles' intended and her father and so many others coming."

"Yes'm. Maybe you sleep tonight."

But the following day Jolly noted that her mistress looked even worse than the day before. She spoke of it with Lacey who immediately took it to Bruneau.

"Bruneau, the Missus is not doing well. You see her lately? You say anything to her? 'Bout what we talk about?"

"No, Woman. I did not. And if I did, I wouldn't tell you. Why you goin' on 'bout so much trouble now? 'Cause you ain't getting' attention? I done told you 'bout making trouble. You want to know 'about Miz Cecily's business, ask her. If she don't tell you, you ain't got no need knowin'."

"You got to be so mean and sassy all the time, *Mister* Bruneau? Missus hear you talking to me like that, she'll scold you. She talk way better to me than you do."

"In front of her I speak well to everyone. Now you better get on about your work and stop trying to stir up a fuss. Fuss enough going on with this do. Got two more days and it will be over."

Lacy almost turned away but then caught herself. She looked back at the big butler and whispered harshly, "Man, why you in such a temper? You right mean to me! You wonder Miz Cecily might already know something 'bout what I told you? What if she do and ain't said a word cause of all this fuss for Mastah Charles. You talk with Mastah Marcus like I told you?" She waited for his anger but this time his reply was more controlled.

"When these doings are over, I'll talk to Mastah Marcus. He will find a solution that pleases everybody. Time Mastah Joseph went away to school."

"So, you didn't. I'm not surprised. You think Mastah gonna send Joseph away and not Tabitha?" Lacey chuckled as she added, "There ain't no end to this that gonna please everybody."

Bruneau's brave front for Lacey hid the fact that he did have an idea that trouble was brewing. He hadn't said anything to Master Marcus, but he was concerned that what bothered Miss Cecily was the same thing that worried both him and Lacey. If it were, there would be trouble. Bruneau did not know what to do except speak with Tabitha. He would bring the matter to her attention and caution her. That night Bruneau knocked on the door to the room that Tabitha shared with Jolly.

"Bruneau, what you want?" asked Jolly. "It late. I gotta be up 'fo sunup to see to the Missus and to help cook. I need my sleep."

"I need to talk with Tabitha."

"Your gal ain't in her bed. She out."

"Out where?"

"How I know? Watchin' bats fly with Mastah Joseph is my guess. Or lookin' at stars. He know some of 'em names."

CHAPTER 8

The drama unfolding at the Durandeaux mansion was not the only problem for the family. At the Perrin household in Charles Town a pretty, young socialite lay prone on her bed while her maid applied cold cloths to her eyes and brow to reduce the puffiness. Julia Perrin had sobbed all night, unable to sleep because of the tantrum she had thrown the evening before when her father, Jasper, had informed her of his determination regarding her future; that she was to marry Charles Durandeaux, the youngest son of Marcus, his friend and business partner. Julia was not opposed to marriage. In fact, she had a beaux already picked out. Her anger was about her father's choice for her. She had shocked her father with her instant reaction...a violent tantrum.

"I will not, Father. I will not!"

"But you must do this, Julia. It is imperative."

"For you but not for me. I will not marry that rube. He didn't even go away to school!"

"He had the best of tutors, and he has other attributes, Julia. He is kind and thoughtful. He will treat you well."

"You can't do this to me, Father. It would be cruel and heartless of you. You reared me in the city and now you want

37

to marry me to a rice farmer and ship me off to a cabin in the swamp? How can you ask that of me? I can't even remember what that boy looks like," she shouted through her tears.

"He is not a boy. He is a man fully grown and ready to have a wife and begin a family."

Julia wailed louder and declared that she would never be a wife to him.

"You will, Daughter. You will because I command it. Now wipe your tears."

Her father's resolve alarmed her. For the first time she felt the weaker of the two and she didn't know how to react. She had always been capable of manipulating him to give her what she desired, but this time, she saw a different Jasper Perrin. She stopped crying, blew her nose, and sat quiet for a moment not ready to concede the battle.

"Why can't I marry Jerome West? He appreciates me and is ready to ask for my hand. If I marry him, we can enjoy all the city has to offer a young couple. I would not mind having a family with him. Can you see me sitting in a hot kitchen churning butter?"

"Julia, my dear daughter, don't you know that I am obligated to the man who made your luxurious lifestyle possible? If we refuse his son, he may choose another match, to our financial disadvantage. He may even discard me and chose another partner. Then you would not have the life he provides. No, child. I am committed to this betrothal and so must you be. Besides, you have exaggerated the condition of the young man. Charles does not live in a cabin in the swamp. There is more wealth in that family than in ours and we are dependent on the Durandeaux for our well-being. You will live in a mansion with more servants than you will need. You will not find yourself churning butter. That I can assure you. Now stop this behavior or you will bring shame on us."

Jasper understood his daughter and he did feel a certain amount of sympathy. She was young, vibrant in a privileged sort of way, and at the age when having fun, enjoying soirees, and learning the new dances from Europe were more important to young ladies than becoming a wife and mother. However, this match must be secured because of the nature of his business with Marcus. Best keep the business dealings within the confines of family. If he must sacrifice his daughter's future happiness, then so be it. He had no choice. In the process of making Jasper wealthy, Marcus had given him none. Perrin was in his debt and the payment was Julia wed to Charles. That night he did his best to explain to Julia what life for a lady was like at the Durandeaux plantation, but she would have none of it. She had her eyes and heart set on Jerome West, an Englishman, a wealthy member of the Church of England, high in Charles Town's society, with aristocratic relatives in England, and a sought-after beaux for Charles Town's daughters.

Julia had met Charles Durandeaux only once, when Marcus had brought him to the Perrin home for the purpose of the young people getting acquainted. Their religious life and social life were in two different parishes, with the Wando river between them. Julia disliked that Charles was too quiet. He barely spoke and had no charming or witty words to amuse her like the young blades in the city. He did not know how to flirt with her to make her feel appealing. He did not notice her attempts at showing her young woman's skill at teasing. When Charles and his father departed, her father had not asked if she would accept the country rube. He had told her she would, which led to her sobs and the unpleasant scene with Jasper.

Today she would, with her father, ride in their shiny new carriage, along with her trunks, to the plantation where she would be betrothed to Charles Durandeaux against her will and her wishes and preferences.

With the help of her maid, she dressed in traveling clothes and tucked her hair under a hat. She watched the footman load her trunks onto the rear of the carriage and saw her father standing by the carriage door. He looked up at her window and motioned for her to come. She could tell that he was already annoyed that she had not come down to breakfast. Her fate was sealed and with dignity Julia descended the curved staircase where she had slid down the banister when she was a child. Taking one last look at their family portraits on the wall in the hallway, she said goodbye to Nancy, their cook and housekeeper, to LuLu, her personal maid who would not be allowed to accompany her, and to Mobley, their manservant. Then she walked away from the home of her youth to enter adulthood, certain that she would be miserable. During the long carriage ride she spoke not a word but clamped her jaws against what she considered cruel and improper behavior of her father. Barred even from taking LuLu with her, she felt that she was going to prison for life.

That was the young lady who stepped from the carriage and refused to accept the hand that Charles offered to help her step down to the ground. Everyone noticed the affront but Charles, who stood with his hand outstretched for too long before dropping it. That this was a match made for business and men's purposes only, was evident, but not unusual for their time and place. It was how things had been done in the old country, and here the custom obtained. It was not exactly a man's world. It was more a father's world.

Cecily greeted her daughter-in-law, for that is how she was considered, and showed her to her room, which had a door to Charles' room. Tonight, the door would be locked, but after the betrothal it would not be locked unless the bride-to-be locked it, even though the official wedding may be days away. After a formal dinner where the family welcomed her, Julia retired went to her room for another night of wakefulness, feeling as though tomorrow she would be slaughtered.

At her best, Julia was difficult. Not a striking beauty, she made up for this lack with her wit and charm, and her love of entertainment and dance. Her mother dead, with only her father and Nancy to rear her through her childhood, neither had had success in taming her tantrums when she didn't get what she wanted; therefore, her father had been indulgent with his only child. Tomorrow Jasper Perrin would see Julia in the care of the Durandeaux family and he hoped that, somehow, Marcus could succeed where he had failed, for he knew that Charles could not. He felt relief that she was safely away from the city, and he could conduct business without having to be concerned about his daughter. Too long a widower, Jasper had no inkling of how devious and determined a woman can be when there is something that she desires or does not desire.

CHAPTER 9

Morning at the plantation came early. The chirping of forest birds, which came before the first glow of light in the eastern sky, woke the barnyard cocks and they announced the new day with vigor. Julia was accustomed to the sound but was not ready to wake and not ready to dress or meet anyone. She lay still, thinking about the day ahead of her. Two occasions to celebrate, her father had said. Charles would be twenty-one and fully adult. Then he would be betrothed to his bride-to-be. All about Charles. Nothing about her. If she had been allowed to wed Jerome, the festivities would have been about her. For the next half-hour she drifted in and out of sleep until a knock on her door and then it opened. A girl entered without being invited. She carried a tray.

"Here's your tea, Ma'am. My name is Tabitha and I'm to help you until we can arrange for your personal maid. Madam Cecily said you should be downstairs and dressed for breakfast soon as you can. Tea is for you while I help you dress."

"I am not accustomed to rising this early. Tell your mistress that I wish to sleep a bit longer."

"No, Ma'am. I can't do that. I must get you dressed and right now."

"What if I don't want to?"

"Master Marcus thought about that. He says that if you don't want to get up, I am to call him, and he will come to get your lazy ass out of bed. That is what he said. Those words."

"Is my father here? Did he hear what that man said?"

"He is in the dining room with Master Marcus and yes, he did hear. They are drinking tea and waiting for breakfast. And for you."

"Father allowed that man to speak of me like that?"

Tabitha, who already disliked the girl, smiled a big smile, and replied, "Yes, Ma'am. He did. Your father just laughed and said..."

"What?"

"I better not say, Ma'am. Just you get up now. Take a few minutes to get you dressed."

All the while Tabitha attended her, Julia thought if she should request that this girl be her maid. Then she could put the slave in her place, but then her own vanity said that Tabitha was too pretty to be seen along with her every day.

"You need to show humility, Tabitha. For a slave, you are much too high-minded."

Tabitha had never been called a slave before...not to her face...and she winced; however, the word did go a long way to reminding her who and what she was even if it pained her.

A thoroughly indignant Julia, her eyes and nose red and swollen from crying, descended the stairs and followed Tabitha to the dining room. She had no idea what to expect from these rubes, but to her surprise, the room was more beautiful than she had imagined it would be. She quickly looked around at the vases of tastefully arranged flowers and the Turkish rug which she knew must have cost a fortune. For the first time since learning of her degradation, she felt a whisp of hope. It soon vanished when Charles loped into the dining room, his boots muddy and his jacket smeared with what appeared to be horsehair and horse sweat.

"Riding so early, Son?" asked Marcus. "Perhaps you should change before coming to the table. Or at least wear a smock when grooming your horse? Sit down and say good morning to your bride."

Charles, who had not seen Julia when he came in smiled his best shy smile. Marcus came to his rescue.

"You will have to forgive Charles, Julia. He is a good young man, but a bit careless with himself. You will be a good influence on him. He rides early every morning. We are accustomed to him, and you will soon be also. Come, sit here by me."

"He should have come in the back door and through the kitchen, I should think," she retorted, not moving toward the empty chair that Marcus indicated. "At his age he should know his manners."

"Julia! Apologize immediately," ordered Jasper.

Julia turned to leave and over her shoulder she said, "I will not. I may have to marry him, but I don't have to apologize for saying what is true. He is a peasant and a bore! I will not sit at table with him."

Poor Charles stood silent as he witnessed the first tantrum of his wife-to-be. He looked to her father and then to his. His brow wrinkled and he frowned.

"You have paired me with her?" he said to Marcus. "I am not sure I want to go through with this. I expected someone different. Someone more to my liking."

"Nonsense. You will accept her. It is necessary and although neither of you wants the other, that is how it will be. There are more important things to consider than the desires of two spoiled young people. It has been agreed upon, the contract has been signed and the dowry accepted."

"As you wish, Father. Always as you wish. Shall I change now or sit?"

"You may as well sit but do not forget this."

"Do you think this will work out, Marcus?" asked Jasper. "It's not too late."

"It is too late. My motto is to marry money to money and religion to religion. That way each family knows what to expect from their blending. With this match, we have accomplished even more than that. We have added business to business."

CHAPTER 10

The appetizing odor of roasting pig filled the air as Reg ran back and forth from the spit to the kitchen on errands for his father. Dubie stood by the great iron pot stirring rice to be served with the roasted pork. Lacey ran to and from lawn to kitchen to see that lighter refreshments were constantly coming to the covered tables set out on the lawn.

By early afternoon the minster had accomplished the betrothal and Charles' birthday had been announced. Julia put on a brave face for her own reputation, but when Charles approached her during the day, she rebuffed his poor efforts at conversation. Her thoughts would not leave the girl who had come to dress her...Tabitha...and she looked for her during the hours of the feasting. Several times she saw the girl bringing food from the kitchen to the tables and then taking platters back with her. Twice she saw her with another young man, obviously a member of the family; Joseph, who had been missing at breakfast, or he may a wealthy guest. She inquired of Cecily and smiled when she was told that the young man was Joseph, Cecily's son. Julia had noticed the way he had looked at Tabitha. A stranger to the scene, she saw with new eyes and knew that she had found something

46

to watch and a game to play to amuse herself during her captivity.

As hostess of the affair, Cecily bravely kept her secret fear to herself throughout the day. Faking a composure that she did not feel, she greeted guests, took a moment to speak lovingly with both Charles and his bride to be. All the while in the forefront of her mind was the subject she must broach with Marcus when they were alone. She caught only a glimpse of Joseph and Tabitha throughout the day and became convinced that her fears were grounded.

That evening Marcus and Jasper stayed late talking about the wedding which would happen as soon as it could be arranged. Marcus insisted on paying for a lavish affair, to take place at Durandeaux.

While the two fathers planned her wedding, Julia, in her bed with the door locked, had no intention of spending the best years of her life living in a swamp and missing out on all the joy and pleasure that life in Charles Town offered young couples. She began to build her strategy.

Cecily knew that good etiquette demanded that she visit Julia's room and spend time becoming better acquainted, but her mind was tormented, wondering how she could have missed the unhealthy closeness between Joseph and Tabitha, or if something had recently occurred to kindle their mutual feelings. Certainly, she had never seen her son gaze at the girl with such intensity as she had now witnessed. Neglecting her duty to Julia, she retired to her room. Jolly undressed her and helped her into her gown and robe. Waiting until she heard Marcus come to his room, she dismissed her maid and gathering all her courage, she knocked on the door that separated their rooms.

"That you, Cecily?" he asked.

"Yes."

"Come on in."

She opened the door and stepped into Marcus bedroom. Drapes were drawn and her husband lay in bed with a book in his lap. Surprised, he threw back the covers, thinking that she wanted to join him. Cecily did not join him. Instead, she stood at the foot of the bed.

"We need to talk about something."

"What? The wedding?"

"No, not the wedding."

"What then? If you don't want to come to my bed and just want to talk, then what about?"

His annoyance obvious, she became more hesitant.

"Woman, what is it? I am reading and have no time for twaddle. What is it?

"Joseph," she said timidly.

"What about Joseph."

"And Tabitha."

"Cecily, please tell me what you want to tell me. I am losing patience. What about Joseph and Tabitha?"

"I fear that they...the two of them..."

"What about them? I only saw Joseph today, but he seemed fine. Is Tabitha ill?"

She raised her head looked directly at him.

"Not ill."

"Then what?" he asked with near exasperation.

"Worse than illness," she replied.

"What is worse than illness, Woman? Speak!"

"They...the two of them..."

It was all she could get out, but then Marcus realized that she inferred the unspeakable. His face flushed and his countenance darkened. She must be wrong. This could not happen with his Joseph, his quiet gentle son who was to be a minister...a man of religion...a man of God and his own half-sister.

"Tell me what you know," he said quietly.

"I saw the way he looked at her and..."

"How did he look at her?"

"Husband, don't make me describe it. You know what I mean."

Silence. She waited for an outburst. It did not come. She turned to go, thinking that he would say nothing. She was relieved. Then his voice stopped her, and she turned.

"With lust? Why are you afraid to say the word? If he looked at her with lust, then say it. Go to bed and say no more about it. To anyone. I'll deal with this in my own way. You go on to bed."

"I hope I did right in telling you."

"You did. Now go to sleep. Leave this up to me. I must think."

Cecily left his room and closed the door between them. Marcus left his bed and donned his dressing gown. He walked to his window and looked down at the garden. On both sides he could see how the wings of the mansion embraced that garden. There was enough moonlight that he could see shapes and shadows among the flowers and bushes and small trees. He stood there and thought. Could Cecily be right? Could the son he thought the least likely to become involved with a woman have proved him wrong? Joseph, the quiet, studious one. But then he brought from his memory the last time he had seen Tabitha. His eyes narrowed and he saw what must have been in front of Joseph for years. A growing, blooming, sultry, light skinned mulatto woman...an innocent orchid just waiting to be plucked. He could not blame his son. Joseph only responded as a normal man would. He blamed those who should have seen and did not, who should have stopped it and did not. He felt no blame for himself as he was busy keeping the family in luxuries. Neither were Charles or George responsible for they were as busy as he. The fault lay with Cecily, with Bruneau, with Lacey. The question of what to do was immediate. No time to lose. And Marcus knew what to do. It would be an immediate solution…the ultimate answer. Tabitha must go but to where. And then Marcus knew.

The next day began as usual. George went about his day with work on the plantation. Charles would spend his day with Julia, which was the way it should be. Soon the newness of marriage would wear off. Julia would be tending a baby and Charles would be back to his bugs and butterflies.

Cecily noted Marcus' calm at breakfast but was afraid to remark on it. She noted that Lacey was not her usual chatty self as she served breakfast, and Bruneau said nothing at all as he stood by, ready to serve. The tension had spread among all.

As soon as Marcus left the breakfast table, without saying a word to anyone, he went to the stable, saddled his bay gelding and mounted. He rode away with no one knowing his destination or when he would return. While he rode Marcus pondered how he could have been so mistaken…so blind. He had always thought of Joseph as being like his grandfather, Francis Battailes; a man of peace and a man of God; righteous, with no hot blood running through his veins. Marcus was well-aware of the condition of Francis' cold marriage bed and that the man did not indulge himself with his slave women. There was that unspoken judgment between them…Francis the cold blood whose goal in life was to do good and Marcus the hot blood who did as his body demanded; neither quite approving of the other. Now, however, he had to see Joseph as blending of the two.

He came to the Battailes plantation, dismounted and a boy stepped from the stable.

"You want me walk him, Mastah?"

"First, you ask someone to go to the house and ask your Master to come out here? Tell him a friend is here to talk in private. Tell him it is urgent. Can you do that? I'll walk the horse."

"Yes, Suh. Trough over yonder," said the boy as he pointed to the water trough and ran toward the rear of the house.

Marcus led the gelding to water, counting the gulps before walking him around the stable yard. In fewer than five minutes the boy returned.

"I tell Miss Rhoda and she tell Miss Trish and Miss Trish tell Mistah Joel, and he tell Mastah Francis. He comin'."

Marcus reached into his pocket, drew out a small coin and handed it, along with the reins, to the lad, who looked with amazement at the gift. The lad took the reins to walk the big bay gelding and Marcus sat on a bench in the shade of a peach tree and waited. He didn't have to wait long until Francis came from the house alone. He walked to Marcus, extended his hand and in bewilderment, inquired, "What is God's name is up, Marcus? Why are you sitting out here? Why not come on in? Trouble at home? Is it Cecily?"

"Can we go somewhere to talk? Privately?"

"Sure. Tack room is the best place for privacy. Follow me."

Marcus followed Francis into a spacious tack room, the walls covered with well-cleaned and polished bridles and saddles. He sat in a soft leather chair as Francis sat in another. Francis waited for Marcus to begin.

"Francis, I have a problem. A big one. I need your help and your promise of silence. Can you give that?"

"Why, certainly, Marcus. We are family. What do you need?"

"Joseph...your grandson..."

"Is he ill? Cecily loves that boy. Not giving you trouble, is he? He's a good boy. Going to be a good man."

"Your grandson is lusting after one of my house maids. Comely mulatto. Playmate with Joseph since they were children and now worse has come to worse. I must get her off the place. I don't want to put her on the block. She is too good for that. Pretty, good house worker. Cecily says she is great at arranging flowers. Vases full of them all over the house. I want you to take her."

"Can't you tell the boy to leave her alone?"

"I can, but she must not be under his nose for temptation."

"You want me to buy her from you?"

"No!" replied Marcus too quickly. "Not buy. I fear that Joseph would wish to marry the girl and I must prevent that. It would be a disgrace on my family."

"I am surprised that he does not just use her. Most men would do that. She belongs to your place."

"Joseph is not like that. He would never take her without marriage. He will be a churchman but has not yet left for seminary. I'll see that he goes soon. I have to get her away from him before..."

"Alright. I'll take her. You are certain that he has not...is she with child?"

"What kind of question is that! Joseph would never...he is to be a churchman!"

"You have just admitted that you misjudged him, Marcus. You have described my grandson to me as a normal man, which I have always found him to be. Besides, churchmen are not perfect, and you say she is comely. And what about you, Marcus? Have you never..."

Marcus held his temper as he replied, "I know this seems strange to you, but..."

"Never mind. I don't want to know your deep dark secrets. Bring the woman. If she stays with you, she will only bring more strife between you and my grandson."

Marcus knew where Francis's thoughts had gone, and he quickly repudiated them.

"She is not the cause of any strife between Joseph and me. It is not a thing of rivalry or jealousy, if that is what you are implying."

"I know you think your son and my grandson pure, but we seldom really know anyone, Marcus, even ourselves, but I can use another well-trained housemaid. Trish is clamoring that she doesn't have enough help. I will take her off your hands. But why me? Why not put her on the block. You are a trader. Should be easy for you to be rid of her."

"I want her here because I know that you do not sell your people. I know that you are kind to them. I know that you will take care of her."

"Thank you," replied Francis, now more than ever convinced that Marcus had already used her. "This is not like you, Marcus. I am convinced that there is more to this than you are divulging," he teased.

"How is your wife?" asked Marcus, changing the subject.

"Unpleasant as ever. Perhaps more-so. I see her as seldom as possible."

"Sorry to hear that."

"No matter. I am used to it. Better solitude than strife. You are blessed with Cecily."

"Amos in Charles Town? I wondered yesterday where he might be. Knew he had returned from France."

"Yes, Amos returned from France more than a month ago and I sent him to the Rice Counsel meetings so I could be here for your celebration. It was quite a festive occasion and I enjoyed myself. Charles' chosen bride is lovely."

"What are his plans? Amos."

"He plans to remain here and run the plantation for me. I am getting too old to sit in the saddle all day riding fields."

"He should marry soon and give you some grandchildren for your dotage."

"No one in sight. He is still angry with me for not allowing him to wed before he went to France. I thought he was too young, and another snatched her up. He has not forgiven me. In love with the girl, he was."

"Another romantic, I see. Wishing to base marriage on love. What a myth."

"How will we arrange this transaction to make it official? For the girl?"

"I'll give you a bill of sale for the charge of one shilling. That will make it legal, and you can keep the shilling. You agree?"

"Sure. I'll take her and we'll have flowers all over our house. Trish will be pleased, and flowers might make the wife smile."

"Francis, is there any way you can keep her presence here a secret? If Joseph knows, he will simply come for her."

"This complicates things."

"At least hide her until I can send Joseph away or find him a bride."

"We have several empty cabins scattered over the property. I'll have one cleaned and furnished. We can manage to keep her presence quiet until you take care of things at Durandeaux. Anything else?"

"Yes. One more thing. I need you to send a carriage for her tonight and I will see that she is put into it. Driver can bring her here to you in the dark of night. I do not want anyone at my place to know, especially Joseph. For that I will be happy to pay …the time and work of your driver."

Francis quietly studied Marcus. He knew beyond a doubt that the man was up to something deeper and darker, but did not think it wise to ask, at least not now. There was simply too much mystery involved.

"What time do you want my driver there?"

"Ten o'clock too late?"

"Ten o'clock it will be. I'll tell him to park outside the gate, not inside. You can bring her there. Anything else?"

"No. Just know that if you ever need me for a favor, do not hesitate to ask."

"Do not worry," replied Francis. "You will be the first I will ask."

"I'll be off now. I must get home. Thank you, Francis."

Francis went out and stood while Marcus took the reins, mounted his bay, and trotted through the gate. Francis waited until he was out of sight before turning and slowly walking back to his house, more convinced than ever that something important had not been shared. Taking the girl under cover of darkness and placing her in hiding? Strange behavior even for Marcus. Whatever the source of the mystery, he would discover it eventually. He only hoped that the girl would not cause trouble in his household. He did not like trouble. Throughout all his life he had strived for peace and contentment.

CHAPTER 11

To the relief of those who sat at table, supper at the Durandeaux mansion was finished. Those not privy to the reason for the undercurrent of tension felt out of sorts. Those few who knew went about their tasks or quietly pushed back their chairs and left the table. Tabitha helped Jolly to clear away plates and cutlery. She removed the cloth and took it to the kitchen door. Accustomed to this tradition, at least a dozen hens, some with broods of chicks, came running to scramble for the crumbs that fell from the large cloth. Folding the tablecloth Tabitha watched the commotion and listened to the squawking hens with amusement until they had cleaned the dirt of their evening treat. Finished with her chores, she walked down the back steps onto the yard. The flock of hens, thinking that she had more treats, surrounded her. She waded through them and walked to the edge of the cleared space surrounding the house. Just beyond that space lay the forest and swamp, a place of danger, a place where snakes, spiders, black bear, wild cat, alligator, and panther prowled for their sustenance. She could hear whip-poor-wills calling back and forth. Sleepy birds chirped as they settled for the night. The direction of the breeze changed, and she could smell the pungent aroma of the marsh that bordered the inlet where Master Marcus docked his ketch when in port. A sudden chill took her and, wrapping the tablecloth around her shoulders, she turned and ran back to the safety of the warm kitchen where she said goodnight to M'aum Sue and Jolly, who sat with tea and brandy for their hard day's work.

Tabitha climbed the stairs to the third floor and the room she shared with Jolly. She intended to get to sleep for Joseph had said they would go berry picking early. He wanted fresh berries with his breakfast porridge. She removed her dress, put on her night gown, and crawled into the wide double bed and was almost asleep when someone opened her door. Assuming it was Jolly finally come to bed, she threw back her covers to make room for her.

Tabitha felt a hand over her mouth, pressing her head into the pillow. Opening her eyes wide, she almost fainted for the person facing her was not her roommate. It was a strange man. He was dressed in black and wore a cap pulled low over his forehead. He quickly wrapped a long cloak around her shoulders and picked her up. She heard someone quietly caution her not to fight as she was whisked down the three flights of stairs, down the hall and out through a side door and into the pitch dark of night. She was too frightened to struggle, knowing that the result of defiance might be punishment. The man carrying her stopped and she heard muffled voices. A carriage door was opened, and the man thrust her inside. He quickly shut the door, the driver instantly snapped the whip, and the horses threw themselves into their harness.

Regardless of the care that Marcus took to keep the affair a secret, Bruneau, still awake and outside for a smoke, heard harness noises, doors closing, whispers. He sneaked closer to the road and hid. He saw the strange coach and Master Marcus standing at the brick wall that separated the manicured grounds from the wilderness road. He saw the strange man dressed in black and the bundle he held and thrust into the cab. He watched in alarm as the man entered the cab and the coachman drove away in haste until they were out of sight. As Marcus turned to go back into the house, Bruneau stepped out into the moonlight.

"Master Marcus, where did you send my daughter? You know with Cassie gone...she is all I got. You sell her?"

"Bruneau, you well know that Tabitha is not your daughter. She is mine. I am her father. When I gave Cassie to you to wed, she was carrying her. Now you see why Joseph and Tabitha...well...you must understand. Even if she were free and white, it would not work. Good night, Bruneau. Try to get some sleep. Tomorrow will bring trouble. I do not know what Joseph will do."

Bruneau was not the only one who had watched the ignoble deed unfold. Joseph had been in the garden looking to identify more stars and watching bats that came out at night to feed on mosquitoes and gnats. He had waited for Tabitha, hoping that she would join him. Only when he heard the same noises that Bruneau had heard did he leave the garden to investigate. He saw Bruneau and his father standing together and heard harsh whispers, and then he heard his father clearly say that Tabitha was not Bruneau's daughter, but his own. Shocked, bewildered at how this could be, Joseph ran haphazardly across the yard, into the house and up to the third floor where he found Tabitha's door open and her bed empty. Joseph knew then that his father had sent Tabitha away...sold her to strangers. He knew also that his father would never tell anyone where she went...to whose auction block she would go. His father's purpose was to separate him from his beloved Tabitha, and he would never see her again. The young man knew his father.

As the coach bounced on the dirt road at almost full speed, Tabitha's first thought, that Joseph was playing a trick on her, quickly changed to terror when the man who carried her did not laugh as Joseph would have done if he were playing. This man was not Joseph. On the long drive from Durandeaux she thought to open a door and throw herself out but knew that it would be too dangerous at their speed. For the first time she felt the truth of her situation; that she was a slave, a truth which she had heretofore been able to hide from her conscious mind. While accepting her helplessness, she endured the long drive, wondering where she was being taken and to what purpose.

After a drive that seemed to take forever, the coach stopped, and someone opened the door from outside. She was taken by someone and hustled across a yard and into a dark cabin. She heard a key turn in the lock from outside. She knew she was alone. In the dark, unfamiliar room, she could see only shadows of table and chairs and in a corner a bed. She could not see well enough to find candle or lamp. With no choice but to wait for daylight, she curled up on the lumpy bed and waited...so frightened that she could not sleep.

Joseph left the house in a daze and wandered about in the dark all night, muttering, and cursing his father's cruelty. Gone were his thoughts of forgiveness and righteousness. He was simply a young and passionate man who had lost the love of his life. He knew that he would never see Tabitha again and he hated his father for it. His heart torn into shreds, he walked aimlessly until sun-up, when he found himself at the river's edge. Tied up at the landing was Old John's rowboat. He loosened the boat from its mooring, pushed it out into the water and quickly climbed in. Picking up the oars, he rowed a distance into the wide expanse of the river and then tossed the oars over the side. The distance was too far to swim back to the riverbank fully dressed and he well knew that. Without hesitation and in a mental state of darkest despair, Joseph let himself over the side and pushed the boat away. The current immediately caught it and carried it downstream. He turned over on his back and let the strong current take him toward the sea. He floated until his wet clothes began to drag him down. He allowed the brackish water to flow over him and envelope him as he went deeper into the black depths until peace came. In his last moments of consciousness, he saw Tabitha's smile, heard her laughter and then he was gone.

Joseph had not thought of the small cabin set back from the river's edge. Nor did he see Old John D standing on his tiny porch holding his fishing pole, with his coon hound at his side. He did not know that the old man had seen his every move. But the old man was crippled with age, he lived alone, and Lacey would not come with his monthly supplies for another week. Joseph didn't hear when Old John sighed deeply and said a prayer accompanied by the mournful sound of the hound's baying: "Fo'give him Gawd cause dat boy he ain't knowin' what he doin'. I needs to tell folk at de house but dese old legs ain't gonna git me nowhere. Lawdy mussy when Lacey comin'?"

The old man, called Old John D by everyone who knew him, was a Durandeaux slave from the days of Marcus' father, Guillaume Durandeaux. Now ancient and crippled with gout, he lived his retirement in a cabin on plantation land, close to the river's edge. Except for Lacey driving a wagon each month loaded with a month's supply of flour, rice, cornmeal, molasses, lard, tea, and a boy to cut his firewood, he lived off the land. Fish and crab from the river, squirrel and rabbit and coon from the swamp kept him and his hound busy and well-fed.

That morning Old John had left his cabin with his hound and fishing pole to hobble the short distance to the rowboat. He was about to step off the porch when he spied the boat already out in the middle of the river. He watched in disbelief and fear when a man, fully clothed, stood up and then let himself over the side. Old John D's fear increased when he saw the man push the boat away, making clear his intention. Realizing this, the old slave became so disoriented that he dropped his pole and hobbled as fast as he could back to his cabin, his hound baying at the excitement. He had just seen a man intent on suicide, an evil, evil thing, and there was absolutely nothing he could do to stop it. And not only a suicide; the man had sent Old John D's boat downstream.

John knew the aftermath of suicide. First, the word could not be spoken. His name could not be spoken. That person now belonged to the Devil. Heaven would not accept him. He could not be buried in hallowed ground. Family would disown him. All records and all mention of him would be wiped away. No one who feared God and his punishments would speak of him ever again and his body would be buried where no one would ever find it. Nevertheless, Old John D knew that he had to tell someone and the only one he could tell would be Lacey. He legs would never take him as far as the big house. He would have to wait until she came with his supplies. He would have to eat his cornbread without fried mullet today. The frightened man closed his doors and

61

shutters hoping that the suicide's soul, which now belonged to the Devil, did not come in to harm him.

CHAPTER 12

After that brutal night Marcus remained quiet at the breakfast table as a sullen Bruneau directed the serving maids in their morning task. Cecily, always aware of her husband's shifting moods, noted that he frowned more than usual but she knew not to mention it. George, his wife, Margaret, and son, Lewis, and Charles ate hungrily but Julia said not a word as she observed everyone. Having grown up in a home with only her father and a couple of servants, this great gathering of family at each meal was new to her. Already she sensed an undercurrent of personality conflicts and behaviors. It would amuse her to try and understand the connections, the problems, the issues with which they all struggled.

Cecily noted Julia's expression and wondered if Charles had again annoyed her. Then she realized that Joseph had not come down and felt that it was a suitable subject to break the silence and her feeling of unease.

"Anyone seen Joseph this morning?"

No one replied and Cecily continued, "He seemed well at supper. I hope he feels well."

"He may have been out late watching bats, Mother Cecily," offered George with amusement, hoping to lighten the atmosphere.

"Have you seen him, Charles?" asked Cecily.

"He mentioned berry picking yesterday."

"Sleeping in, I suppose," countered Julia, and then she added with a sly, suggestive smile, "I haven't seen Tabitha yet either."

"Julia, eat your breakfast and don't imply things about which you know nothing. Speak when you are spoken to," came the sharp admonition from Marcus, her future father-in-law.

Julia lowered her head to hide her sudden tears and then pushed her chair back and ran from the table.

"Papa, did you have to do that?" asked Charles as he stood to go after his fiancé and comfort her. "She is already unhappy here! Don't undo all my efforts to make her feel at home."

"You are in a tiff this morning, aren't you, Husband!"

With that unexpected remark from Cecily, Marcus had enough and left the table, his plate still full of food. George, Margaret and Louis, remained at the table with Cecily to finish their food in silence. One by one they went about their daily callings and duties and left foul-tempered Marcus alone.

Lacey had waited for the chance to speak with Bruneau and as soon as her mistress finished her tea, she motioned to the butler to follow her from the dining room. They both went through the kitchen and stepped outside onto the back porch. Lacey looked up at Bruneau and voiced her opinion.

"Something going on, Bruneau. What is it? Mastah in a fit and both Mastah Joseph and your gal not here for breakfast. Who know where they is? You know something I don't know?"

"Woman, keep your mouth shut. Don't go messin' 'round with things you got no business knowin', like Mastah told Miss Julia. Do your work and let Mastah handle what comes. Nothing we can do...you and me."

Bruno turned quickly but not before she saw his tears. He left Lacey standing and went outside to find a place where he could cry and scream and curse Marcus Durandeaux. Marcus had taken away his daughter twice: once in reminding him that she was not his own daughter, a fact that Bruneau had almost managed to forget, and then for sending her away. Bruneau felt doubly injured and vowed that someday he would take his revenge. If it were true that God was punishing him for something his ancestors did, and if he could not take revenge on Marcus, he would take revenge on God.

Bruneau never knew if the Bible was correct or not where it was written about how God punished sons of Ham to wipe out the sins of their fathers. Bruneau never understood it and never accepted it, but he had to acknowledge that he must be a son of Ham. He was a slave because his parents were slaves, and if he tried to...there his thoughts ceased because he knew the futility of it all. He wondered how many generations it would take to wipe away all those sins of their fathers. Meanwhile, he accepted his fate and never attempted to run. Where would he go? He had never been to Africa and simply was not brave enough to suffer the penalty of being caught and punished. He had to admit that he had a comfortable life where he was and most likely would not find a better place even if he did escape.

His mind turned to Joseph...wondering where he might be and getting a sick feeling. Had Joseph watched as he himself had, in the dark, when Tabitha had been taken away? Joseph would not wish to live without Tabitha. Bruneau knew that deep in his soul, but he would never, ever express that to anyone.

The morning passed and no one mentioned Joseph, although some wondered where Tabitha might be. Midday came and still the two missing had not shown themselves. One by one, the adults began to fear that something dreadful had happened. Supper time came and while sitting the table, Louis poked his father and asked permission to speak.

"Go ahead, Louis. What do you have to say to us?" asked George.

"Papa, there is a rowboat at the river. Sometimes I go fishing with Joseph and Tabitha. We catch mullet and perch and get big blue crabs off the dock. M'aum Sue knows because Uncle Joseph gives her the catch."

"Are you suggesting that Joseph and Tabitha went fishing?" asked George. "That's a long time to sit with a pole in the river."

"Something may have happened?" asked Cecily. "Send someone to the river and see if the boat is still tied up. Can we do that?"

"I'll go myself," said Marcus, now extremely worried about his missing son.

"I go with you, Mastah Marcus?" asked Bruneau. "You might need some help."

Marcus studied the butler, feeling animosity coming in waves from the man, but he replied, "Yes, you come. Have the buggy hitched. We may have to drive down our side of the river for a way."

"Can't go no further than a mile or so. Swamp takes over and trees all the way to the riverbank."

"Isn't there a ferry station?" asked Marcus, who seldom traveled by land.

"It's upriver from our boat landing. Where the big road between us and Battailes goes down to the river."

"Let's go."

On the drive to the river Marcus and Bruneau remain silent, neither wishing to begin a conversation that might lead to harsh words. Both knew that life was not fair. Some flowers reach for the heavens and find sunlight. Others find themselves seeded under wide rocks and beat their heads on the hard surface until they give up, shrink, and die.

"We should have seen this coming, Bruneau."

"We should have."

"You think maybe Joseph saw the same as you? You think he knows that I sent her away?"

"If I saw it, he might have. He out a lot at night. Like Mastah George said. "Lookin' for stars. Watchin' bats fly.""

Marcus gave him a long look before saying, "You know I sent her to a good place. She will be taken care of. It's a good family. Maybe she will find a young man and marry and be happy."

"I reckon you did."

"Did my son really love her?"

"If that wasn't love between them two, I don't know what love is. It was a good love. A pure love. I saw how your son looked at her and took care of her. I never feared that he would hurt her."

"But you know...Cassie explained to you...told you..."

"Yes, Mastah, I know. But I never knew that Cassie was carrying when you let me marry her. She never let on until Tabitha came. Then she told me. Said she wanted me to trust her to be honest with her. I know that Tabitha your daughter since she came."

"I knew I could trust you," replied Marcus.

Bruneau withheld the fact that Cassie had never allowed him intimacy. He doubted that the master would believe him, and if he did, it would only swell the man's ego. Let him think that he had Cassie as well.

The same realization occurred to each of the men as they rode together on the buggy: they were talking to each other as equals, as two men with a problem. Speaking of Tabitha sparked a bit of tenderness in both their souls, but their brief spell of camaraderie only served to give importance to their vastly different status. That one owned the body of the other was suddenly unspeakable. Equally embarrassed, they grew quiet as the river came into view.

"Boat not tied up at the landing. John D must be out fishin'. You want I drive down the bank as far as we can, Mastah?"

Suddenly the word irritated Marcus. Annoyed, he turned on Bruneau, "Why do you call me Master?"

"What else I gonna call you? That is what you are. I can't call you by your name."

Chagrinned, Marcus realized that he was unreasonably taking his fear and anger out on Bruneau.

"Right about now, you could call me...never mind."

A tiny bit of a smile quivered at the corner of Bruneau's mouth, but it quickly vanished when Marcus said his next words and expressed his greatest fear.

"You think Joseph would go out there in the river and go off the boat? Do you think that he would do that terrible thing to us?"

Bruneau wanted to say what a terrible thing Marcus had done to Tabitha and Joseph. Instead, he said, "That a terrible thought. He might have rowed to the other side. He might have gone to the city and we don't know yet that he came here."

"There's that."

"We can ask Old John D," suggested Bruneau.

"He still alive? He lives out here?"

"Got a cabin set back from the river. Lacey comes ever month to bring him supplies."

"Well, go ask him if he saw anything."

"He most likely got the boat out fishin' but I'll go see."

Marcus waited while Bruneau left the rig and walked back to the cabin which was half hidden by tall bushes and shrubs covered with honeysuckle vines. He knocked on the door and Old John D's hound dog came from around the back baying lazily.

"Old John not to home?" Bruneau asked the hound.

Back at the rig, Bruneau told Marcus what he believed to be the case; that Old John had the boat out on the river.

"Mastah Joseph might still be around somewhere. Don't think the worst until ain't nothin' else. Let's go home. We'll get the word out that he is missin'. Tell Sheriff Williams to get men out lookin'. They'll find him or he'll come home. He out just broodin' now, I think."

Soon after Marcus and Bruneau left the river, Old John opened the door to the outhouse which sat a way back from his cabin and stepped out, pulling up his trousers and pulling his suspenders up over his shoulders. He reached down and scratched his hound's ears and asked, "What you howling 'bout, you old coot? You smell a 'coon?"

A storm hit Marcus when he and Bruneau returned to the mansion. The storm was Cecily. As soon as he entered the house, she accosted him.

"Where is my son? Did you find him?"

Marcus was in no mood for hysterics and called loudly for Lacey to come.

"Take your mistress to her room and give her a spoon of laudanum. I can't have her screaming at me all day."

Cecily futilely hit out at Marcus and screamed, "I won't go anywhere until you tell me what is going on, Marcus Durandeaux! I have a right to know where my son is. I have..."

Lacy came quickly and placed an arm around the hysterical woman's shoulders. She led her, still screaming at Marcus, up the stairs to her room.

"Damn it!" exclaimed Marcus as Bruneau stood by.

"It will get worse, Mastah. You sure you did the right thing?"

The look that Marcus gave Bruneau was a warning that he should back off. Their brief bit of manly camaraderie was long gone. Bruneau knew that he had come close to committing the unforgivable, improper behavior from a slave to his master, but he had at least said what he wanted to say. He went about his work, leaving Marcus to face the aftermath of his own doing. Bruneau would miss Tabitha, but still felt pain that he had been used as a scapegoat for Marcus Durandeaux's philandering with his slave women. Bruneau had long ago judged his master and could not look upon Marcus with any sort of respect for a man who earned his wealth and more, by buying and selling men, women, and children.

CHAPTER 13

Morning brought enough sunlight through the cracks under the door and through the edge of the shutters for Tabitha to see the inside of the cabin. She left the bed and tried the door. Still locked. She tried the shutters, but they were also locked from the outside. She looked around the cabin. Small fireplace with iron hook for kettle. Small table and two chairs. A shelf for tin plates and cups. A coffee-pot. A brush broom. Although freshly swept the place felt as though no one had lived here for a long while.

Tabitha was hungry and thirsty and wondered when someone would come and who would it be. She lay back down on the bed and had not long to wait when she heard a key in the lock and the door opened. An old black woman entered. She carried a basket in one hand and a jug of water in the other. She set them both on the table.

"I'm Bessie. I brung you food and some wawta. Soon's Trouble come he can chop me some wood so I can cook. Can't cook wid no wood. Mastah Francis, he say you stay heah. He busy all day and come see you afta his suppa. He don't want you outside, you heah? You keep yo' nose inside and don't make him mad."

Tabitha then knew where she was, but not the why or way of it. Master Francis could only mean Francis Battailes. The man must have bought her from Marcus Durandeaux but why the secrecy? Why the wild night ride? And then she knew. Surely Joseph did not know what his father had done. She must be sold and sent away in secret for the father would not wish to face his son's wrath.

Bessie departed without another word and Tabitha heard the click when the old woman locked the door. Hungry, she looked in the basket and found two cold biscuits filled with ham and two boiled eggs; enough to last all day. She felt relief that, at least, she would be fed, although what else would happen, she had no idea. Would she stay here, or was this only a stopover before she would be sent farther away? She sat down to eat. Her hunger satisfied she lay down again. There was nothing she could do but wait. Soon she slept again.

Francis Battailes, tired from the hours he had ridden his fields, stopped for the day. With little daylight remaining, he rode into the stable yard and halted his aged chestnut gelding. He wished for his son, Amos, to return from Charles Town, for at fifty-seven years, he was simply too old for so much work. He was about to dismount and then remembered that he had one more errand. Before he could go home, remove his boots, eat his supper, and go to his bed he must visit the cabin where he knew the slave girl had been taken. He wondered what aberration of mind had caused him to agree to taking a young female slave trouble maker on his hands. He turned his gelding away from the stable and entered the road that led to the rear of the big house and the near cabins, still wondering why he had allowed himself to be involved in this nasty business. He always prided himself on keeping out of the affairs of others and keeping his slate clean of worries. How had he allowed Marcus to talk him into this? Would he send the woman to Trish for work in the house or would she go to the field quarters?

Twilight had come and with it came the night noises: crickets chirping, frogs croaking, Mockingbirds singing to claim their spot and settling for the evening. He allowed the gelding, as tired as himself, to walk quietly until they came to the isolated cabin behind. He dismounted and left the reins hanging to the ground, knowing the horse would not take a step. He walked to the door and gently knocked. If Bessie were here, she would hear and open the door. If not, he had a key on his keyring. He was anxious to get a look at the young woman who had caused so much trouble to the Durandeaux. When no answer came to his knock he reached into his pocket and pulled out his ring of keys, looking for the key that matched this door. He had not used it for years, but it was there. He put the key into the lock and turned it. The door opened of itself. He stepped inside the dim interior and looked around. His eyes went to the bed in the far corner, and he saw the girl who lay sleeping, the quilt pushed to the bottom of the bed. He walked closer and studied her.

Small body, her lower legs and bare feet exposed, she lay on her back with one arm outstretched and the other behind her head with her face turned to the wall. She still wore the nightgown that she had worn when suddenly taken from her room. Not since Cecily had married and left home had Francis seen someone so vulnerable and who looked so innocent.

"My, oh, my," he whispered. "A real beauty. Now I know why he sent her away."

Tabitha, half asleep and about to awaken, sensed that she was not alone. She opened her eyes to see a man standing at the foot of her bed. She sat up, frightened, and quickly pulled the quilt over herself.

"Don't be frightened, Tabitha," said Francis softly. "I know the way you were brought here must have been terrifying, but it was the order of Marcus Durandeaux. No one will harm you here."

"I want to go home," she said clearly, not even understanding what he had said.

"Well, you do speak well. He said you had been taught with his son."

"I want to go home," she repeated, becoming more frightened.

"This is your new home, Tabitha, and you will live here. Your Master Marcus sent you to me."

"Did Master Marcus sell me to you?"

"In a way, he did. For only one shilling but the agreement is that you will remain here at my plantation."

"Why? Why did he sell me for so little?"

"You must have some idea, Tabitha. Think it over for a while. Now I must leave you to Bessie. She will come every day to see that you have what you need. I will visit you again. Now I am tired and hungry. Is there anything you want to ask before I leave?"

"I believe this is a prank played on me by Joseph. Will you tell him that he is not funny? How did he get you to play with him? Is Master Marcus a party to it?"

"Tabitha, this is no prank. Marcus wanted you away from Joseph. You are never to see him again. Your master's orders. Joseph will be sent away to seminary and his father will find him a wife."

"All this is not in fun? You mean what you say?"

"Yes. I know this must be difficult for you as it was for me when your master asked me to take you. You have been sold away to protect Joseph and their family. Marcus was kind enough to send you here and not put you on the block. Be thankful for that. I agreed to keep you here on this plantation. I must leave you now. Ask Bessie for anything you need. She will be here every day."

Francis Battailes left the little cabin and his new slave with strange feelings. He had been exhausted and now he felt renewed energy; however, his heart fluttered, and his knees felt weak. He thought that he had ridden too long in the hot sun and had overtired himself. Best get his supper and to bed and to rest. Amos would be home from the city soon.

Francis lay in his bed wanting to sleep, but sleep played tag with his mind. Instead of the usual quiet and peaceful rest he enjoyed after a hard day's work and a hot meal, tonight he tossed and turned in his bed. Try as he might he could not rid himself of the memory of Tabitha lying on her bed, all youthful beauty, innocence, and guilelessness. He was further surprised to feel heat is his loins, a feeling from his youth that he had lost long ago and believed he had lost forever. He questioned what that encounter with Tabitha had done to him. He considered himself to be a kind and good man, but within his manhood lay possibilities of which he had forgotten. He clearly recalled her face, her body, and her soft and gentle voice, replete with fear and doubt. He finally fell asleep, a troubled sleep with feelings of guilt and desire arguing with each other for dominance in his dreams.

The following morning and throughout the day, as Francis went about his tasks, he was thoroughly intrigued by his continued feelings and desires. The vision of Tabitha would not depart from his mind. He felt as he had felt in his younger years, before he had been emotionally castrated by his cold, dry, wife. He completely understood a man's attraction to her, and the reason Marcus had sent her away. Francis also asked himself why Marcus had not kept her for himself in an out-of-the-way place. He answered his own question by presuming that Marcus *had* done as he wished and had only sent her away to keep her from Joseph. Francis was aware that his son-in-law did indulge his baser nature with whom he pleased. Slaves talk and female slaves talk even more. Knowing all that did not help Francis. It only made his desire the more uncomfortable.

The next evening Francis removed his dirty boots as usual and left them on the kitchen porch. On his way through the kitchen, he encountered Bessie.

"Mastah, kin I axe you some questions?"

"Of course, Bessie. What?"

"You got anything to tell me 'bout that gal? What you gonna do with her? She do housework or field work? Where she come from? Where she belong? Why I gotta mind her? She skin and bone. Don't hardly eat nothin'. She gonna dry up and blow away. 'Sides, I'm wore out runnin' back and forth from dat cabin to heah and back again carryin' food and stuff."

"Bessie, you are to care for her as long as I say. Trouble can drive you there and back. He can chop wood and bring water. No one else is to go in and she does not come out unless I am there. You cook for her and clean for her. Do her laundry like you would your mistress. Take her whatever she asks you bring to her. Everything but freedom. She belongs to me and me alone. Do you understand?"

With a knowing look and in total shock at the strength of his words, Bessie replied, "Yes, Mastah Francis. I do. I do indeed."

Bessie was not the only one who questioned his words and even his sanity. Francis, himself, wondered from where those words had come.

During the next few evenings Francis avoided seeing Tabitha, leaving her care to Bessie and Trouble. By day he worked but while riding his fields he allowed his imagination to roam. He envisioned evenings where he and the girl could innocently walk forest paths in the summertime and sit by the fire in winter. Remembering that Marcus had said she was well educated, he imagined conversations about current events, discussions about books, and things he could teach her. He had thoughts of companionship that been denied him for all these years. He thought that he might even take his meals with her. With Amos returning any day from Charles Town, he would not need to work so long and hard. He would have more time to relax, and he might enjoy such imagined, pleasant evenings with Tabitha.

CHAPTER 14

Marcus and Bruneau kept the terrible suspicion concerning Joseph's disappearance between them. It was a burning torch for both and demanded that each hold his tongue and temper when conversation came to either of the missing young people. The rest of the family suffered as more days passed with no sign of either Joseph or Tabitha. Searchers ceased to comb the woods and swamp for bodies and returned to their farms. No one raised questions for there were no answers.

Marcus was not one to allow himself a range of feelings; rather, he thought that a display of any emotion other than anger to be ridiculous and useless. He considered a nuisance and vulgar those who displayed all their sentiments. Nevertheless, faced with his recent actions and the fall-out, he felt exhausted due to the pain and turmoil demonstrated among others in the family and household. Not willing to bear more, he sought peace in the sanctuary of his study. He placed his forearms on his desk, laid his head down and closed his eyes.

Whatever agony he might have felt, he pressed down deep inside. He wanted the throbbing in his head to cease. He wanted to not hear Cecily's sobs. He wished he had never gone to the river with Bruneau, for now Bruneau saw him more as a man and less as a master. He questioned how he could bring peace back to his home, especially to himself. When he heard the knock on his door he shouted, "Go away! I don't want to talk with anyone. See to yourselves."

"Father, it is I, Charles, and I must speak with you," declared his son as he opened the door without permission.

Charles entered the room, which to him had always felt the way a coffin would be. Everything solid, unbreakable. Oak for walls, oak for his father's gigantic desk, chairs, and tables...nothing at all light or insubstantial. Even the drapes were made of dark, heavy satin and the two vases on the mantle over the fireplace were blown from dark, thick amber colored glass. He remembered his father telling him how his grandfather had brought those vases from Nantes to England and then to the Colony. This room was made of the stuff that would last for generations and had always made him feel insecure and insignificant rather than protected, just as his father had made him feel.

"I don't want to talk with you or anyone," said Marcus. "I am tired, and my head is roaring! Now go away and leave me alone."

"No, Father."

Marcus looked up wearily at his son. "Is this a sit conversation or will you stand," he asked.

"I better sit. It's about Julia. We must address the way you spoke to her. You were rude and hurtful. She is heartbroken. Has been in tears and I want you to apologize."

"You choose now of all times to show courage, Son?"

"Yes, Father. I am to be a husband and I must defend my bride-to-be. You have already frightened the poor girl half to death."

"I doubt if I could frighten that young harridan half-way to anywhere! You want me to apologize to her? It will never happen," retorted Marcus, raising his voice.

"Then you must allow me to leave with her and live in Charles Town with her father."

"I must what?" Marcus asked, even louder.

"You heard me, Father. Julia said that if you will not apologize to her and promise to treat her with the respect she deserves from now on, we will live with her father."

"Julia says? And you agree with her?"

"I do, Sir. I certainly do."

"Then pack your trunks and take your spoiled brat of a fiancé to her papa and live happily ever after! You both will see that the Perrins depend on me for their bread and tea and at any time I can direct that effort elsewhere."

"I have no idea what you mean. Julia said that her father is a wealthy man in his own right. Very well, Julia and I will prepare to leave and soon we will be surrounded by luxury in a townhouse in the city where there are pleasures to be had for a young couple. Julia has told me all about what we are missing. We will wed in Charles Town. Will you come?"

"Leave me alone, Charles. Just leave me alone."

When Charles left him alone again, Marcus mused on the new development. From the beginning he had been inclined to annoyance with Julia, which led him to having already considered the advantage of having his son living in town. He had been unsure of how Charles would take the idea but he certainly could be of more use to their business there than here on the plantation. Marcus had often wondered if he could trust Perrin as much as he did. Was the man doing anything untoward in their joint endeavors that may harm the Durandeaux? With Charles living under his nose, seeing who comes and goes and then reporting to his father, Marcus would be in a more securer position in their partnership. He decided to be as helpful as he could with his son's venture. He would make it serve his own purpose and given the circumstances, the move would tempt Charles to settle down and pay more attention to the earning of money rather than the spending of it.

Julia knew that her attitude since she had arrived at the plantation had only served to raise tension in the household and to increase Marcus' irritability. Determined to return to the city, she had whined and pouted until she declared that it was the only way she would agree to marry Charles. Charles had begun to feel lucky to have such an attractive young bride, and not willing to lose her, agreed. He relayed to her his conversation with his father and that he agreed to allow them to move to the city. She wrote to her father that Marcus would allow them to live in Charles Town and awaited her father's reply.

Jasper Perrin read the letter with relish. He had wished for this marriage but had missed his daughter more than he had expected. He also wanted to maintain his business relationship with Marcus Durandeaux and for her to bring Charles to the city was the best way he could imagine to maintain the business and familial connection. This match between his daughter and Charles had been a long time coming and difficult to achieve. Jasper knew his daughter quite well and, not certain if Marcus had willingly consented, and hesitant to offend Marcus, he wrote to Julia asking her to relent and to accept her obligation. He received a reply from Marcus, himself, saying that he gave his blessing to the move and that Charles was to be involved in their joint endeavors. He was to be given responsibility for keeping account ledgers on certain elements of their trading transactions.

Julia lost no time in getting herself and Charles to the city and the Durandeaux household were not unhappy to see her go. At least, while she made her new husband unhappy, Marcus would not have to be a witness nor to be a referee. Cecily was relieved that the couple would marry in the city and the responsibilities for the festivities would fall to Jasper, for Cecily wished to devote all her energy to efforts to finding her son. Not knowing what had happened with Joseph and Tabitha had driven her to the brink.

CHAPTER 15

Lacey's kitchen calendar marked the days since she had delivered supplies to Old John D. The time for a new delivery had come. While she busied herself filling sacks with flour and corn meal, cannisters with tea, a jug with molasses, and a can with lard, Dubie and Reg came in through the rear.

"Miz Lacey, can me and Dubie go down to the quawtas and go fishin?"

"You done finish your chores?"

"Yes'm. I done swept de porch and Dubie slopped the sow and pigs."

"You sweep steps too or just the porch?"

"All steps got swept. Can we go?"

"You leave the sweepin's on the ground right off the steps or did you rake 'em off side?"

"We lef' 'em on de groun', but we'll rake 'em off."

"Well, I gonna take Old John D his supplies. You wanna go ride the wagon with me or go fishin'?"

"Naw, Ma'am. We went with you last time. Today we promised to go fishin' with Rudy and Jug. We bring M'aum Sue some mullet."

"Well, guess I'll have to drive out there all by myself," Lacey said with a pout.

"Ole John got moonshine, Ma'am. You come home happy?"

"Git on with you! You got no manners a'tall. "Fo' I come back you get that rakin' done!"

Reg and Dubie ran toward the field quarters where they would spend the bigger part of the day. Lacey loaded the sacks and cannisters and tub of lard onto the wagon all by herself. She hitched the mare and started her drive to the riverside cabin, singing gospel songs while the mare plodded along. It was a pleasant drive. The sun was out but not too strong. The air smelled of brackish water and marshes that she loved. She was well, she had a stomach full of food, a warm bed at night and pleasant work to keep her busy. She was respected as a member of the household. As such, considering all her blessings, she felt better off than poor young Charles, who would marry a woman who didn't love him; one who was only obeying her father as he was obeying his. Lacey sang louder to emphasize her contentment with her lot in life.

While she drove the wagon, she looked forward to sitting a while, sipping moonshine, and listening while Old John D told her stories from the days when he was butler for Marcus' father. When the old master had passed away, Marcus, knowing how much his father and the old butler cared for each other, and in a rare show of generosity, had given Old John his choice. He could retire to his old cabin in the house quarters and spend his days as he wished, or Marcus would have a place built for him on the river's edge. Old John, full of gratitude, chose the cabin by the river for that is where he had spent all his free time when younger. He had lived on the river, alone, for near to ten years since he retired from work. No one knew how old he was, how he had lived so long, or how he had remained so healthy, except for his old bones aching. He said it was due to living in solitude and Lacey thought he might be onto something.

"Some peoples got it worse. I sho' wouldn't want to be Miz Cecily," she said aloud as the mare, by now accustomed to their monthly drive, stopped at Old John's cabin. As soon as the mare halted and Lacey struggled to get off the seat and down to the ground, she heard a hoarse shout coming from the cabin. She turned to see Old John hobbling out with his cane.

"'Bout time you come," he shouted as loudly as he could. "I been waitin'."

"You done et all that food I brung last time?"

"Naw. Not 'bout food. 'Bout dat damn fool man I seen. Been wantin' to tell somebody, but no body come and nobody to tell."

"What fool man? Somebody been bothering you? You want I should send one of the younguns to stay here with you? I kin send Dubie and Reg."

"Naw, Woman. It dat man what took my boat out to de middle of de riba, and I seen him get out and shove dat boat away. I seen it!"

"When you see that, old man? When?"

"Dunno. Days past. Maybe week or mo'. But I seen it."

"You see who it was?"

"Naw, Woman. I can't see far. You know?"

"You telling me that a man just rowed out in the water all by hisself? You know what you sayin', Old Man? You sayin' somethin' awful."

"I seen him," insisted the old man.

"Let me get these bags inside. Then I must get on back home. I got to tell Bruneau what you said. He won't like it."

"You ain't gonna set a while? I got co'n likker from de ferryman. He come and brung it and set a while back."

"Naw, Old John. Not dis time. I come again soon. Best I get home and tell what you said."

"Bruneau, I got something to tell you," Lacey whispered when she arrived back at the mansion and located the butler.

"What is it? You been to Old John's?"

"I scared to say. It's bad. Real bad."

"Lacy, what is it? Can't be that bad."

"Bruneau, it what Old John D said he saw."

"You took his supplies?"

"Just got back."

"So, what did the old man see?"

"You might sit while I tell you."

"That bad, Lacey? Alright, I'll sit. Now say it!"

"Well, Old John saw a man step off his rowboat in the river and push the boat away and he never come up. That is what he told me he saw."

Bruneau stared at Lacey for what seemed like an eternity as the image stuck in his mind...a man stepping of a boat in the middle of the river and not coming up.

"When?"

"Ole John said he ain't sure, but days. He don't know how many. You know Ole John, he lose track of time."

"Me and Mastah, we went out there. Old John not to home and boat gone...we figgered he out fishin'."

"We have to tell Mastah."

"I don't know what Miz Cecily gonna do. Just don't know. Where Mastah now? You know?"

"Said had business to do today. Said he'd be home before supper. He rode out early."

"We can't tell Miz Cecily. He have to do that."

"We better have Doc here when he tells her. I'll send a rider."

Marcus returned home before supper. His clothes and boots soiled and rank with the smell of swamp, he came in by the rear door. He removed his boots and hung his jacket on the hook and entered the kitchen in his stocking feet. Marcus immediately felt the tension in the cook's expression.

"Something wrong, M'aum Sue?" he asked.

"Mastah, you gotta go talk wid Lacey and Bruneau. Right now," she replied, nodding her head.

Marcus felt adrenaline well up and he felt dizzy. It could only be news about Joseph. As he left the kitchen and walked into the hallway, he saw Bruneau and Lacey coming toward him.

"You have news about Joseph."

"Maybe, Suh. But it ain't good."

"And it might not be him," added Lacey.

"What have you heard?"

"Lacey, you tell him. You heard it."

Lacey proceeded to tell Marcus what Old John D had told her. While she spoke, Marcus remained silent, listening carefully.

"You sure that's what he said he saw?" asked Marcus, his only reactions were more furrow to his brow and a darkening of expression.

"Yes, Mastah Marcus. That's what he saw. Now they ain't no way to prove he saw Mastah Joseph!"

"It had to be. Who else at that time and that place?"

"Mastah, we already know Miz Cecily gonna need de doctor, so we sent a boy to tell him to come," said Bruneau. "He be here soon."

"Good thinking Bruneau. Yes, she will need her doctor. We will wait for him before we tell her."

"You tell me what you want us to do."

"I need to change now. I helped to round up cattle from the swamp today."

Although Bruneau well knew that his master would never stoop to rounding up cattle in the swamp, he said nothing. Dubie and Reg had already come home telling how, while fishing at the inlet, they saw the master boarding his ketch which then sailed out of the inlet into the bay and then returned a while after.

"Yes, Suh," said Bruneau, wondering why the master had lied.

It fell to Marcus to inform George and Charles what Lacey had learned from John D. After he had related what he knew, George asked only one question.

"He saw a man go in the river and not come up?" George repeated as though he either could not believe or did not want to.

"That's what he said. He saw the man push the boat away."

"You believe him?"

"I do," replied Marcus. "John is old but still has his wits."

"If it is true, that is an absolute horror," said Charles.

"Yes."

"Did he see a girl with that man?" asked George

"No. No mention of a girl."

"So, Tabitha didn't run off with Joseph."

"Seems that she didn't," replied Marcus.

"Does Mother Cecily know?" asked Charles.

"Not yet. We sent for Doc Scott. We will tell her when he is here to care for her."

"Wise," commented George. "She will not take this easily. Joseph and Tabitha were her life."

Not a soul in the household doubted that the man who went into the river and pushed the boat away was Joseph.

After seeing to the care of his horse and cart, Doctor Scott came into the house with George, who had heard his arrival and had gone to meet him.

"You will want to speak with Father," said George.

"This is something very serious? Can you say what? Your messenger only said that had to come to see about Miz Cecily."

"My father should tell you."

"Then I will speak with Marcus in private before I see Cecily."

"Let's get this over with," said Marcus to the doc. "The study?"

"Good as any," replied Marcus, leading the way.

Once sitting together Scott began, "What is the situation?"

"You know that Joseph is missing? My youngest son?"

"I am aware. You have never found him?"

"Not found him, but perhaps we know what happened. An old, retired retainer lives at the river. We take care of him. Lacey drove to his place today to deliver his supplies and he told her that he saw a man step off his own rowboat in the middle of the river. The man did not come up. We all think that the man in the boat most likely was my son. Can you imagine, Doc? Do I have to spell it out?"

"He had cause?"

"He thought he did."

"Is it the worse? His body found?"

"No. It is better this way."

Scott remained silent while he thought of the proper words to say and then asked the obvious, "Anyone else see him?"

"I think not. Only Old John."

"You believe him?"

"I do. He is not given to tall tales. My father's old personal servant."

"Your son had enough reason?" Doc repeated.

"You had to know Joseph. He did or thought he did."

"Care to explain?"

"No. That is private and it is not necessary for Cecily to know what I just told you. I merely want you to be here when we tell her that Joseph will not come home. With all that means, with no body for her to bury and mourn over, she will lose her mind. What should I say to her?"

"You must tell her the whole truth just as you told me. Nothing else for it. Shall we go up?"

The two men climbed the stairs and knocked gently on Cecily's door. Jolly, who had been sitting with her, answered and opened the door for them to enter. Marcus sent Jolly away.

"Doctor Scott here? Is someone ill?" Cecily asked.

"Cecily, Marcus has something to tell you and we know it will disturb you. I am here for you," said Scott gently.

She sat up in bed, alarmed and wary. What is it? Have you found Joseph? Is he hurt?"

"Joseph will not be coming home, Cecily," said Marcus. "He is gone."

"What do you mean...gone? Gone where? He left no note or letter to say where he went?"

"He went into the river, Cecily," explained Marcus. "And he didn't come up."

Cecily gazed at Scott, whose expression showed his sympathy, and then at Marcus.

"You are lying," she said simply and quietly. "You are lying to me."

"No, Cecily. We are not lying to you. It is true," said Marcus. "Someone saw him."

Then the dam broke. Crying aloud as a hurt animal might, she attempted to leave the bed but stumbled. Scott caught her and tried to lay her back on the bed, but she fought him. She cursed Marcus. She cursed Scott. She cursed them both with words that otherwise would never have come from her mouth. Marcus called out to Lacey and Jolly, and they immediately came into the room for they had been waiting just outside her door.

"Lacy, here, see if you can calm her," said Marcus.

"No, Marcus, you hold her while I give her laudanum," said Scott. "If I can get it down her throat...she will calm down. We must or she will hurt herself."

Marcus and Lacey together held the struggling Cecily while Scott tipped the spoonful of the bitter opioid between her teeth and then held her mouth shut until she swallowed. Lacey managed to get her to lie on the bed again and sat with her until she began to cease struggling.

"Will she recover, Doc?" asked Marcus.

"Don't know. Might. Might not. Might recover a little, but not all. Have to wait and see."

"Not much encouragement there."

"You need truth now. Not false hope. I don't know the why of what has happened because you prefer your secrets, but this woman has been damaged. Shock has affected her, and I doubt she will ever be the same. I don't know what brought about this tragedy and I won't pry but you have to know that she is in danger."

"Danger of what?"

"She may try to harm herself. She is that desperate. In danger of being mad; of losing her mind and her reasoning. She will need to be closely watched for a while. Now, where can you find a bed for me. I'll stay over and see her tomorrow morning before I leave. We can leave her now. Let her maid stay with her. She must remain awake, and she can wake me if necessary."

"I'll stay here with her all night," offered Marcus in an unusual show of concern. "Let Jolly and Lacey sleep."

His offer caused Lacey to doubt her master's intentions and her mistress' safety. She replied, "Mastah Marcus, betta you get to sleep," said Lacey. "We all might need you tomorrow when she wakes up."

"Very well. Suit yourself."

"While you decide that, I have had a full day and I missed my supper," said Doc Scott. "Will someone take me by the nose and lead me to food and then a bed?"

Lacey's expression and offer told Doc Scott all he needed to know. The undercurrents among those present made it obvious that this family had more to deal with than a suicide. They were dealing with the thing that had led to that horrible end for Joseph Durandeaux. It might be better for Cecily not to recover.

"Come on, Doc. I'll show you to the kitchen."

"Lead on, Marcus."

"Mother Cecily? How is she this morning? You told her?" asked George of Marcus when they sat at breakfast the following day.

"Yes. Last night. Doctor Scott gave her laudanum. She needed it. He gave her more before he left early this morning."

"By now he has washed out to sea," George offered. "Or his body may come up on a bank."

"George, we will not speak of this again or of Joseph. He took his own life and committed an unforgivable sin. He selfishly brought shame to our family. We must forget him and wipe out all trace of him."

Marcus now had only two sons whom he publicly recognized as such, although there were others in the quarters. Far from being a religious man, he did hold to superstitious and some teachings of the Church. From this day forward it would be as if Joseph had never lived. Marcus didn't even wish to speak with Old John D for he knew in his heart that the old man had spoken truth, and that the old man would wonder how the boy's father had erred.

When night came and Bruneau lay in his bed, he had a thought return...a question...a wondering. Why had Master Marcus lied about rounding up cattle when the boys said they saw him at the ketch. Everyone knew that he traded in slaves and everyone also knew that if one wanted to inspect a new cargo of slaves, it was more reasonable to sail from the inlet around to the harbor than to travel by land. He did it regularly, so why lie this time? Bruneau drifted off to sleep and sleep erased his wondering.

CHAPTER 16

Francis Battailes, like Marcus Durandeaux, was a Protestant by religion and culture, according to the customs of his time. He had enriched his inherited plantation, had fathered a family, and was respected as a man of means and ability by men and women of his class. He had used slave labor as did all successful rice planters, for they knew of no other way to successfully cultivate rice, the crop that grew best in the land and clime. A man of education, a compulsive reader and student of history, he had read widely and had found mention of slavery in books written about the distant past. Greece and Rome had slaves from all races. When battles were won, the losers were taken into slavery. Various countries took slaves to row their galleys when fighting their wars of conquest, and raided villages to capture young women for harems. At least one of these slave girls had become legal wife to a renowned Turkish sultan. Francis knew that slavery had existed since one man proved stronger than another. The world still considered slavery a normal custom and Francis indulged, although doubt and a modicum of guilt constantly nagged at his empathetic mind.

Tabitha Tragédie et Triomphe

Francis Battailes felt a captive of his era, his family, his way of life, and therefore of his slaves. Everyone in his religious and social circle trusted the minister's sermons when he said that God permitted slavery; that God had punished the black man for sins from the distant past and had assigned the white man to aid God. Now, however, regardless of the lofty words and thoughts from the men of God, at an age when he should show mature judgment, Francis found his conflict continuing. Wonder and question all he may, he could not change a thing without disrupting his world and for this he neither had the will and courage nor the motivation. But the thought and the question concerning the right or wrong of slavery lingered, bringing him to leaning more toward the thought of the equality of master and slave rather than what he had been taught.

Even without the pleasures of a wife, never had Francis considered bedding one of his slave women. The mere thought of it was abhorrent. He had always been a man of his word and had made a vow in the house of God to remain faithful to his wife until parted by death. That vow he had kept no matter how difficult it had been during his younger years. However, now, with the addition of Tabitha to his life, he found himself questioning his resolve.

Francis judged Tabitha as the most desirable female he had ever seen... the epitome of womanhood. He began to cut short his afternoon work to give him time to spend more time with her. He did it simply for the pleasure that seeing her brought to him. He admitted to himself that he had begun to feel old and feared that his joy in life was finished. The young woman had changed that as she continued to affect him in such a way that he had rarely experienced. At fifty-seven years of age, standing at the threshold of old age, he desired Tabitha as a man desires a woman. He wanted to see her smile at him. He wanted her to be comfortable when near him and he wanted to wipe away her expression of apprehension and fear. More than all of that, he wanted to touch her. He wanted to feel her lips on his, his mouth covering hers. His desire to feel this girl's body beneath him became intense.

When away from her, examining his own thoughts and desires, he thought he might be going mad. He didn't know what had happened to him...this change. If he had ever harbored any doubt at all whether skin color determined anything, that doubt vanished. If Tabitha, that delectable, desirable, beautiful creature was not human and fully so, then neither was he. Francis didn't know it yet, but he had fallen deeply and sincerely in love with her. The fact that she belonged to him never left his mind but he could not...he would not...he was surely not a copy of the lecher, Marcus Durandeaux.

CHAPTER 17

"Blister my bunions if dat man ain't gone plumb crazy. Picnic my ass," Bessie grumbled under her breath. "I do declare, he done left he mind. Why he want to go and eat on the ground when he got a big ole dinin' table to eat off."

"What you say? What you grumblin' 'bout now, Woman?" asked Trouble, who drove the wagon toward Tabitha's cabin with Bessie sitting on the seat beside him, a basket in her arms, supplies for the cabin and a bundle of clothes for Tabitha in the wagon bed.

"I said dat man go crazy."

"Whut man?'

"Mastah Francis. Das who."

"'Bout what?" Trouble shouted.

"'Bout dat gal. He gone crazy 'bout her. Don't talk so loud. She heah you."

"We ain't even close to her. How she gonna hear? What he do now?"

"She sleep late every day'! He spoilin' her for sure. Fust he brung her to her own cabin and not to de quawtas. Den he makes us tote and carry and do fo' her. She too good fo' de quawtas?"

"Bessie, don't go tryin' to figger out Mastah. I gits to live in de house quawtas, too, and now I don't has to go to de fiel'."

"I know what he up to. He gonna lolly 'round wid her."

"No, Woman! Mastah, he don't lolly 'round wid any gal in de quawtas. If he did, we'd know. He don't lolly 'round wid nobody. Talk is he don't even lolly wid de missus."

"Dat true but dis gal she ain't in de quawtas and he got lolly on his mind, fo' true. He tell me last night he want me fixin' a basket with food and have it ready dis mo'nin'. Want a cloth to spread on de ground. What he gonna do sittin' on a tablecloth on de ground wid dat gal but lolly?"

"He don't want nobody knowin' he bidness. He a good man. Dis gal his secret. Dat mean you and me, we can't tell."

"Joel, he say we gotta tell him everything what happen on dis place 'cause he say Mastah Amos want to know what all goin' on. Old Man, you gonna hide what you know?"

"I ain't scared of no butla. Mastah Francis want me keep secret, I keeps it. And you betta, too."

"No matta we do or we don't, Joel gonna fin' out anyway. Best we tell 'im."

Bessie shrugged her shoulders as if to say she might and she might not. She did not like being on Joel's bad side.

"So, what you put in de basket? Fried chicken taste mighty good on a picnic."

"How you know? You eva been to a picnic?"

"I et fried chicken! Lot o' times. Sometimes at de Church house dey got picnic some Sunday and table fo' us in de back. One time I fill up a plate and took it to a gal, and we set in de grass and et off dat same plate. I even touch her hand."

"Where she now? She live heah?"

"Naw. 'nother plantation. Got married and Mastah Francis he let her go wid her man. I had my eye on her, but she got gone. All I got from dat picnic was a few ticks from de grass."

"Dat what happen at church dinnas. Gals meet mens off de place."

"How you know he ain't takin' de missus on de picnic?"

"You crazy, Trouble? Lak you said, he don't lolly wid de missus. I done tole you what Mastah up to."

"I reckon you right."

"Miz, she don't even talk to him. Dat's what I heah."

"Dat why he takin' de new gal?"

"Didn't I say he fallin' fo her?"

"What you mean, fallin'?

"Fallin' in love, Man. You know…love! De kind dat don't let go."

"You eva had dat?"

"Naw, but I seen folks what did. Make 'em crazy. Act lak damned fools."

"So, what you got in dat basket?" he repeated.

"I put in some biled eggs. Peaches off de tree. Cornbread and ham. Dat should fill dey bellies."

"No fried chicken?"

"Ain't gonna kill one now. Ketch me a pullet in de mo'nin' and kill it and get de feathers off it and I'll fry it up."

"Love, you say? What make you say dat?"

"Dis picnic fo' one thing. Mastah Francis he a good man. Ain't lolly 'round wid gals. But now he gonna."

"Mastah ain't old. He still got what it take," said Trouble with a chuckle as he halted the horse in front of the cabin.

"Go on wid you, Trouble. Yo mammy sho give you de right name. I gotta git dat lazy gal awake. Massa gonna make her so she ain't no good fo' nuttin'. Nobody gonna want her

99

when he toss her out. I got to wake her up and git her dressed 'fo he come. He sent a bundle o' dresses and shoes and stuff. Some purty, too. Mus' be missus' dresses she don't wear no mo."

"Why he do dat?"

"She got to wear somethin'! She come heah in her night shift, don't you know. Middle o' de night. Somethin' real fishy 'bout dat, but I ain't figgered it out yet. I brung her one dress so she could get outta de bed, but now she go to a picnic...gotta wear picnic dress. I reckon."

"What a picnic dress?"

"Aw, Trouble, you tires me out. He'p me git this stuff inside."

CHAPTER 18

"Sun been up long time, Miss. You wake?"

"Yes, Ma'am. For a while."

"Well, Mastah Francis, he say fo' me to git you dressed in one of dese dresses. He comin' fo' you and take you somewhere. I ain't know where. What dress you want?"

"If I don't know where I am going, how will I know which dress?"

"Don't you sass me, young'un. You a slave jis lak me, so don't talk uppity. I pick de dress."

Bessie rummaged through the pile of garments and pulled out a brown frock.

"Heah. Put dis on. You goin' on a picnic, so you won't get dis one dirty. I got to do yo' washin'."

Tabitha reached for the dress and held it up to herself. Seemed to be the right size.

"Heah a under skirt. Now hurry and dress. He gonna be heah directly."

While Tabitha dressed Bessie grumbled under her breath.

"I need you to lace the back," said Tabitha, turning around so that Bessie could lace the ties while she silently grumbled. "What are you grumbling about? I didn't ask to come here and if you are angry with me, tell me why?"

"You young, Gal, but you slave so I reckon you know what Mastah Francis about."

"What do you mean? I barely know him so how should I know what he is about?"

"He don't lolly 'round wid gals in de quawtas. Dat why he put you in dis cabin away from ev'ything. He made me fix up a basket so you two could go on a picnic. Alone. What you think he gonna do wid you out in the grass somewhere alone? Same thing what them other men done."

"What other men? Did what?"

"Neva' you mind," said Bessie quickly, realizing that she may have said more than she should. "Mastah Francis don't know, but dey ain't no secrets in de slave quawtas."

"What secrets?"

"We knows you was brung here in the dead of night from Durandeaux and we knows why."

"Then please tell me."

Bessie looked at her long and then asked, "You don't know? You don't know dat Mastah Durandeaux wrap you up and put you in Mastah Francis carriage and he driver brung you heah? Cause dey a mess wid Mastah Marcus and Mastah Joseph fightin' ova you? You playin' wid two mens? You a purty, high yella gal and now you gone and got t'ree men in a fix. Playin' yo' games wid 'em. You talk fancy but you a slave jis lak me and you done got sold from one mastah to notha. Mastah Francis, he got a bill o'sale."

"How do you know all that?"

"I told you. De driva what brung you, he tell Joel and Joel tell Trish and Trish tell Rhoda and she tell e'body. No secrets 'tween slaves. Walls got ears. You wanna keep on de good side of Mastah Francis, you do what he says. Don't back talk. He say jump, you jump. You be fine for a while den he git tired of you. Den you go to de slave quawtas wid all of us."

"No one fought over me."

"Why else Mastah Marcus sell you away? He don't want nobody else lolly 'round wid you but him. Mens is jealous. You causin' trouble."

"I was not *lollying* with anyone. I grew up with Joseph."

"You ain't bedded by Mastah Joseph and Mastah Marcus?"

"No. Not by either. And no one else."

"You ain't neva.... neva...?"

"Never, Miss Bessie. There are no secrets among the slaves at Durandeaux either, and that includes me. Since I was old enough to comprehend, I have known that Master Marcus Durandeaux is my natural father, and that Joseph is my half-brother. The housekeeper, Lacey, thought I should know. My mother served as personal maid to the master's wife, and Master gave her to the butler to marry. Master sold her away after I came. The butler never let on that he knew Master Durandeaux was my real father. He treated me like his own daughter. No one told Joseph the truth and I knew better than to let the secret out. Joseph did not know that I am his half-sister and that must be why master Marcus sent away. Joseph loved me. Now you can tell that all over the house and the quarters; however, I doubt that Master Francis would be happy."

"Mastah Francis, he know all dis?"

"I don't know what Marcus Durandeaux told him, but I doubt if he told him the truth."

"Lawdy, Missy. E'body say you little tramp playing bad wid yo' family. And now you gone and got Mastah Francis in a fix."

"I have done nothing to Master Francis. Nothing."

"Missy, he in love wid you jis lak yo' Joseph. Why else he keep you heah and not in de quawtas and why me to come heah ev'y day to take care of you?"

Tabitha had no reply for Bessie. She simply shrugged her shoulders.

"Well, Missy, dis yo' home, now. You git dressed. Mastah Francis, he on de way."

Tabitha finished dressing in silence and in fear of what the afternoon might hold for her.

All night Francis could not sleep. He tossed and fought with his covers. His loins ached. His heart pounded. He soaked his bedding with sweat. He got up from bed and walked downstairs to the kitchen. He opened the pie cabinet and found a peach cobbler, still warm from supper. He took a spoon from the container on the long worktable and dipped it into the cobbler. After two spoonsful, he could swallow no more, returned the cobbler to the cabinet and went back to his bed and more tossing until sun-up. He dressed in a good suit before going to a light breakfast. He ordered his butler to get word to the stable to have his double buggy hitched and ready to go by eleven, sharp. Nervous and anxious, he nibbled at his food.

Francis treated his slaves with as much compassion as any man could. He did not abuse them. He kept families together. He showed kindness and generosity to those who had been with his family long enough to be considered members of that family. Now, for the first time in his life, he would do knowingly something that he considered abuse. Francis had made up his mind. He had decided, for good or bad, for better or worse, and would take consequences for what he planned to do. He simply could not endure another day or night like the past week. He had been a man out of his mind.

He arrived at the stable at eleven o'clock. His favorite carriage horse stood hitched to the double-buggy. He climbed aboard and drove from the stable yard, down the long drive and turned into the narrow road, shaded by pine forest on each side. He drove to the far end, around a bend and stopped in front of the cabin where he had placed Tabitha. He halted the horse and stepped out of the buggy. Completely beyond his own wise counseling, he had come to the edge of wisdom and had entered that no-man's land of extreme desire. He suffered as a man dying from thirst with water within his reach. His heart raced. He paused to catch his breath. On shaking legs and weak knees, he opened the door to the cabin and entered.

Tabitha stood by the table and Bessie stood behind her. Francis had eyes only for Tabitha and missed that Bessie attempted to send him a silent message with her expressions.

"Bessie, is the basket ready?"

"Yes, Suh. It ready. Anything else you need?"

"Perhaps a blanket to sit on?"

"You come wid me and pick de one you want?" she asked, hoping to get him alone to warn him that Tabitha had not been used.

"No, you choose," he said, not taking his eyes off Tabitha. "Any will do."

Bessie came back with a folded blanket and handed it to Francis.

"Tablecloth folded on top de food."

"Let's go, Tabitha."

Without a word and without a backward glance at Bessie, Tabitha left the cabin with Francis, took the hand he offered and mounted the step to the buggy where she sat stiffly.

105

Francis stepped up on the other side, took the reins and clucked to the gelding. He drove the buggy along a bumpy back-woods road that wound through a tangle of scrub oak until he came to a clearing. He halted the gelding and looped the reins. His hand shook as he offered it for her to take and step down. He dared not look into her eyes for fear that she would fathom his intention and that she would run away. He needn't have feared. She accepted his hand and stepped down, remembering the words that Bessie had said.

He took the blanket and the picnic basket and waited for her to follow him. Setting down the basket he spread the blanket on the damp grass and then the bright colored tablecloth. He motioned for her to sit and she obeyed. His plan had been to talk with her...to draw her out...to lessen her unease; however, he could not. He lost control. Driven by days and nights with the agony of unrelieved physical desire, with a hoarse voice he spoke words that he would regret for the remainder of his life.

"Stand up, Tabitha."

Slowly she stood.

"Take off your clothes. All of them. Down to your skin. No one will see you but me."

The reminder came again: *I am nothing but his slave. I obey or get punished.*

She unbuttoned the waist of her skirt and dropped it to the ground. She stood in her underskirt.

"Top, too."

"I can't reach the laces," she croaked, now shaking in fear.

Francis stood at her back. He unlaced the bodice and as it fell away from her shoulder, he did not resist the urge to kiss her bare, smooth skin. He then pulled the bodice down around her waist and before he could restrain himself, he pushed her to the blanket, pulled up her underskirt, and held her with his weight until he could unbutton his trousers and free his demanding manhood. Using his knees to pry her legs apart, before he entered her clumsily and roughly, he said, "I know you must be used to this. I do you no harm."

She screamed in pain and too late he realized his mistake, but he could not stop. Driven by the primitive urge, he could not withdraw until he finished. Seconds later he rolled off her body as she lay sobbing, her hands over her face. To the surprise of them both, Francis, too, was reduced to tears. Emotional release, physical relief, guilt, regret, his sobs came louder than hers. He attempted to hold her, but she turned away and used her skirt to cover herself.

Francis tried to believe that he simply had been too rough because of his long years of abstinence. He could not easily accept that Tabitha came to him a virgin; that he had done her harm. He fully assumed that both Marcus and Joseph had used her and that she would be the perfect woman for him until he grew too old. Now he sat up and looked at the devastated young woman. He did not know what to say and Tabitha used his silence as permission to stand and put her clothes on. Francis glanced at the place where she had lain and saw a red smear on the tablecloth. He knew then that he had raped a virgin. He had raped the woman who brought love into his life. He had defiled that love and he knew that nothing would erase those moments of unbridled license that he had allowed himself.

"I am sorry. I am so sorry. I thought that you and...that you were not...Marcus...Joseph...I thought..."

"You didn't think, Master Francis," she spat at him, forgetting her position in life. "If you had thought you would have asked me. You don't have to think. You are a master of slaves, and I am only one of them. Bessie warned me."

"Bessie warned you?"

"Bessie is a woman, Master Francis. She is a woman who has lived longer than I and she understands men better than I. I know only Joseph who is my friend. He is kind, gentle, encourages me to learn. Don't blame Bessie and please do not punish her. She only tried to prepare me."

"God help me, if I had known..."

"Who is to say you would have done any differently? Surely not God, who says what you white men do is just fine with Him!"

Francis had never been spoken to like she spoke to him, and he knew he deserved it. He did not reprimand her but remained silent. He had no excuse. He could say or do nothing to undo what he had done, as shame and remorse came on him much stronger than had his prior physical torment.

"Will you take me back to Bessie, Master Francis? Your picnic is spoiled, or perhaps it wasn't."

"Not Master, Tabitha. Do not call me master."

"What shall I call you? You are my master and you just proved it to me."

"Please call me Francis. Will you do that? When I am with you, I want to be Francis. Simply Francis. Will you?"

Her silence spoke mountains of words as she pulled her unlaced bodice up to cover her breasts and walked to the buggy, where she climbed up and sat. Francis gathered the tablecloth, the blanket and the basket and took them to the buggy. All the while on the ride back to the cabin they both remained silent. Francis wanted to go to his room, lock the door and drink himself into a stupor. Tabitha wanted to bathe and take away the rank odors that had come from Francis. When he halted the gelding in front of the cabin she jumped down and ran inside before he could help her. Francis's head held low in his own dishonor, he could not bear to face Bessie, and drove away to his mansion to face his shame alone.

When Billy, his valet, came to call him to supper, he found his master fully clothed, stretched out on his bed, an empty bottle of Single Malt by his bed. The valet removed his boots and before covering Francis with a blanket lest he take a chill in the night, he caught the unmistakable odor of sex. The valet returned to downstairs and whispered to Joel what he knew. Before locking the doors that night, as usual, Joel told Trish what the valet had told him. Trish told Rhoda and before noon the next day the entire population who resided in the upper quarters, and who were of an age to understand, knew what Master Francis had done to Uppity Tabitha, for that is how Bessie had earlier described her to everyone.

Francis woke with a head the size of a watermelon; his throat dry and parched. He had a moment before he saw the empty bottle and remembered what he had done the day before, which had led to his night of terrible dreams. He rolled over, still in his rumpled clothes, got up and rang for Billy.

"I need you to draw me a bath."

"Yes, Sir. Anything else, Mastah Francis?"

"Yes. Whatever you saw last night and this morning, keep to yourself. Say nothing to anyone."

The valet nodded his in agreement while knowing that he had every intention of reporting to Joel that Mastah Francis had required a bath and the supposed reason why: this the butler required of him because Master Amos would want to know.

Only after his bath and a bite of breakfast did Francis feel anything like human, but still a huge cloud of remorse hung over his head. He had done wrong. He had somehow to make it right...or at least better. He thought and thought and then it came to him. The small home where his old mother lived after she became too violent for the house servants to manage sat empty and idle. Francis had built the comfortable place for her and had moved her in with her maid, cook and a man for cutting wood. There Francis' mother had remained for a decade until she passed away. The house had stood empty since then. He would give it to Tabitha as her own, with servants of her own. It would become his home away from home.

While Francis thought how quickly he could ready the place for her and who he would send to care for her, a realization struck that shook him to his core. He now knew that Tabitha had been a virgin and if she became pregnant, the child would be his. HIS, without question. Another son or daughter to bring up to brighten his elder years? He needed to hurry to give Tabitha a better home; to somehow make up for his dastardly act. He hoped and prayed that she would be with child. He may have done her a wrong, but good may come of it yet.

CHAPTER 19

"Dis mo'nin' Mastah say he gonna take us all to dat old house where he Mama stay when she got old and crazy and didn't know who she was," said Bessie to Trouble.

"Why dey send dat ole lady out de house? De big house got rooms what got rooms."

"Old Lady she got mean. Had fits. Scream all de night long keeping e'body 'wake. Don't know nobody. Not even Mastah Francis. Hit anybody come close. Throw food and her own mess at de help. Mastah had to get her out de house. He built a place and moved her in 'til she died. Dat cabin been empty since."

"Well, I declare. You say we movin' in, too?"

"Yes. You and me. Dat house got rooms for help. It got t'ree sleepin' rooms and a big kitchen and a big table and in a corner got chairs to set and talk. Mastah Francis give Missy dat, he in love!"

"How dey picnic go?" asked Trouble. "She say?"

"Don't you even ask. She come in all dirty face from crying. Her dress half off. Mastah Francis never come in. He jis drove away."

"Why she cryin'? You axe?"

"You that dumb, man? You ain't know why she cryin'? I ain't had no need to axe. I knowed anyway. She come in and ran to her room and shut de do'. Den she calls me and say she want de bath full up. I carried wawta and put in de tub and she tell me to go."

"He lolly wid her?"

"Keep yo mout shut, Trouble. You ain't know what you talkin' 'bout. Ain't fo' you to know."

"I jis wonderin'. He love her? I ain't never knowed Mastah Francis to love nobody."

"Me, neither. Love is a land where Mastah ain't never been befo' now. I guess dey's things can happen dat we don't know. You love dat gal at de picnic behind de church house?"

"Naw, but I loves you, Bessie," he said with a grin across his face.

"Go on wid you, Trouble. Stop messin' wid me. I got work to do."

Trouble caught a glimpse of a tight smile at the corners of her mouth.

Francis allowed two days to pass before he managed to gather enough courage to call on Tabitha. That instant when he considered her his slave had passed, and with it all the passion and desire he had known. Those feelings had been intrusions on his natural being and had brought him to a state he had never before experienced. He relegated them to a dark corner of his mind where he both cherished them and hated them, remembering always what had happened in his time of weakness. Or had it been finally a bit of strength showing? After a while he would feel his old self again and only wanted to enjoy Tabatha for her company alone...if only she would allow. That she may not, he knew quite well and would understand. He prayed that she would understand and forgive his injurious behavior as an aberration to his normal self. He could only try.

Francis steeled himself as he dressed in his best trousers and waistcoat. He stood still while Billy tied his cravat, handed him his cane, and held the door open him.

"You look mighty fancy this afta'noon, Mastah Francis," said Billy. "Look lak you goin' cou'tin'. Pity ain't no young ladies close."

Francis gave the man a long, serious look, trying to fathom if the man meant anything untoward by the comment or if he simply meant to give a compliment. Deciding the latter, he descended the stairs and made his way to the stable, while the valet went directly to Joel.

"Where Mastah go now, Bill?"

"He go see that gal again."

"How you know?"

"He told me to get out his best trousers and the fancy waistcoat he got last time he went to city. I told you what I smelled before, and I bet you I'll smell it again."

"We'll see. Mastah Amos not gonna be happy 'bout all this messin' with women. No, he ain't. I do hope he come home soon."

Francis halted the gelding and jumped down from the buggy. Faking a calm attitude though his heart pounded in his chest, he knocked on the cabin door instead of opening it and walking in as if he owned the place. If Tabitha was to be his companion, he must treat her with respect. He was surprised when Bessie opened the door.

"Suh, you come on in."

"You still here? I thought you would have left by now," he said with a bit of disappointment in his voice.

"Jis' waitin' for Trouble to come and carry me home."

"Step outside for a minute?"

"You got somethin' you wanna say?"

"Yes. I want to ask after Miss Tabitha."

"Well, when you brung her back here she 'cryin' if dat what you mean. Her face all smeared, and she don't talk nothin' but asked me to fill that bathtub you give her. I did and I called her for her suppa, but she ain't et nothin'. What goin' on, Mastah? Somethin' I should know?" asked Bessie boldly, pretending ignorance and deliberately omitting that Tabitha's clothes were torn.

"Nothing you need to know," he replied rather curtly. "Is she dressed?"

"She is. Got on one of the frocks you give her."

"Will you tell her that I wish to take her for a ride?"

"Where you takin' her?" asked Bessie with a bit of rancor in her voice. It was a question that she should never have asked but thought she had earned the right.

Francis gave her stare for stare until Bessie dropped her eyes in defeat. Only then did Francis reply to her question.

"It's time you all get into a bigger cabin. You need more space. You will all move into the old cabin where my mother lived when she was very ill. You won't have to go back and forth each morning and night to the mansion. You and Trouble will be staying with Tabitha in your own rooms. Tell Trouble to help you pack what you need. I'll make sure you all get the things to make the place comfortable. I've had it thoroughly cleaned inside and out. Now go fetch her."

Bessie must have told Tabitha that the master would take her somewhere, for she came from her room with her head up. Not willing to show feelings in front of Bessie or to sound weak to Francis, she walked briskly by him, out the door and climbed into the buggy. Since her talk with Bessie, she had been thinking about what he did to her, why he did it, and the way he did. She knew now that Master Francis had believed her to be little more than a mulatto trollop and had used her accordingly. Marcus had not explained anything to Francis and he had assumed too much in error. As much as she had been hurt both physically and emotionally, she faced the truth and blamed her father, Marcus Durandeaux, not Francis Battailes.

They rode quietly for a short while and then Francis turned his face to hers.

"I want to apologize, Tabitha. Sincerely apologize for...I had not intended...something came over me...I could not control...oh, I am so ashamed," he said as he lowered his head.

She said nothing.

"If I beg you to forgive me, will you? Please."

She wondered what to say...how much to tell him...how to answer...to forgive or not. Her basic good nature won the emotional battle.

"Master Francis, what Master Marcus did not tell you is that he is my real father. He got me onto a slave woman and when she told him that she was with child, my father gave her to the butler to marry. When I was born, my mother was sent away, and I was brought up with Joseph. We were children together. We played as brother and sister play. We learned together. Then we grew up and I think Joseph wanted more. He wanted to marry me. That is why my father sold me to you as he did, just as he had sold my mother after I was born. Joseph and I are half-brother and half-sister, but no one told him. We were not allowed."

Francis had remained silent during her words, but he turned his face to her.

"Oh, My God," he whispered when he could find his voice. "Why didn't he tell me that?"

"It didn't really matter to him, what happened to me. He didn't want Joseph wed to a mulatto slave and he could not wed his half-sister. Don't you see? As it is, I cannot fault you for what you did to me. I am your slave and must obey."

"Tabitha, if I had known any of this, I would done differently."

"Are you certain?"

Francis had to think and to recall his emotions, his need, and his lack of control when he had seen her standing tall in front of him, half naked. Would he have done differently?

"I don't know. I honestly don't know. I know I would have wanted to do differently, but I don't know."

"That is honest at least. And now you want me to forgive you. Forgive you for what? You did as you are allowed by law. And by God's law."

"Please don't let yesterday to make you bitter, Tabitha. In truth, I love you. I am completely and truly, for the first time in my fifty odd years, in love. I can't wait to see you every day. You are the first thing on my mind when I wake, and in my dreams while I sleep. I want to have you all to myself. I want to touch you and I want to have you in every way. This morning I said a vow to God that I will love you until the day I die. I am taking you to a surprise that I have readied just for you and Bessie and Trouble.

The surprise was the cabin. Inside she explored the larger space: three sleeping rooms, a separate kitchen, and a sitting room. A verandah finished the front of the house and sported a swing and two rocking chairs with a tea table set in between.

"You are to live here now. Bessie and Trouble will live with you. They will take care of you."

"Why not send me to work in the mansion? I am capable of work."

"Never. You will never go into that house. Never as long as I live."

"As you wish, Master."

"Francis, please. I forbid you to call me master."

"Why do I have this cabin?"

"Because you are my secret. My very own secret and that is all I know. I don't want anyone else to know or see you but Bessie and Trouble. I don't expect or ask you to understand because truly, I don't either. That is how it is. The place is ready for you. Bessie and Trouble will come before night. I will leave you here and you can become acquainted with your new home. Now tell me what I may I bring you to pass your time until I come at night, and I will bring it."

Tabitha thought and recalled how she and Joseph painted watercolors with Cecily in the garden. She looked around her and saw only trees and sawgrass and tangles of vines. Hardly flower blossoms, but she could at least keep busy.

"Joseph and I grew up at Miz Cecily's feet, watching her paint in watercolors. I would like to do that again. To paint."

"Cecily is my daughter, whom I gave to Marcus. I'll get what you need from the city. It will take a while. Now I must leave. Ask Bessie for anything. She is your servant."

With that he left as Tabitha stared after him, wondering what had occurred to change her life so. She did not hate Francis for being a man. Not a man like Joseph, for no one else compared to Joseph. She kept in her heart her childhood memories and knew that she had begun another phase in her life. She had no choice but to accept it and do her best. She would not consider it a tragedy, but a challenge.

CHAPTER 20

Worrying for Cecily occupied Marcus mind more than usual and more than he liked. It prevented him from concentrating on his work. It appeared as though the poor woman had settled into a pattern of long sleeps broken by hours of sobbing. She no longer fought but seemed to accept the tragedy and simply waited for her own end. He wondered if he should send word to her father. He decided not. Let the sleeping remain asleep. Why stir up trouble now. Francis would ask questions he preferred not to answer, and Tabitha should not know about Joseph either.

Marcus used the days of quiet to recollect, think, and then put people and happenings in their order of importance. With Cecily quieted by regular doses of laudanum, she dropped from first place in his attention. Charles and Julia had gone to her father in the city, bringing relief to the entire household. Marcus missed his son but felt such joy that he did not have to listen to Julia complain at every meal and to hear that she attempted to create discord among the servants. Now, at least, Charles could keep a close watch on Jasper Perrin's accounting practices. Charles would be able to report to his father if he caught Jasper in underhanded moves. Long had Marcus suspected that Jasper had his own way of skimming profit off the top for himself, before reporting it to the account ledgers.

Slave trading brought wealth and the Durandeaux and Perrin families had grown rich in the practice. Perrin knew the ins and outs of their various enterprises, and Marcus trusted him only to a certain degree. Having Charles living in the same house with Jasper, observing his actions and learning the accounts, would relieve him of concerns.

Marcus then considered George: what information to share with him, knowing that whatever he told him, would be repeated to Margaret, George's wife. A good woman and good wife, but still a woman and in Marcus mind...a risk. George ran the plantation but knew nothing about his father's other endeavors. Having noted a little too much of Joseph in George's make-up, that desire to act in good faith, which permeated both their personalities, he had not considered it necessary or even wise. Best not to burden George with certain bits of knowledge best kept to himself. Within a month the household had settled into another smooth pattern and life for Marcus continued as he wished.

CHAPTER 21

Amos Battailes, home from his three weeks of meetings in the city, woke before the cocks crowed and enjoyed the quiet of the country. In the city he had grown accustomed to the sound of wheels on cobblestone streets and the cries of early morning street vendors pushing carts of fish, oysters, or shrimp just taken from the sea. Back home, he had to adjust to the silence. Forcing himself out of bed he dressed for work and descended the stairs to the kitchen.

"You up early, Mastah Amos," remarked Rhoda. "Brekwus gonna be a while. Dat boy left de wood box too close to window and rain come in and got all de fat wood wet. He gone to get some dry wood."

"Then I'll go for a ride and be back in time for eggs and ham. Oh, I didn't see Papa last night at supper. Is he visiting Cecily?"

"Mastah Amos, you best talk wid yo' Papa 'bout where he go of a evenin'. I ain't one to tell tales. Betta...you axe Mistah Joel. Dey a lot goin' on dese past few weeks you don't know nuttin' 'bout."

At the stable Amos saddled Blackbird, the Spanish mare he had brought back with him from France along with

Snowbird, the stallion. He rode out of the stable yard onto the long drive leading away from the mansion. Here, in his element, he wished to immerse himself in the land around the plantation again and wash the city away from him. At thirty-one years of age, he had relieved his father by taking over much of the business of the rice growing; especially that part that involved the city, the warehouse, shipping schedules and meetings with the rice council...a group made up of the prominent rice growers in the Low-Country. He left the desk work to his father.

As he rode, he took deep breaths, threw his head back, relaxed his shoulders, and breathed in the damp air pungent with the smell of sea and marsh. He began to whistle. Amos's own relaxed body and his whistling in musical time with the hoofbeats, calmed the spirited mare.

He and Blackbird had circumvented the length of the path that surrounded the land in cultivation and had returned to the road that led back toward the mansion, when Amos came up on the rear of the house where his grandmother had lived in constant care before she passed. Thinking to see it in bad shape from non-use, he was surprised to see the surrounding yard newly cleared of intruding bushes and smoke coming from the chimney. He dismounted and led Blackbird closer. Rounding the corner of the cabin, he saw a woman sitting in a chair outside, with a pad on her lap and paints on a small table beside her. She heard the mare snort and looked at him in alarm.

"Who are you?" They both said at the same time.

"You first," said Amos. "Who are you?"

"I am Tabitha Durandeaux."

"I know the Durandeaux. I never saw you before. Why are you here? You waiting for someone?"

"No. Who are you?"

"I am Amos Battailes. Francis Battailes is my father. He bought you from the Durandeaux? Are you the one who cleaned up the place?"

"I did not. I am to live here."

"Why? Who told you that?"

"Ask your father. He will tell you. I am afraid I cannot."

"I certainly will ask him."

Amos turned away in a bit of annoyance, mounted the mare and put her to the gallop toward the stables. Until his father's lack of concern had cost him the girl he loved, he had always thought that he and Pricilla would live there, alone together, for a year or two when they wed. Now, finding someone in the cabin did not add to the pleasure of his homecoming. He would see to it that the slave moved to the quarters. Was this one of the things to which the cook had referred? Surely, he would speak with Joel.

After putting his mare away, Amos went directly to find the butler. When he had found him, he confronted the quiet, stern butler who ruled the household servants with a strong voice and soft heart.

"I rode by my grandmother's old house. A woman is there. Mulatto. Must be a new slave? I want her moved to the quarters for I have decided to have that place for my own private home. I plan to add on to it."

"Master Amos, I can't do nothing or say nothing about that woman. You have to see your father about her."

"You can't tell me about this? I give you money...to be my eyes and ears. For you to keep me informed. Now tell."

"Your father bought her and put her there. If you want her out of that cabin you will have to convince your father."

"What is going on? I was only away for three weeks."

"Lot can happen in three weeks, Suh. Lot can happen. Now whatever I say, don't you say to your Papa that I told. You promise?"

"Have I ever betrayed your trust?"

"No, Suh, you haven't. You might not believe what I say, but I'll say it. You been gone not more than a few days when, during the night, she got brought here from Durandeaux plantation. Kidnapped and brought here. But seem like Mastah Marcus sent her. He give her to your Papa and he done and gone and be in love with her."

"Who's in love?" asked Amos, as though he had not understood.

"Your Papa is who."

"He what?" Amos shouted.

"Mastah! Somebody gonna hear," whispered Joel. "Talk low. Now, I know from Bessie and Trouble that Mastah Francis been going to see Tabitha, that her name...Tabitha...every evening. And he already...well...you know...he...they..."

"What are you trying to say, Joel?"

"You want to know everything, Mastah Amos?"

"Of course, I do."

"Well, Mastah Amos, yo' Papa and Tabitha, Bessie say they done lolly 'round."

"By lolly 'round, do you mean what I think you mean?"

"I think I do."

"Well, I'll be damned. I never would have thought..."

"Yes, Suh. We all thought Mastah Francis, he don't do that. But that Tabitha, she do look kind of sweet."

The glare that Amos gave his butler and confidant could shrivel a soul, and Joel quickly backtracked.

"Don't mean no insult, Mastah Amos. I mean Mastah Francis he got a good eye for a lovely woman."

"You're getting in deeper, Joel. Better you tell me what else you know."

"Well, I think I already said he eat his supper with her and stay and talk. Some nights he comes home to sleep and sometimes he stay all night. We used to it now."

"It will take some time for me to be used to it," said Amos. "Hard to imagine my father in love. Always thought him quite bloodless."

"Yes, Suh. That all I can say, Mastah Amos. You want to know more, better ask your Papa. Can I go now?"

Wisely, Joel had withheld the one thing that he knew but could never say...that Master Francis had taken Tabitha by force. For Amos to know that would destroy both father and son. He had sworn Bessie to hold her own tongue on pain of being sent to the field quarters to work rice. He knew that she would rather have her tongue cut out than go to the quarters and do field work.

After speaking with Joel, Amos lost not a moment in finding his father. He went to the study, opened the study door, and entered without permission; he was that irate. Francis looked up from the account books and ready to voice a pleasant greeting when met with Amos' sudden question.

"Hmm, Son, good morning. You missed breakfast. Out riding?"

"Who is she, Papa?"

"Whom do you mean?"

"The young woman out at Grandmama's old house. I saw her today on my ride and she would not say why she is there."

"Did she say her name?"

"Tabitha Durandeaux. You bought a slave from them?"

"I did."

"For what purpose? She does not act like a servant, and she speaks as well as you and I."

"She is my personal companion..."

"Personal companion? Papa...with Mama upstairs in her room..."

"Your mother prefers her room over mine, and she has not allowed me near her bed since before you were born! Now leave this alone and do not ask me about it again. Son, I do not need to answer to you. I enjoy this woman's company. She will live in that cabin, and Bessie and Trouble will live with her. You will not interfere, and you will not speak of this to your mother or anyone! Do you understand?"

Amos had never seen his father take such a stand. He wanted to ask more but saw that he would just drive his father into further stubbornness.

"Alright, Papa. You are not the first man to bed a slave and you won't be the last. You didn't know that I wanted that cabin for myself. I planned to enlarge it...to build on wings."

"I did not. You will have to find another. I have a while yet to enjoy it and when I am gone it will belong to her."

Amos took the measure of his father and saw someone who had suddenly come into being. This was not his old, mild, kind father speaking. It was a man determined. He could see that his father loved the woman. Amos knew the signs. He backed off.

"As you wish, Father. When do you wish to know the results of my work in town? I suppose you are still interested in our business?"

"Your sarcasm is not welcome, Amos. Certainly, I wish to know. We can talk tomorrow. I will be away after supper."

"Then I will see you in the study after my breakfast tomorrow."

"Son, please try to understand," said Francis with a bit more gentleness. "It has been a long, lonely time since you were born. You know your mother and you know how she feels about..."

"That is between the two of you. I understand your needs. I am a man, too. But a slave?"

"Who else, Amos? I am legally wed to a living woman. Tabitha is as different from a slave as a girl can get. You have the advantage of visits to the city. I do not."

"I will try not to judge you, Papa."

While Amos ate his breakfast he thought on his conversation with his father. After the explanation for the girl in the cabin, why did he feel angry still? He brought back an image of her and as he saw her in his mind's eye he realized that in spite of his displeasure at finding her there, he had been attracted to her. Recalling her golden skin against a frock the color of the sky and eyes of the darkest blue added to the impact. She could be an artist's model. She seemed much too young for his father, and much too beautiful. His anger was based on envy. Amos knew he desired her for himself.

At early evening his father departed the mansion and Amos went to his room. He tried to settle down to work organizing all the documents he had brought home for his father to read and file away, but he could not get his mind clear. Imagining his father and that girl together became too difficult. He shoved the papers aside and left his room to go to the parlor for a brandy. He saw Joel locking the heavy front door and called to him.

"Yes, Master Amos?"

"I have spoken with my father, and he has told me who the woman is and why she is in that cabin. Now I want you to tell me all that you know. Everything. Is that clear?"

"You want the whole story?"

"Yes. All that you know. Complete. From beginning to now."

Starting with the driver who drove Tabitha to the Battailes plantation, through the information that Bessie and Trouble had brought to him, Joel related to Amos all that he dared. He hung his head so that Amos would leave him, but it didn't work. Amos pressed on.

"I see there is more. What else?"

"Well..."

"Tell me. All of it."

"I can't say no more, Mastah Amos."

"Then our private deal will be finished. No more coins."

Joel looked up in surprise and knew that the young man meant what he said."

"Time to decide your loyalty, Joel."

Without hesitation Joel spoke, "Bessie said he defiled Tabitha."

"Defiled?"

"Yes. That is the word that Bessie used, and I know what she meant."

"What, exactly, did she mean?"

"Master Amos, she meant that your father took advantage of Tabitha, and she never been touched before. That is what Bessie said. Said it right to me. Bessie asked me how a slave woman could fight her master off. Then she said that Master Francis didn't know. He thought she had been used before."

"That is not like my father. Not at all. I can't imagine him forcing a woman. Not even a slave woman."

"I know. I have never seen him like this. He fixed up that old place of your Grandmama's and he keepin' her there with her own help to look after her. Looks to me like he has gone and got in love. She told Bessie that Master Marcus Durandeaux is her real father. She was brought up as the butler's daughter but as a playmate and companion of Joseph Durandeaux. That means Miz Cecily's son, Joseph, was her half-brother, and Tabitha wasn't used by either of them. That is what everyone thought when she came like she did...like they were getting rid of trouble. But Bessie said Master Marcus knew Joseph in love with her and didn't know they had the same papa. Now I hear Joseph is gone."

"Gone where?"

"Don't know. Just missing. Nobody has seen him since the night she came here."

"Joseph is my nephew but I didn't' know him well. Just that he is a quiet young man. Cecily said he was to be a churchman. Very studious. So, he is her half-brother...in love with her...she is taken away...now he is missing. Wonder why Cecily did not tell us. She could have written. Hmm..."

"Where you think he went, Master Amos?"

"I have no idea, Joel. Where would a young man go when thwarted in love? What would he do?"

"You think...well...Tabitha must be a powerful woman. Makes a body wonder what..."

"It does, indeed...."

"Master Amos, you want me to keep on getting information from the help?"

"I do. I want to know everything. Bessie is living with her? How often does she come in?"

"Trouble drives the buggy in every day and brings Bessie in to get food and things for the cabin."

"Good."

"Good night, Master Amos. You sleep tight."

Amos went to his room and took off his dressing gown. He lay on his bed and closed his eyes, hoping to drift off to sleep now that his curiosity had been quelled. However, he did not sleep. He lay with eyes wide open until early morning. He had to see for himself why his memory of her kept him awake.

The sun not yet up, he dressed for outdoors, went to the stable, saddled his mare and mounted. Riding down the long drive he said to the mare, "Blackbird, tell me what makes a woman able to turn a man's world upside down, for that is what she has done."

The first glow of morning lit the top of the pine forest as he rode quietly toward the little house, built far enough away from the mansion that the demented screams of his grandmother could not be heard by the family. He approached the cabin from the front but remained just inside the trees to be hidden. He waited to see if his father came out. His mare, not yet tired, anxious for a longer run along the sandy road through the pines, began to fret and snort. Her snort was answered by another from the small stable. Looking closer Amos could see his father's buggy parked by the stable. Beside it stood another buggy with horse still hitched, which he assumed would be for Trouble. He attempted to quiet his mare by dismounting and placing his hand over her nose, but having heard other horses, she snorted louder and shook her head in annoyance.

Just then Amos heard voices and saw Bessie and Trouble come out, Bessie carrying an empty bucket. Trouble followed her to the well and then beyond, where he stacked an armful of kindling from the woodpile. They both returned to the house. Soon smoke came from the chimney and Amos smelled coffee. His mare had continued to toss her head up and down, demanding her morning run. He had not seen his father or Tabitha yet but mounted and with difficulty, kept the spirited mare at a walk until they reached the sandy road. He continued for a distance and then doubled back, anxious to discover what he could. He approached the house again and was rewarded for his patience. The horse had already been hitched to his father's buggy; a task obviously completed by Trouble. Amos watched from the shelter of the pines when his father opened the door and with Tabitha bidding him good day, he put on his hat, walked to the buggy, and drove away. Blackbird wanted to follow the buggy and Amos had difficulty in keeping her quiet. He wanted to see Tabitha before he left and remained in hiding as his mare stamped her foot in the sand and needles of the pine forest floor.

Tabitha came from the house into the front yard. Dressed still in her night clothes and covered by her robe, she threw back her head and breathed deeply of the smells of the forest. She held out her arms and stretched. Her dark hair tumbled down her back. Watching her, Amos could not imagine a more sensual scene. The manly part of himself that he kept under control wanted to break free, to walk to her, take her into his arms and kiss her until neither could breathe. He asked himself, what if I didn't control myself? Then, is this what happened to my father? The woman was a temptress without even knowing it. Innocent yet deadly. Beguiling yet perilous. She was the sort to capture men's hearts without knowledge or intent, and to make a lover mad with jealousy.

The mare's patience had ended. She wanted her run. She stamped her foot, snorted loudly, and shook her head.

Tabitha heard the noise. She turned and ran back into the cabin. The magical scene was gone but Amos knew that he would remember it forever. Both his understanding and his animosity toward his father grew strong. This woman should belong to a young, vigorous man, not an old man who had to take by demand. The primitive urge to consider his father a rival welled up in his mind but was countered by the good will that they both had always shared with each other. They faced a true case of finder keeper, looser weeper. Fair is fair. His father had met her first but Amos knew that every morning would bring him here on his ride and every evening he would drain Joel of any new information. If he could not have and do, he would at least know. If his father ever abused her again, he would answer for it to his son.

After giving the mare her head on the sandy road through the pines he allowed her to gallop as she wished until she returned to a trot and then a walk. Giving her rein so that she could stretch her back, he made for the stable. He untacked her, let her have a few gulps of water and then he walked her until she had cooled. Handing her over to the stable boy, he went to breakfast. He calmly exchanged greetings with his father and exchanged a knowing glance with Joel but no words. He ate, drank his tea, and stood to leave the table.

"Son, what are your plans today?"

"I plan to ride the south field, Papa. The acres that front the river. I want to see how the crop is doing and to see if the workers need anything. I'll check in with the new overseer, Rogers what's his name. Do you know when someone rode it last?"

"Abner Rogers. He rode it last."

"What did he say in his report?"

"I really don't recall what he said. Nothing must be wrong, or he would have made it a point."

"How long since you hired him?"

"Soon be a month."

"Not as good as Timothy Anders, is he?"

"Not sure yet. But Timothy was excellent at his work for certain. Too bad he is gone."

"You did get good references on the new man...this Rogers, did you not?"

"Certainly, I did. Excellent references."

"Where from?"

"Plantation in Georgia. Family name of Sturdevant."

"Why did he leave them?"

"Said he had relatives in our Low-Country and wanted to be closer."

"I'll make certain to watch him closely for a while. That is the main reason I will ride the South field. It is the farthest and most difficult to reach around the saw grass."

"You will be out all day and I will not be in for supper. I'll see you tomorrow."

"Yes, Father."

All through the day's ride Amos could hardly keep his mind on his work. Try as he might his mind continued to bring him various mental pictures. He instantly shut down those of his father with beautiful Tabitha but allowed the mental fantasy to play out when he pictured her in his own arms. A conflicted and sad young man returned to the mansion at the end of the day. More annoying was that he had been unable to locate the new overseer. No one he asked seemed to know where he was and their replies were more sullen than helpful.

Amos ate supper alone and went directly to his room to change into his night shirt. He wrapped himself in his dressing gown, poured a double brandy and without his slippers, walked barefoot out onto the small balcony. Change was in the air. Leaves on hardwood trees had turned to full color and had begun to fall. From his second-floor bedroom he could gaze across the field and through the thinly wooded area and see the roof of the house where, at this moment, his father lay with Tabitha. His feet now cold, he downed the brandy in one gulp, closed the balcony and climbed into bed.

Amos had believed that he would never love again after having lost Pricilla but found himself with the same feelings he had for her and the same desires. Both times his father had been the obstacle to his own amorous fulfillment. He would need to work harder tomorrow to keep this out of his mind.

CHAPTER 22

Trouble came through the back door into the kitchen with an armload of firewood. He dumped the wood into the wood box and brushed the residue of chips off his shirt.

"Don't you do dat in my kitchen. You go outside to brush dirt off'n you," admonished Bessie.

"Why you always fussin', Woman?"

"'Cause fussin' come easy. Braggin' on you don't. You don't lak my fussin' you can go right back to de fiel' quawtas where Mastah find you."

"Dat new man, he won't let me in. Say I don't belong in his quawtas no mo'."

"You tell him you come see yo' brother? Dat's what you told me."

"He say I ain't got no bidnes. Tell me to git back where I belong."

"Dat ain't right. I gonna tell Joel. You been goin' to see your brother ever since you move up heah. Dat man ain't s'pose to change no rules lessen Mastah tell 'im! Missy, she outside wid dem paints. You watch over her and get her what she need. Stay heah 'till I gits back. I gonna fix dis!"

134

Bessie walked the distance to the mansion, went in the back door and met with Rhoda.

"Where Joel? I got to talk wid 'im."

"You look put on. What goin' on?" she asked. "Gal runnin' you ragged?"

"Somethin' goin' bad down at de field quawtas. He got to look into it."

"He 'round somewhere. Go look. You find 'im."

Bessie found the butler clearing up and folding newsprint in the study.

"Mornin', Bessie. What you want?"

"Trouble, he come back from de field sayin' he warn't 'lowed to see his brother. He always see his brother ev'y now and again and ain't nobody stop him. Now dis Rogers man, he say no. Mastah Francis say that so? He change anything?"

"Not that I heard. I'll ask Mastah Francis or Mastah Amos, whichever comes in first. Tell Trouble to come talk to me tomorrow and he can go try again. Anyway, I'll know what they says."

"Alright, den. Trouble, he worried. His brother ain't none too well. Older'n Trouble, don't you know? He need checkin' on reg'lar like. I gotta git back to dat gal."

"How is she doing? Mastah still go every night?"

"She doin' fine and Mastah he still come. Dey sit by de fire talkin', drinkin' tea, and starin' in the fire. Den dey go to bed and den dey git up and he come home. Payin' more 'tention to dat gal dan to his farmin' and his peoples."

"Do they...does he...she tell you..."

"Joel, you mind your rat killin' and 'low Mastah Francis mind his own. What dey do or not do ain't gonna cross my lips."

"Well, all right. You want to be that way," Joel replied with a pout. "But you know Mastah Amos, he wants to know everything going on."

"Well..., I only know what she say next mornin'. She say dey lay in dat bed and he don't make no move. None a'tall. She say after what he done, he so 'shamed he can't do nothin' but sleep."

Joel chuckled quietly and under his breath he muttered, "what a waste." But aloud he said, "Yeah, sounds like Master Francis. He good to a fault."

"Well, you keep it to yo'se'f. I got to git back. You tell Mastah Amos what goin' on at de fiel' quawtas."

"I will. Good thing he came back home. Only gone three weeks, and then that gal come, and things go to pot."

"Looks like things went to pot since that Rogers, he come. I gotta go."

Joel heard Amos when he came in through the kitchen and hurried to meet him. There were things he had to say and to ask before the master went out again.

"Mastah Amos, you got a minute?"

"Sure, Joel. We need to talk anyway. What have you heard about the new overseer? Anything?"

"Well, funny you ask. Bessie just now left. She came to tell me that Trouble went to see his brother like he always does, and that Mister Rogers sent him away and said he didn't belong there."

"Time I met this Rogers and find out what's going on down there. I went down to meet with him but he was not on the place. No one knew where he was...said he sometimes left them working alone. I'll have to tell him our rules. Seems that Father has been too busy."

"When you going, Mastah?"

"I might as well go now. This can't wait."

If Trouble could be believed, the new overseer had already overstepped his boundaries and it was time to set things right. Besides, the overseer should ask permission before leaving the workers alone in the fields because accident sometimes happened. Amos wanted no difficulty in either of the quarters. He preferred to be a peaceful man but could rise to the occasion if the opposite were required.

His family had always avoided buying slaves who came off the ships directly from Africa. If they had to buy, they chose second generation workers. They took great care to see that their workers had the basics of need and care, were not overworked, and when their assigned tasks finished, they had time for themselves. The Battailes saw slavery as a necessary evil and did what they could to make up for their own participation. They kept families together, encouraged marriage and allowed their elders to teach youngsters their traditions and skills. As a youngster, Amos had gone to the quarters to play with boys and to fish in the river. He had eaten at their tables, joined them in their dancing and festivities, and until he had gone to Paris for college, he had been accepted in friendship. This had been their way for as long as Amos could remember.

Both Amos and his father knew their field workers by name and they gave respect to each other. They attempted to settle differences before they came to violence; even so, they never knew when a young field slave might believe that he could make a run for freedom or when an issue of jealousy would erupt. The overseer's task with fieldworkers compared as Joel's to household servants; to maintain peace, to make certain that chores were accomplished, and to report any disturbance or injury, all within the rules laid down by the Battailes. Finding an overseer who understood the Battailes' approach was not easy and now it seemed that this overseer did not. He had hardly been on the job long enough for the workers to know him and already he had made unpleasant waves. Time had come for a confrontation.

After his dinner Amos rode Snowbird out to the south field, the field closest to the quarters. He was surprised to see men and women still at work in the fields this late in the afternoon, and unlike previously, they did not look up at him and wave, but kept their heads down as they worked. He instantly felt their blended anger and knew that the problem may be worse than he had assumed. He continued to look for Rogers. He rode the complete path and still had not seen the overseer, but something did catch his eye. A man he knew as Thomas, who should not be in the field at all because of his age, looked up briefly, a frown on his face. His eyes sent a message to Amos and his message was clear. Thomas quickly lowered his head and continued his work, but Amos knew that he had received a silent warning. There was trouble. Thomas was also frightened. If not, he would have stood and spoken up like a man. If Thomas felt afraid, then the others also felt afraid. Amos's question was, afraid of what. Or afraid of whom. On long rein he allowed Snowbird to pick his way further down the path toward the quarters. Amos rode into the center of the square of cabins. Women were still winnowing rice, not weaving their lovely baskets, or sewing. They kept their heads down. Children, usually playing tag or stick and ball, were not in sight. He stopped in front of an older women he knew.

"You all still at work, Johnsie? Your tasks not finished yet? Where are the children?"

"Mastah Amos, I can't talk wid you. Let me be."

"Why not? You and I always talk when I come."

"Dat new man. He don't 'low. We got task all day."

"Rogers said?"

"Yes, Suh. He said. Dat Rogers. We don't git no time fo' our own. And dat ain't all, but I ain't sayin' no mo."

"Where is he now? Do you know?"

"No, Suh. Some afternoons he leaves. Just goes. He come back 'fo dark. Most nights he on de bottle."

"How long ago did he make the changes?"

"'Bout two weeks."

"Where is your man?"

"He in de field."

"Children?"

"We hide 'em," she whispered. "Dey inside our cabins. Dat man he put some to work."

"I'll see about this. You do as he says until I put sense into his head. I run this plantation, not Rogers."

Amos left the quarters and galloped back to the stable. Leaving Snowbird in care of the stable boy he went in search of his father. Finding him in the study with paperwork, he burst in on Francis.

"Father, I have just come from the field quarters. Do you have any idea what is going on with Rogers? Has he talked with you about his changes?"

"What changes?"

"His changes. Something dreadful is going on and you don't know?"

"What is going on?"

"Something is wrong there. People are frightened and Rogers has taken away their free time. Makes them work all day. Leaves them no time to tend their gardens or do for themselves. Did you give permission for that while I was away?"

"Of course, I have not," replied Francis with indignation. "Why would I do that?"

"Have you ridden to the field quarters? Have you gone to see how the new overseer is getting along? Our workers?"

"No. Yes. Not regularly. Not every day. I rode the north field mostly," Francis replied with a certain amount of guilt in his tone.

"Begging your pardon, Father, but you have been giving all your attention to that young woman. She is all you have on your mind."

"You are right, Son. I am an old man in love, reaching for the stars and missing by miles."

"Missing everything, it seems," replied Amos; however, his father's ready admission to his slacked attitude concerning the plantation immediately deflated Amos' pompous anger.

"Then sit down and tell me what Rogers has done?"

Amos repeated to his father what he had discovered involving work related changes that Rogers had made, and then he told what Johnsie had said about having to hide their children.

"Why are they hiding the children?" asked Francis, the innocent.

Amos, a bit more worldly than his father, just shook his head and decided it was time his father was introduced to reality.

"Father, why do you think? Why would men and women hide their children from a strange man?"

Francis required a full minute to absorb his son's meaning and then, horrified, he rejected it.

"No. Can't be. Men don't...children...never..." he said, almost choking on his disgust and rising from his chair. "Boys and girls?" he whispered harshly.

"Yes, Father. Men do. And worse. Since ancient times and even before that. Men do."

"Fire him. Find out what you can and then fire him!" said Francis, full of righteous anger.

To Amos shock, Francis broke into sudden racking sobs and sat back down in his chair. He put his hands over his face as though to hide from himself. He had remembered himself pulling Tabitha down to the tablecloth and forcing himself on her. He dared not look up to his son, for he was certain that Amos knew what he had done. His son was describing him, and he was no better than those men of ancient times, who took what they wanted, with no care of their own souls.

Watching his father sob, Amos did, indeed, realize what his father's tears meant. Those were tears of guilt and shame. His father had broken his own code and had done the unthinkable. Amos saw his father with new eyes and even he saw Tabitha differently. She was a victim not a siren. His father ...Amos didn't want to think any further.

"Will you give him a dressing down, or shall I?" Amos asked, expressing a bit more anger than he had intended. "Have you written to verify his employment and reference? Did you write to the Sturdevant family?"

Francis shook his head and whispered, "The reference seemed genuine and..."

"You were busy with your new woman."

Francis looked up at his son and replied, "Son...please...don't..."

"Call you out on your lack of attention to the crops and our people? I certainly will. You taught me that our people come first because without them we have no livelihood."

Francis hung his head as he said, "I am ashamed."

Normally, Amos would try to console his father, but how, he pressed on in his own anger.

"To say the least. Your mind is elsewhere. I will take over running the plantation. I'll come to you for advice when I need it."

Still with his head hanging low, Francis replied in a barely audible whisper, "If that is what you want, I won't stand in your way." He raised his head and looked at his son, "You are not lacking in age or experience. I do find my mind and my mind leans in another direction."

Backing away from his anger, Amos asked, "Father, what is it about Tabitha that has you entranced? I have never seen you like this. You have always put the plantation first. This is not like you."

"Amos, if I knew I would tell. Truth is I don't know. She has taken over my heart and my soul."

The son looked long and hard at his father. He saw not the man he knew a month ago, but someone strange. After Francis's tears of guilt and shame, at the mention of Tabitha, his eyes glowed, a smile flitted about his mouth, his body at ease.

"I see, Father. I will take care of Rogers and I will find the Sturdevant family and write to verify what the letter of reference stated. I am now considering that it may not be legitimate."

"As you wish, Son. As you wish. Now I must finish my toilette and dress. Tonight, I sup with Tabitha."

"I sit alone at my meals now?" he asked before leaving his father, shaking his head in disbelief. How could a man change so quickly? He was about to think, and with so little cause, when a vision of Tabitha came to him. Her deep blue eyes against her golden skin...that may be cause enough.

Who was he to blame his father when he, himself, felt the pull of her? That night Amos wrote a letter to a college friend who lived in Savannah. He asked about the Sturdevant family and requested a hasty reply.

CHAPTER 23

The following morning Amos ate an early breakfast, tacked the stallion, and rode toward the field quarters. He had a mission to accomplish, a mystery to explore and a man to set back on his arse. The new overseer had gone too far. He may be accustomed to the ways of the Sturdevants in Georgia, but he would adapt to new ways or move on. Again Amos noted that men and women who usually looked up and smiled when he rode by, now worked with their heads down. Only a few looked up when he rode by. None greeted them but their message was loud and clear. They were angry and expected him to repair the damage done to them.

Amos rode on to the overseer's cabin at the far corner of the field quarters. He dismounted and looped the reins on the hitching post. He opened the cabin door without knocking and stepped into the dimly lit cabin, finding Rogers sitting at his table drinking coffee. Startled, the man stood so quickly that he knocked his coffee over and it spilled on his trousers.

"What the hell! Why you barging in like this?" he demanded. "Who are you and what do you want?"

"Why are you lingering when men and women are out in the fields? And why have you taken it upon yourself to change the rules which have been in place for years and have worked quite well. To answer your question, I am your boss."

"Boss? Then...then...you are...must be..."

"Amos Battailes, Mister Rogers. Son of Francis Battailes and now in complete charge of this plantation."

Rogers stood quietly and absorbed what he had heard.

"Please answer my question."

"Sir, I only hoped to increase productivity. I saw how your slaves only worked part time for you and the rest of the day they dawdled. That is not productive."

"It is for me to decide what is productive, not you. The work our people do in the fields half a day is enough to keep the farm going and to keep food on our tables and new boots for me when I need them. The remainder of the day they work their own gardens, feed their own pigs and fowl and work at crafts which they send to the city for sale. This activity takes the burden of supporting them in all and every way away from the plantation. They maintain pride by doing for themselves. They have time for their families which we keep together. Do you understand? We may not do things the way the Sturdevant family did in Georgia, but it is our way, and it is the way you will treat with our people. And another thing. Where are the children? In the afternoons they should be out either playing, watching little ones, or helping their parents. When I came yesterday, I saw none. You will return to the rules as my father gave them to you and you will ride the fields every hour they are working," he said as he turned away.

Rogers was not happy. In fact, Amos could see rage building and decided to retreat and allow the man's rage to show itself so he could see. He left Rogers, mounted the stallion and rode a short way before doubling back. He found a place where he could watch and listen. Soon Rogers came from his cabin muttering under his breath. With no man or woman within reach for him to hit, he kicked an unlucky hound that lay in his path.

Amos' instinct was to accost Rogers, but he remained quiet. He had only wanted to see for himself Rogers' basic nature. He had seen and now he knew that the trouble may go much farther than he had supposed. Rogers was a bully; a cruel, heartless man and such a man overseeing people in bondage was a disaster. Amos needed to find someone in the field quarters who would talk with him. How to do it? It had to be in secret and, among the people. With them, Amos would stand out like a magnolia blossom in a pine tree. Then it hit him. Joel. He would dress Joel in work clothes and send him to the field quarters to get information.

"You want me to do what, Master Amos?" asked the surprised butler.

"I want you to dress in field clothes, go to the quarters at night, and speak with someone. Man, woman, doesn't matter. Find Trouble's brother. Convince someone to talk. What is Rogers doing other than stopping the task way. Ask about the children...why they are hidden. I suspect he is up to more than just changing work rules. I want to know if I am right or wrong. I need to be sure. Will you do that?"

"Why not send Trouble? He already wears work clothes, and he knows the field people."

"Trouble is not strong enough. He is old. I can't depend on Trouble to ask the right questions or to remember what he hears. Trouble is a good man but a simple man; not the man you are. I can depend on you. Can't I?"

"I reckon, Master Amos. I reckon. When do you want me to go?"

"Tonight. You go tonight. I can't wait another day to know what that rascal is up to."

"Alright. Where do I get the clothes?"

"That's easy. I'll send someone to get clothes from Trouble. You only need trousers and a shirt and I'm sure that you and Trouble wear the same size. By the time you get there on foot your boots will be dirty enough."

"Trouble's clothes will be dirty, Mastah Amos? I don't like dirty clothes. He wipes his nose on his clothes!"

"I hope they are dirty in case someone sees you."

"Oh, Mastah Amos, I'm gonna be scared. Your Papa didn't school me for this."

Dark fell. Joel donned Trouble's dirty clothes that Bessie had pulled from the basket of clothes set aside for washday. Holding his nose against the smell, Joel and Amos left the house on foot. They walked together until they came to the edge of the main rice field.

"You go on. I'll wait here for half an hour. That will be time enough for you to find out what else is going on if anything. You are not back by then, I'll come looking for you. Go now. You are on your own."

With trepidation, Joel stepped out from Amos's shadow. He stooped low and crept along the side path until he came to the quarters directly ahead. He slowly stepped forward, stopping at the first cabin. His heart pounding and his brow covered with sweat, he scratched on the door.

"Who you?"

"I come from Master Amos," whispered Joel. "He sent me."

"What he want?"

"Answers. Open the door so I can come in."

Joel waited what seemed like an endless minute when the door opened a crack. Afraid that the door would slam in his face Joel put his foot inside and then he pushed the door open further and quickly slipped inside the dark cabin.

"Before you ask, Master Amos thinks something bad is going on here and sent me to find out. You willing to talk?"

"Man, you lucky you hit my do' fust. Dey's dem what works wid dat man and you knock on dey do' you ain't seen no mo'."

"What do you mean?"

"One man done gone 'cause he say he gonna tell Mastah Francis."

"Gone where?"

"You get word 'bout man got snake-bit and died?"

"Yes. But he is not gone. He is accounted for."

"No snake never bite him. He ain't had a bite anywhere on he body. Mens what seen tell me. Dat Rogers, he got him kilt 'cause he gonna tell Trouble when Trouble come to see he brother."

"Ahhh, so that is why Rogers kept Trouble away."

"Keep yo' talkin' low. Dat ain't all. We got two little gals missin'. Not dead. Jist gone."

"Two gals? When?"

"Las' week. Mammies cryin'. Two li'l gals playin' and watching babies. Then they gone."

"Where they go? Anybody see?"

"If they did, nobody sayin' a word. We think we know but we all scared of Rogers."

"What do you think?"

"I tell you, who you gonna tell?"

"I'll tell Master Amos. He is the one sent me tonight."

The man's voice lowered to a barely audible whisper as he said to butler, "Some of us thinkin' Rogers sell them li'l gals on de market and pocket de money, or else he doin' it fo' somebody big. Dat man what die, befo' he supposed to got snake-bit, he say he hear Rogers talkin' wid somebody 'bout li'l gals. Well, he talk too loud and men what help Rogers, dey fix him. Rogers workin' fo' somebody and it ain't Mastah Amos. Somebody buyin' dem gals. We hear tell of li'l boys, too."

"Do you know who all helps Rogers?"

"Naw, Sir, not fo' certain, but my reckon is one o' two new mens he bought off de auction."

"He bought?

"Yessuh. He gone one day and come home wid two new mens. Say he got 'em at auction."

"Without Master Francis? Or Master Amos?"

"I don't know. Just know he brung two here. Strange men and dey do anything what he axe 'em."

"My, oh my. This is just what Master Amos wanted me to find out. I'll tell him all that you said. What's your name?"

"My name Brutus. Brutus Batailles. My pappy was Caesar Batailles. He work for old Mastah. You tell Master Amos what I say. It de trut. He betta fix dis mess quick fo' mo' li'l gals goes missin'. And he betta come talk wid dey mammies and pappies. Dey is mad as a wet settin' hen. Dat man, Rogers, he bad stuff. Now you git on back. I need my sleep. Gotta be up and workin' 'when dat sun come up."

Joel sneaked from the cabin, hardly breathing, enveloped in fear that one of Rogers' men would see him and stop him. He hurried faster than he should, but nothing could have made him stay any longer. He found the path easily and ran all the way to the top of the field. He was out of breath from fear when he found Amos waiting for him.

"Good man. You made it there and back. What did you hear? Who spoke with you?"

"We got to go back to the house before I tell you. Too dangerous here. Let's hurry."

Amos had to run to keep up with the frightened man and when they reached the grounds of the mansion, he stopped his companion.

"Can't you tell me anything?"

"In the house, Master Amos. They might be coming behind us."

"And that is word for word what Brutus told you?" asked Amos as he sat with Joel, still shaking with fright.

"I told you all he said. Every bit."

"Even to bringing his own men?"

"Yes, Sir. He either brought his own men or he bought them at auction. Doesn't matter which, does it, Master Amos?"

"And the man who got snake-bit didn't get snake bit? They killed him?"

"That's what Brutus said. What you going to do with that Rogers, Mastah Amos?"

"He must be tried in the courts and go to prison, so I can't just run him off. Somehow I need to capture him and turn him over to authorities."

"What about more little girls? Every day he might take another."

"Then we must be fast. Tonight, we organize our men to capture Rogers in his cabin before daybreak. One of you will ride to the parish sheriff, explain to him what is happening and ask him to send deputies. How many men can we scrape up?"

"Well, three from the stable. Simon and two grooms. Trouble. You and me?" suggested Joel.

"What about the groundskeepers?"

"Yeah, that makes two more."

"Simon can ride well so we'll send him for the sheriff. That leaves seven. We ought to be able to keep him locked up until Sheriff comes. You go and let them know and I'll get Simon on his way. Tell them to bring a jug of water or coffee and bread and sausage. We'll be there for a while. Tell them to meet in the tack room at nine o'clock."

"How we know Rogers gonna be in his cabin?"

"I'll go in a while and make sure I see a light in his window."

With Joel out speaking to the men, Amos went to the stable and found Simon. Blackbird was his fastest horse and Simon would have to ride her.

"Simon, you ever rode Blackbird?"

"Why, naw, Suh. She yo' hoss! I jist takes care of her. I ride dem other hosses what needs exercise."

"Can you ride her to the sheriff and give him a message?"

"Well, Suh, if she let me git on her, I ride her."

"That is settled, then. You go on over and tack her up and we'll see that you get on her. I'll draft a paper for you to give Sheriff Williams. Then you come on back with them. You can do that?"

"Yas, Suh. I do it."

"You'll have to take the ferry. Here is money for the ferryman, both ways."

"Blackbird been on that ferry, Suh?"

"She has. She will be fine."

Blackbird sensed excitement in the way the men talked while tacking her up. Amos handed the paper to Simon and watched him tuck it into the saddlebag. When Amos held her bridle and Simon stood close to her near side, the mare knew something was up. She half-reared but Simon was quick and skilled. In one swift motion he took the reins from Amos, grabbed a fistful of mane, put his foot in the stirrup, threw his leg over her, settled in the saddle, and turned her toward the road. The mare was off like a rocket, throwing Simon backward. He quickly gained his balance as the mare galloped out onto the long drive. By the time the two hit the road on the way to the settlement, Amos could hear Simon laughing aloud.

"At least this will be fun for one of us," commented Amos as Joel joined him.

"Everybody on notice for tonight, Mastah Amos. I told 'em to meet in the tack room at nine o'clock."

"I'll go now and see if Rogers is in his cabin. I'll be back as soon as I am sure."

Eight forty-five came and men began to gather in the spacious, oak paneled tack room. That they were apprehensive was apparent. Not sure what they would find, or who they would face, had them feeling both excited and anxious. By nine o'clock they had all gathered.

"What we gonna do, Mastah?"

"We will lock the overseer in his cabin and hold him for the sheriff. Simon has already left on Blackbird to fetch Sheriff Williams. You all listen carefully. We will go as quietly as we can. We will surround his cabin and I will place a lock on his door."

"What if he climb out de winda? What if he got a gun? We don't have none. How we gonna take 'im down?" asked Jeb.

"We will take our hammers and nails and as soon as you are all in place you will nail his shutters closed. There is one window on each side of the cabin and two in front. There is no back door, but there is one window. Five windows and five men. I'll be at the front with the lock. That makes six. Everyone understand?"

"Yas, Suh," they all replied in unison and then Riley said, "Dis gonna be fun!"

"What if he ain't in he cabin a'tall?" asked Jeb.

"Somebody gotta peek in a winda and see," suggested Riley.

"Dem windas high. Who gonna reach it?" asked Lisle. "'Sides, shuttas latch on de inside, too."

"I know he is inside his cabin because I was just there," said Amos. "I hid and watched while his candles burned. I saw when he snuffed them out and the cabin went dark. He is there and by now he is fast asleep."

"What we do den?" asked Jeb.

"We stay there and keep him surrounded until the sheriff comes. That is why Joel told you to bring something to drink and to eat. We will be there for a while. Any more questions? None? Then let's go. Remember to keep your voices low and totally quiet when we reach his cabin."

Heads nodded in acknowledgment as the group, high on fear, excitement, and adrenaline, set off for the field quarters and the overseer's cabin.

Amos' plan succeeded. The group crept up on the dark cabin and each man went to a window, with hammer and nails in his pocket. When they were in place Amos climbed the steps to the front and quietly slipped a heavy lock onto the outside latch. He snapped it shut, left the porch, and waved to one man on the side, who began to nail the shutter. At that first sound Rogers woke and called out over the din of the other hammers.

"What in hell! What's going on here?"

They heard him stomp across the room to the front door and attempt to open it. He found that he could not. He attempted to open a window but found that he could not. He cursed and cried out a name, but no one came. He called another name, but no one came. He was a prisoner and did not know who had captured him. He initially feared that the slaves had taken him prisoner. He continued to curse and call out names until he realized that no one would answer him.

By that time, the entire population of the field quarters had awakened and had come out to observe the commotion. When they realized that Master Amos had locked their hated overseer in his cabin, they cheered, laughed or cried.

"You don't have to go to the fields tomorrow," announced Amos to the crowd gathered. "We will wait here for the sheriff to come. While we are waiting, prepare yourselves to tell what you know about his behavior, the one of your own who died and the two missing children. The sheriff will want to know it all and I will vouch for you. You may as well go on back to bed. Sheriff won't be here until early tomorrow morning."

"Naw, Suh. We gonna wait right heah till dat sheriff he come. We got to see dis," said Brutus.

"Right now, I gonna make you all de biggest breaftus you eva et," promised one of the women.

"Make enough for the sheriff and his men," said Amos.

Sheriff Williams and three deputies followed Simon and Blackbird down to the field quarters. The men who had sat up all night to guard Rogers cheered their arrival. Amos went to meet them.

"Glad you got here, Sheriff Williams."

"Can one of your men take our horses up to your stable? They are tired and thirsty. We rode hard."

"Certainly. Simon, take them all up and give care."

"Will do, Mastah. Blackbird done good," said Simon, a wide smile on his face.

"I am glad that you got along with her. Take her up and let her rest."

"Yas, Suh," replied Simon.

"Pleased with yourself, are you?"

"Yes, Mastah Amos. I'll ride her any time you need," he replied with a wide grin.

From behind him, Amos heard Williams' voice.

"You are Mister Battailes, I presume?"

"I am, Sir. Amos to you. You are Sheriff Williams?"

"Owen Williams. I'm tired and I'm thirsty, Amos," Williams declared. "Where is this man you say is evil?"

"He is in that cabin. Locked in."

"What is the problem with him that you have him locked up? Must be bad to bring us down here on the run."

"Not positive, but it could be murder and theft for legal matters, and for work related matters it is total disobedience. I'll take care of the latter, but the others are for you."

"What's his name?"

"Rogers. Abner Rogers. Anyway, that is what he says and what is on his letter of reference."

"How long as he been here?"

"Not much more than a month."

"Where did he come from?"

"Said from Georgia. The Sturdevant family."

"And he killed someone?"

"I believe he killed one of my people. A man who was about to speak up about his bad ways. We were told the man died of snake bite, but others here do not agree. Said he had no snake bite on him."

"What was he planning to say about Rogers?"

155

"Two young girls were missing. Simply gone. That man was going to suggest that Rogers was behind it. Selling the girls away."

"You didn't give him permission to sell them?"

"I did not. We do not sell our people. They live here. This is their home. I rarely buy and I don't sell. Their grandparents were bought long ago by my grandfather."

The sheriff gave Amos a long look. He knew the type. Compassionate. Guilt-ridden. Thinking that slavery was bad yet participating anyway. But murder was murder and theft was theft, and he was too tired to get into a philosophical squabble. Perhaps another time he would plumb the depths of this Amos Battailes. Now he felt the excitement of seeing Amos' captive.

"His real name is not Abner Rogers. Unless I miss my guess, your overseer is a criminal by the name of Angus Church."

"Angus Church? That is his name?"

"Among others. He has gone by numerous aliases; worked at various plantations; kidnaps children on the orders of someone very high on the food chain, who then ships them to various ports to be sold to wealthy men. Steals young boys, too, if they are attractive enough. There is always a special market for youngsters. Boys and girls."

"Who is the man at the top who sells the children everywhere?"

"You mean men. Have not been able to identify them. So many blind connections between men like Angus Church and the power behind him. So many ships and ship's captains and first mates. So many ports in so many countries. None of the sheriffs in other parishes have been able to discover the man in our colony who controls Church. We have a suspect in mind but no proof yet. Perhaps if your captive is in a co-operative mood, we might discover a name or two."

"If not?"

"He will be tried in the courts and sentenced to hang, or he will spend his life swabbing decks under a whip and living in a cage in the hold of a ship."

"You have known about this for how long?"

"We received word from Charles Town, from Philadelphia, from Jamestown, Beaufort and Savanah. Beautiful young children missing and not always slaves. This Angus Church is wanted in all those places for the same thing. It is a lucrative business."

"In Paris I learned about this practice. Children used by men, but I thought we left it in the old world. Never thought it would come to the new."

"Where there are men, you will find this curse. It may be one of the oldest sins and crimes of the human male. Not only black children but white, mulatto...color does not matter and neither does gender. And I thank you for catching Angus Church for me. Now, I can ask him who buys the children, which ships they sail on and to what ports. Not that it will do any good. He will be too frightened to talk. Wealthy criminals know how to keep their secrets."

"At least he won't be able to continue," said Amos.

"Mister Battailes, a dozen...a hundred just like him...will take his place. What you learned in Paris is still true. This sort of slavery has been with us forever and will continue. Since Greece and Rome, and even before...Sodom and Gomorrah...men have enjoyed sex with children. Boys and girls. Whichever suits their proclivities. Wake up, Mister Battailes. Pull the wool from your eyes and see the world as it is, not as you wish it to be."

"You are a cynical man, are you not," stated Amos.

"No, Sir. I am a realist. I am a sheriff. I work with criminals. I know how low a man can go and still I know he can go even lower. Men who think they are above it all have no idea of what they are capable, given enough passion or greed or even reason. Men whose depravity is sex will do anything to live out their fantasies and men who crave money or power will stop at nothing to acquire more. I want to strip the belly skin off and expose the guts of this travesty. In the mental house where we dwell, most men live on the bottom floor. Seldom do we learn enough to climb to the top."

"I never want to be that cynical, Sheriff Williams, and I am sad for you."

"I'm tired, Battailes. A good rest and I'll be chipper and happy again, thinking the world is a wonderful place, all men are holy, and all women are angels. I'll feel better after I see this one put away."

"You have enough evidence?"

"Letters to those cities I mentioned, and their replies should do it. Plus, we have ways of getting confessions. But I am sorry to say that there is hardly any chance of getting your girls back. They may even be on their way to Europe by now. Or Africa. Asia even. The Mediterranean. Men everywhere...all over the world. Corrupt men exist everywhere."

"Yes, I am beginning to see," said Amos.

"Mister Battailes, I know one good man and I would like to tell you about him. He is a rice planter on the coast near Charles Town. He was a sea captain. Scion of a wealthy family in England. He inherited the place here and came ashore to run the plantation. Of course, there were slaves doing the work of growing rice. Do you know what he did?"

"What did he do?"

"He gave the slaves their freedom. Every one of them. He told them they were free to go or stay. If they stayed with him, they would be paid for their work. It was a gamble for certain."

"What did they do? Did all run away?"

"Only three left him to be close to women who had been sold away. To the others, man, woman, and child, he gave their papers, and they chose to remain with him. From what I hear, the place is profitable and the people happy. Just a thought."

"It is something to consider. Now...what about the two men collaborating with Rogers, or whatever his name. Brutus said that the overseer bought them at auction, but perhaps they were his men before?"

"If they are his men, they will stay with the two missing girls, and others that they have kidnapped, until they put the children on board a vessel. Then they will fade into the swamp and look for more children at other plantations. I smell breakfast, Amos Battailes. Lead me to it before my deputies finish it all. I am usually not so long-winded."

"My men and I, we have a march ahead of us."

"I wish you could stay longer, Sheriff. Won't you rest a bit longer? I have enjoyed our conversation and would like to continue."

"Later, perhaps. Now it is best that we put this rascal in chains and lead him to his prison. We hope to get useful information from him...names of those who run this iniquity. If no names, at least I can be certain that he will not enjoy his punishment."

"Sounds good to me. I am pleased that we met Sheriff Williams."

"As am I, Mister Battailes."

CHAPTER 24

"Papa, we must find another overseer. Someone responsible, who will respect our people. How did you find that rascal, Rogers, or Church as his name really is?"

"Marcus sent him to me. Said the man came to him looking for work, but Marcus didn't need him. He sent him on to me to see if I could give him work. I was grateful."

"After this unpleasantness we just experienced, I am wary of hiring someone from a distance who might have a false reference. I would rather hire someone less experienced whom we could trust. Not that difficult. A new hire will come to me for work orders, assign tasks and report to me any unrest or problem. I ride the fields to make sure all is going well. I am thinking of choosing a black as overseer. Do you agree?"

"It might be a promising idea. Do we have anyone in the quarters who would fit?"

"I would prefer someone from outside. Might stir up jealousy among the young men if I chose one of them."

"I see. Then why not ride to Durandeaux and ask Marcus if he has someone on his place he could spare. He will ask a fair price so be prepared to pay."

"I'll do that. I'll ride over today if you have nothing for me."

"Go ahead. I have enough to do to fill my day. See Cecily while you are there. We need to know how she is faring. You will return this evening?"

"I will. Will you be at supper?"

"I will have my supper with Tabitha, as usual."

"Papa, I am curious. What do you do..."?

"We have our supper together and then we talk."

"About what? What do you have in common with her? I don't understand it at all. A man of your age and your knowledge and education..."

"She is educated. Same as Joseph. We talk about what we do during the day. I read Shakespeare to her, and she shows me her paintings. She is quite good, you know, and vastly more knowledgeable than you might think."

"And then...you take her to bed? It's not like you. I've never known you to use our women."

Francis's face grew red as he recalled his shame. He felt embarrassed that, because of his unforgivable act, he could no longer perform as Amos supposed, even if he wished.

"We lie together quietly, and I do not abuse her. We have the kind of evening that I would like to have had with your mother, who was unwilling to be a comfort to me."

The thought of his father lying beside Tabitha brought sudden jealousy to Amos and in anger he retorted, "Father, I know that you bedded her and how. There are no secrets here."

Francis' face turned pale, and Amos thought his father would faint.

"You will never again speak of that to me! It is none of your affair!"

Amos immediately left his father, wondering why he had spoken as he had. He realized full well that he had come too close to uttering unforgivable words but he knew also that he could not bear the image of his father and Tabitha coming together in the biblical sense or even lying side by side in bed. When he pictured them, he felt a knife blade in his gut. He decided that in future he would do his utmost to avoid the subject. It was fraught with too much explosive emotion on both their parts. He hoped that his mission to Durandeaux to find an overseer would clear his mind of unpleasant thoughts and visions.

Amos went directly to the stable and saddled Blackbird. He mounted the mare and from habit she turned to the drive. When they approached the narrow sandy road that led toward Tabitha's house, Blackbird attempted to turn into it, but Amos kept her on the drive until they came to the narrow road that led to their neighbor's plantation. While on the ride Amos regained his composure and found himself remembering what Sheriff Williams had said about the planter on the coast who had freed all his slaves and then hired those who remained. He wondered how it would be if he and his father did the same. He was in deep thought about that possibility when he approached the honeysuckle vine-covered brick wall that surrounded the Durandeaux mansion. He turned the mare into the yard and immediately a young stable hand came to take Bluebird.

"She has had a long ride. You know what to do?"

"Yes, Mistah Amos, I do. She a beauty! Where she come from, Suh? Chas'un?"

"From France."

At the boy's quizzical expression, he explained.

"France is a country across the big ocean."

"I ain't neva' seen no ocean. I seen the inlet. It big enough fo' me!"

"She is a Spanish mare. Take her, then."

"She not a France mare?"

Amos smiled at the boy and dropped a coin in his hand.

"Mastah Marcus, he not to home," the boy said with a grin. "Been gone for a while. Mastah Charles, he in Chas'un. Mastah George in de house. Jis' go on and knock. Mistah Bruneau, he let you in."

"Thank you. I'll go on in."

"How you do, Mistah Amos?" greeted Bruneau. "It good to see you. You come on in, Sir. You come to see Miz Cecily? I'll go tell Mastah George you here. You go on to the drawing room and he'll be there shortly."

Amos did as the butler had suggested and waited for George Durandeaux, whom he knew from their familial relationship through Cecily. They also had occasion to meet at the same church services and at Rice Council meetings. They shared more than a passing acquaintance even if they were not close. He waited only moments before George arrived.

"Well, well, if it isn't Amos Battailes," George said in his hearty greeting. "Hello and welcome. I was surprised when Bruneau told me that you had come. Have you come to see your sister?"

"Hello, George. Good to see you again, and yes, I hope to visit with Cecily, but I really came to ask a favor."

"Mastah George, you and Mistah Amos want refreshment?" asked Bruneau from the doorway.

"Tea, coffee or something stronger, Amos?" asked George.

"I'll take coffee, thank you."

"You heard the man, Bruneau."

The two men settled in their comfortable leather chairs and then George asked.

"A favor? I hope I can accommodate you."

"Yes, but first, how is my sister? I have heard unpleasant news regarding the family. Has she been affected?"

"I imagine you *have* heard talk and none of it good. If so, I will confirm that gossip. You sister is not doing well. Not well at all. I did sent word to your father, but I have not heard from him."

"I am sad to say that my father seems to be preoccupied lately with personal matters. It's good that I returned from Charles town when I did. Speaking of which, I didn't see you at Rice Counsel meetings. Do you not attend?

"Sometimes I do but often Jasper Perrin attends. He is our partner and resides in the city. Relieves me of the necessity of travel to the meetings."

"I see. Then what can you tell me? I sense a difficulty has come about and is affecting Cecily negatively."

"You would be correct," replied George, lowering his voice. "Our house has been turned upside down. Of course, you are aware of Tabitha, are you not? Although my father will not say, I am certain that he took her to your father. Is that correct?"

"She is there...at Battailes, but my father has said little about how or why of it."

"What did he say?"

"What he said hardly made sense to me."

"Joseph is missing. Has been since Tabitha went away. We don't know where he went or if he is still alive."

"No word at all from him? What happened? Can you say?" Amos asked cautiously.

"We suspect that he may have gone into the river. The young, damned fool wanted to marry her. Tabitha. It was forbidden," whispered George. "When she was sent away, I suppose he fell apart. And now I have said too much."

"Oh, my God," whispered Amos.

"Does Tabitha know?"

"I do not know. My father spends time with her while I am busy running the farm."

"Your father with Tabitha?"

"As a companion only, he says. They read and talk," he said, trying not to implicate his father in anything untoward.

George's doubtful expression told Amos that his host did not entirely believe him. George thought that Amos was hedging the truth. Amos quickly spoke to assure him.

"Not the way you think, George. My father would not..."

"All men would," interrupted George. "Especially with a woman like her."

"You sound like Sheriff Williams. He is of the same opinion. My father gave her a place of her own and a man and woman to care for her. She wants for nothing."

Amos did not mention what he knew...what Tabitha had told Bessie about Marcus and Joseph. He wondered if George knew that Tabitha was his half-sister. At least George could understand if Francis had become besotted with the girl.

Not wanting to pry into that relationship for fear of what he may learn, George reverted to the original subject.

"So, what is the favor you would ask?"

Amos explained the circumstance surrounding Abner Rogers and his group of child stealers and his capture. He ended with a question.

"Have you had children missing? Young boys and girls? A few here and there?"

Dorothy K. Morris

"I really don't know. I leave the quarters to the overseer."

"Just as I did until one of our men got word to the house about what was happening. But now I have no overseer. Until I can give my full attention to hiring another I wonder if there is anyone of your people who could take on the job of temporary overseer. I need someone from outside our plantation. Young man...twenty to thirty years? On loan for a few months?"

"By my people, you mean our slaves. Men in the quarters?"

"Yes, that is what I mean."

"You want a black overseer? A black to ride herd on blacks?"

"Not exactly ride herd, but to work between me and the others. If you have someone you are willing to part with for a short while, I'll pay you for his time."

"Someone of that caliber will cost you," replied George with a smile, thinking of his men and instantly one coming to mind, and a way to kill two birds with one stone.

"I do have someone. Grew up here."

"Would he be willing to come to us?"

"Willing? Amos, if I tell him to go, he has no choice."

"May I speak with him?"

"Certainly. Let me tell Bruneau to send someone to fetch him. Won't take but a short while."

"While we are waiting, might I see Cecily? Father will wish to know how she is faring."

"Certainly. I'll ring for her maid."

Amos followed the maid to Cecily's room. She opened the door and motioned for Amos to enter. Amos stepped into a dark room. Shades and curtains closed; the heavy, complex odor of laudanum gave Amos all he needed to know. He looked around the room and found Cecily sitting in her rocker, rocking back for forth, her face expressionless. He called out to her.

"Cecily? It's me. Your brother, Amos. I've come to visit."

Cecily turned her face to him but did not speak. Stifling his shock at her appearance, Amos walked close until he stood in front of her chair. He knelt, noting her alarming weight loss. He gazed into her faded blue eyes underlined with dark circles. He reached for her hands and took both in his.

"Why didn't you come?" she whispered. "I needed you to find Joseph. No one here cared. They did not search long enough, or they would have found him."

"Cecily, I did not know what was happening here until days had passed. There was nothing I could do."

"No one here knows what I feel. No one cares. Both the children gone. Tabitha and Joseph. Where are they?"

Amos was surprised that no one had told her where Tabitha had gone, nor the family's thoughts on Joseph. Protecting her, he supposed.

"Surely Marcus knows and cares?"

Cecily turned her face away and murmured, "Marcus cares only for his women. Don't you understand?"

"Understand? Marcus? What women?" Amos wondered if she were imagining things.

"I know all about his women. And his children," whispered Cecily with a voice close to madness, and then she clutched her brother's hands and began to speak rapidly. "I tried to be a good wife. I gave him a son. He fumed and said he already had two sons and wanted a daughter. He never held Joseph when he was a baby and then one day, he brought me a baby girl. A beautiful tiny baby girl. Skin a bit dark and a bit light. Obvious that she was his own daughter from one of his women, but he gave her to me."

"Why do that?"

"She was the daughter he had wanted. He wanted her reared with Joseph. I took her in my arms and from that moment she was mine, too. And now he has sent her away. He took both away from me, my son and my daughter."

"Does Marcus know that you know all this?"

"Of course, he does. Everyone on this plantation knows and understands how he gets children on his slaves. If I had known, I would have asked Papa not to give me to him as wife."

"If Papa had known he would not have."

Amos did not know how to comfort her, and he remained silent.

"He is away now. On one of his long trips. Says he sails to the Caribbean on business. To visit his trading clients along the islands and coastal towns, but I think he has a woman in Charles Town. Maybe Beaufort or Georgetown."

"He sails away often?"

"Business he says. But I don't believe that. He has a woman somewhere. Now my Joseph is gone, too. He may have..."

"Never mind, Cecily. George told me."

She lifted her eyes to his and he saw her pain.

"What am I to do, Little Brother? What am I to do?"

"Will Marcus allow you to return with me? Our home is still your home. Father would be delighted."

"No. I have asked to be released from this marriage and he has refused. I am to remain here as his wife. His prisoner."

At that moment, a knock came from the maid who informed Amos that Master George had sent for him.

"I must go now, Sister, but I will return to you before I leave."

"No, Amos. There is nothing you can do. Take care of father and send my love."

"Cecily, do you know where Tabitha is?" he asked as an afterthought.

"Marcus said he sold her away. She is gone."

Amos left his sister wondering how Marcus could do this to his sister. Then the alternative came. Was it better for Cecily to think that Tabitha had been sold away, or for her to know that Tabitha was now in the arms of her own father? Marcus was only trying to protect her. Unable to be of any help or comfort to his sister, Amos went downstairs to meet George in the study.

George had spoken with the young man and date was set for their transfer and a price determined for the young man's time.

"Did you have a good chat with your sister?"

"I would not say it was a good chat. She seems quite unhappy."

"With reason, I am sure. I discussed with Father that she may be happier with you and your father, but his answer was no. She is to remain here. My wife, Margaret, visits her every day and Jolly takes good care of her, but she is so listless. No conversation. Just sits there. Sad. I do hope that things will improve for her. She is a good woman and deserves better," admitted George. "She was a good stepmother to Charles and me. Often gave me good advice when I got into trouble with my own wife."

"I, too, asked if she would return with me. Same reply."

"Won't you stay for dinner?" George asked. "You could say hello to my family? I am sure they would like to see you. You could stay over."

"I have enough light to get home if I leave now, but I am grateful for the invitation. Perhaps another time?"

"Certainly. Come more often and I'll try to get out your way soon. Young man's name is Christopher. I'll send him on to you."

"Thank you for your help, George. I'll be expecting him soon. Where is Charles? Did he marry the Perrin girl?"

"She spirited him off to live with her father in the city and they married there. I miss Charles but am happy to see that one leave our home. She was intolerable. Charles will be helping with the joint business affairs of her father and ours...accounting and appointments with shipping and trading. He will be on site for rice council meetings also."

"Very good. I hope the young couple are happy."

Over a firm handshake George leaned in and whispered shocking words, "Promise you will take care of my sister? Joseph would have wanted that. I'll watch out for yours. It is the least we can do for each other."

"Your sister?" asked Amos, quite at a loss over his plea. "Tabitha?"

"Yes, my sister."

Over a shared tragedy the two had bonded.

On the ride back to his home Amos' thoughts centered on secrets. Family secrets. It surprised him to realize that there were none. Someone always knew and someone always told. He did not know how George had become aware that Tabitha was his half-sister or when, but one thing was certain. In that household it was not a secret. He thought then about his own household and knew there were no secrets there either. Secrets buried deeply or not were inevitably uprooted, causing pain, sorrow, and often, the ultimate tragedy.

CHAPTER 25

"Rhoda, call Joel back heah," whispered Bessie from the rear kitchen door. "I got somethin' to tell."

"What you gonna tell?" whispered the cook, maintaining the clandestine attitude.

"I tell fo' Joel, not you."

"Den go git him yo'se'f," the cook replied loudly, "I makin' a pie and I ain't yo' step 'n fetch it."

"Oh, git on wid you. I'll go find 'im and I'm tellin' Trish how you sassin' me."

Bessie left the uncooperative cook and entered the hallway that led through the length of the house. She found Joel polishing a table in the foyer.

"What you want, Bessie?"

"I got somethin' you want to know."

"What? Hurry up and tell me. I got work to do."

"Dat gal...dat Tabitha...," she hesitated.

"What about her?"

"She miss her you know what."

"What? Who does she miss?"

"Not who. You know--her time. She done gone and miss."

Joel stood quiet. Perplexed.

"Woman, I do not know what you are talking about, and I do not have all day."

"She got a baby in her belly!" Bessie declared much too loudly.

The butler stood, stunned, no expression unable to say a word.

"What you expect?" continued Bessie. "Her and Mastah Francis...they been..."

"Hush up, Bessie. Don't you say another word. You get on back to that cabin and do your work and don't go carrying gossip. Don't you say another word, you hear?" he repeated. "Now get on."

"Well, I jis'...ain't we s'pose to tell you?"

"I know, but now get on."

"Next time I won't tell you nothin'," whined Bessie as she left Joel. "You'll wish I did."

When she had left the room, the butler absentmindedly continued to polish the table, whispering to himself, "Mastah Francis gonna be a papa. He gonna be a papa again. I have to let Mastah Amos know before that sassy Bessie tell 'im. Mastah Amos not gonna be happy."

Joel tucked away the dust cloth and set out to find Master Amos. He searched but could not find him in the house anywhere. He went to the stable and found him putting away Blackbird.

"Evening, Joel."

"Evenin', Mastah Amos. You have a good ride to the Durandeaux?"

"I did and a successful mission. What's for dinner? I am starved."

"I think she fixin' fried chicken and collard greens, roasted yams, biscuits, and a pie, but I can go tell her to fix what you want."

"I could eat a whole hen about now. Fried chicken sounds good. Rice, too?"

"Yes, Mastah Amos. Always rice," he replied with a grin. "Always rice."

Joel stood quiet for a bit while Amos continued to brush Blackbird's saddle sweat.

"Something on your mind," asked Amos.

"Yes, Suh. Something powerful I just heard from Bessie."

"Speak up. What did you hear?"

Joel leaned in closer and whispered, "She said that Mastah Francis' woman in the family way and it Mastah Francis."

Joel backed away as shock showed on Amos' face.

"My father?" he stammered.

"Remember when I told you what Bessie said after that picnic? I know it sounds bad, Mastah Amos, but Bessie, she told me she saw that tablecloth and what was on it."

"What tablecloth? What was on it?

"De picnic. Dat's where...when...Mastah Francis...he... you know."

"I asked Father and he said they don't..."

"Maybe don't but did. One time for certain. Ain't nobody been 'round her but Mastah Francis."

"Thank you, Joel. You know to keep this quiet."

"I do, Mastah Amos. I do."

Anger hit Amos like a great ocean surge, the devastating flood after an earthquake. Thinking that his father had deliberately avoided the complete truth; that he was indeed enjoying the delights of Tabitha, was more than he could stomach. His father had violated an innocent girl and then had misled his own son. Knowing this about his father caused his son to see him in a different way; not as the saintly man Amos had always believed him to be, but a man willing to take what he wanted, like any other, just as Sheriff Williams had described. Then for the briefest instant, he felt unreasonably angry at Tabitha as though she had somehow betrayed him. That anger quickly faded and for the first time since his awareness of the young woman, Amos saw fully her position. She was truly helpless. Defenseless. A slave; sold to his father. She could not say no. She could not struggle. She could not oppose him. He asked himself, what if she had said no to his father? What if she had fought to protect herself from unwanted advances. The next questions set his mind into a turmoil. Had she wanted to protect herself? Or had she desired his father's advances? What if his father were pleased with himself? What if he were proud to sire another child? If Tabitha's child had been sired by his father, as Joel assured him it was, Amos would find himself in the same boat as George...half-brother to a slave woman's child. He wondered in how many households this happened and knew that the answer would be in more than a few. Then he wondered if his father knew.

So upset was Amos, sitting alone at the long dining room table, that he hardly could swallow the fried chicken, the smell of it bringing him near to nausea. He picked at his rice and greens, but his throat was too tight to swallow. He had never felt so sick at heart since he had lost his beloved Pricilla to another. He fled the table and hurried to the stable. He saddled the stallion and rode to Tabitha's cabin, halting while still on the road. Candlelight glowed from the cabin windows and smoke rose from the chimney. He walked the stallion a few steps further and he could see in one of the windows. His father sat in one chair by the fire and, close enough for their hands to touch, Tabitha sat in another. A peaceful scenario: man and woman silently enjoying the company of the other. Or did she enjoy his father's company as his father enjoyed hers? Amos felt that stab in his gut and then angered at his own feelings and thoughts, he turned the stallion and galloped back to the stable.

Amos hardly slept all night and was already awake when he heard his father return home early the following morning. He arose from his bed, dressed for a day of riding the fields and went down to breakfast. While on his first cup of tea, his father joined him, a calm smile on his face.

"Good morning, Son. I hope you had a good sleep. Can you tell me about your visit to the Durandeaux? Did you have success?"

Amos did not reply, but silently selected from the platters of food laid out on the sideboard. His father followed suit, knowing his son was in a mood. They both sat to eat. Francis, being pleased with himself and happy to be alive, pressed.

"Did you find a suitable overseer at Durandeaux?"

"I did," Amos replied but said nothing else.

"You plan to tell me about him, or shall I wait in suspense?"

"Father, we have to talk."

"Ahh, I see. You are upset. Then we will talk but first I eat. I am hungry."

Francis's cheerful calm annoyed Amos until he could no longer sit, again leaving his plate of food untouched.

"I'll meet you in the study, Father," he said sternly and left the dining room for the study, where he sat and paced, sat, and paced.

Francis, wondering what was afoot, thought that Amos' mood was a result of his visit to their neighbor. He leisurely finished his breakfast and, taking a cup of tea with him, he went to meet his son.

"Please close the door, Father, and you might take a seat. What I have to say you will not find pleasant."

"Hmm," Francis murmured. "Unpleasant you say? I have done something to displease you?"

"You lied to me."

"I lied to you? About what? Is this about your mission yesterday? How did I lie about that?"

"Father, I have one question and I hope you can answer it truthfully this time."

Francis's quizzical expression gave Amos permission to pose his question.

"Is Tabitha's child yours or was she with child when she came?"

Francis looked blankly at his son, hardly comprehending what Amos said. He had been expecting something different.

"Tabitha has no child," he replied and then recalled Amos' visit to Durandeaux. "Did she leave a child at her home?"

"Father, do you not know that Tabitha is with child right now and I am asking if it is your child," replied Amos with a bit too much strength.

If Francis had been standing, he would have sat. Instead, he was sitting and immediately got to his feet.

"What are you sayin?"

"You are not aware, Father?"

"Aware of what? What child are you talking about," sputtered Francis as though he could not absorb Amos' message...that he was to be a father again.

Then as suddenly as he stood, he sat again, while Amos paced. Francis looked up to his son, his face gone white.

"Yes, Father. You are going to be a father and you lied to me."

"I didn't know. I didn't know."

"You certainly knew that it was possible, didn't you? You lied to me, letting me believe that nothing was between you and her but simple chatting over tea by the fire!"

Even though Joel had already informed Amos of certain happenings, Amos could not reveal what he knew. He had to protect Joel. The shock of Amos' words addled Francis's brain. His thoughts went in every direction.

"How do you know this? Have you seen Tabitha behind my back?"

"Oh, Father, why would I do that? How could you think..."

"Then how do you know? From Bessie? She should have told me!"

"I knew what happened between you and Tabitha the day I returned from Charles Town," shouted Amos, losing control of his temper. "I have ways of knowing what happens on our land, Father."

"I know you are jealous!" Francis shouted, also beside himself with confused emotions. "I see it in your eyes and hear it in your accusations. I know that you are jealous of my finding a bit of happiness in my old age, when you cannot even find happiness in your youth. Why are you not wed and surrounded by children? Now you envy me and my love?"

To Amos, this accusation was digging too deep. His father should have known not to bring up this subject, which had smoldered in his heart for over a decade.

"I am alone because you refused me the bride I wished until it was too late. You knew that I loved Pricilla Allard and that she loved me. You hesitated to speak with her father until it was too late...until she was betrothed to another. I begged you, Father. Remember? You said we were too young and that I should wait another year? Remember? And when that year had almost passed, I heard that she was to marry another? Remember, Father?"

Francis stared at his son, remembering his failure to adhere to his son's wishes; knowing nothing of love and thinking that his son needed to mature more before settling down. He thought Amos should sow his wild oats, not realizing that his son was not made of wild oats, even as he himself was not. Since then, he had tried to encourage Amos to find another young woman and fill his life with family but had met with his son's refusal and anger and accusations to the point where he ceased to mention it.

"I do remember, Son. And I am sorry, but why have you not moved on..."

"Because I will not marry just to have a family. I do not need children to be happy. I need a woman I love, and she was Pricilla. I have found none to take her place in my heart."

"Then you must understand what Tabitha is to me!" he shouted, again coming to his feet. "She is my heart. You are not the only one who feels deeply. I know...I never felt that with your mother, or ever before with anyone, but I do now. If what you say is true, that she is with my child, I am overjoyed. And I wish you would be as well."

"You can be happy bringing another slave child into the world? Like Marcus Durandeaux, who uses his women for his own pleasure, and is not at all unhappy if a child comes to increase his quarters? You felt pleasure, but what did Tabitha feel? Did she come to you willingly, for her own pleasure, or did you force her? In that moment was your mind on consequences? Your behavior was not what you have taught me, Father."

Francis stood speechless. The accusation was as unexpected as it was true, and he could think of nothing to say. He had not considered this consequence. As mother, so is the child. A child of Tabitha would be a slave. At that crucial moment he had not thought. He had only acted. His knees gave way and he sat hard in his chair.

"Of course, you could free her. Give her liberty to go where she wishes, but then you would lose her presence and the comfort you derive from her, is that it? You will continue to have her if she enjoys you or not? Will you tell her that Joseph, the man *she* loves, may have done the unthinkable to himself because he lost her? And your own daughter is suffering mightily for her loss of both? I have just returned from Cecily's home and you have not yet inquired as to her well-being!"

"What are you saying?"

"Must I? Tabitha did love someone. You must know that because it is the reason she is here. Now he is no more. Will you tell her? Will she welcome you now?"

"Where did you...what did he do? Did you see Cecily?"

"From George Durandeaux. He risked offending God by telling me what little he could, but the message was clear. *The river* he said. That is all he could say. His brother loved Tabitha more than his own life. She came directly from that to you. Do you care how she feels? Did you ask her? Before I left, George pleaded with me to take care of *his sister*. And he would watch over my sister, whom you gave to that

180

disgusting Marcus Durandeaux in marriage. I promised that I would."

"Enough, Son. Enough. Please leave me. I can bear no more of this."

"Gladly, Father. Gladly. I have fields to ride and work to do," he said, knowing that his father would immediately go to Tabitha.

In Tabitha's cabin another emotional scene unfolded.

"But, Bessie, there was only that one time," cried Tabitha. "How can I be..."

"Only take one time, Miss Tabitha. Only one time. But you say you ain't done it mo'? Jus' once?"

"That's right. After that one time he didn't...couldn't..."

"Serve him right!" chuckled Bessie. "But dat don't help you none. You jus' as messed up. You gonna have Mastah Francis' baby in, let me see...might be little mo' dan sebem months. You want I should tell 'im?"

"No, Bessie. I will. You think he will be pleased or not?"

"Well, I think he gonna be mighty pleased. If a boy, Mastah can name him after his self. Mastah Amos, he got named to his Mamma's Pa."

"He would name a slave Francis?"

"He might. He don't think on you like he think on me. You nothin' but his woman."

Francis, unable to erase his son's harsh tirade from his mind, felt intense shame for the act that had brought the child. Having his son surmise how the child must have been made caused his guilt to be heavier to carry. He had done a dastardly deed. Worse still, he had gone against what he had always believed and what he had taught his son; all for his personal pleasure; to indulge himself. He thought to cease his evening visits to Tabitha's cabin, but then he knew he would not. He could not. Sinful he may be, but he wanted to be with her every evening to watch his child grow. He would not enter her bed again, but he would not dessert her. He would be with her until the child came and thereafter. He must see her and know the truth.

Straightaway, Francis rode his gelding to Tabitha to discover if Amos was correct. In his heart he knew his son had not lied, but had he been misinformed? That Joel was Amos' source for gossip was easy to guess and he would deal with Joel later. Now he had to know the truth. He halted the horse and left his reins looped through the hitching post, not expecting to be long. He knocked and entered to find Tabitha alone.

"Welcome, Master Francis. You are early today."

"Tabitha, are you carrying my child?" Francis demanded to know, unable to be patient.

Tabitha did not hesitate, "Bessie says I am."

"Bessie would know."

Francis was torn by mixed emotions. His son's words still rang in his head...the accusations...the harsh inditement, which he knew he deserved. He wanted to take Tabitha in his arms and embrace her but he could not. He was overjoyed and at the same time he was ashamed of the way he had gotten the child into her belly. His thoughts became confused. He felt dizzy. He tried to lift his arm to put his hand on her shoulder, but he could not reach her. Instead, he felt himself falling to his knees. He knew that she tried to help him, and he heard himself call her name. Then all went black.

"Master Francis?" she cried. "Can you get up?"

Francis did not move.

"What de matta wid Mastah Francis? What you done, Gal?" asked Bessie, who had just come through the rear door with an armful of sheets from the clothesline.

"He fell, Bessie. He was talking and then he reached for me and then he fell. He won't answer."

"Lawdy mussy, Mastah Francis, what you gone and done!"

Bessie threw the sheets on the kitchen table and ran to her master. She looked for signs of life but found none.

"You stay heah, Missy. I gonna get help. Gotta fin' Mastah Amos."

"Is he dead?"

"Look so to me, but Joel, he'll know."

Bessie took her shawl and threw it about her shoulders. She ran from the cabin and saw the horse tied to the post. She decided that no one would be angry if she rode for help and quickly untied the horse, led him to a tree stump, climbed up and hefted herself into the saddle. The horse immediately turned toward the mansion. Bessie had not ridden for years and held on to his mane as the gelding galloped for his stable where he stopped short, almost sending Bessie over his head. She dismounted and ran to the house to find Joel or anyone who might know the whereabouts of Amos.

"What you yellin' 'bout, Bessie?" called Rhoda from the back door of the kitchen. "You gonna wake the dead!"

"I wish I could," said Bessie, still trying to catch her breath. "Where Mastah Amos? Joel?"

"How I know, Woman? I lives heah in dis kitchen. You go fin' 'em. Why you heah, anyway?"

"It Mastah Francis. He done fall down and I don't know he gonna git up. Got to git Joel."

"What is it, Bessie," asked Joel, who had heard the ruckus and had come as quickly as he could.

"Mastah Francis...at de cabin...he fall...where Mastah Amos?" said Bessie.

"What you mean, he fell?" asked Joel.

"On de flo'! Right dere on de flo' he fall down. He ain't got up. Dat what I mean! Now where Mastah Amos?"

"He's out riding the fields. Left in a state, he did. He won't be in before dinner time."

"Then send somebody to go git 'im. He gotta come to his Papa."

"I'll send Simon to find him and tell him to come to Tabitha's cabin. I'll go back with you. Let's go"

A half hour had passed before Amos arrived at the cabin. He had been difficult to locate among the fields, but when Simon told him that something urgent had happened at Tabitha's house, and not knowing what to expect, he had ridden as fast as he could. He dismounted, left Snowbird standing and entered the cabin to find Joel and Bessie waiting for him.

"Master Amos," began Joel, "I think Master Francis..."

"Father? This is about Father?"

"Yes, Sir. It is. I picked him up off the floor and put him on the bed. He's in there," said Joel, pointing toward a bedroom.

Amos went to his father's bedside. He felt for a pulse. He felt none. He leaned down to feel breath. He felt none.

"What happened?"

"Bessie, she can tell you. Or Miss Tabitha. They were both here when he fell down."

It was only then that Amos noticed Tabitha standing in a corner of the room, her face showing her terror. He hesitated to ask her anything for fear she would crumble.

"Bessie, what happened?"

"Well Suh, I come in with a bundle of dry sheets off the clothesline. I did the washin' yestiddy, don't you know, and I saw him talkin' to Missy and he reach for her, and he fell down. She try to get him up. But no... he ain't got up. I seen dead folk befo'. Den, I ride and go fo' help. You ask Missy. She tell you."

Amos looked to where Tabitha still huddled.

"Tabitha, what did my father speak of when he came?"

Tabitha looked from one face to another and another, not knowing if she should reply or not. Her hesitation brought a comment from Bessie.

"Missy, Mastah Amos, I reckon he know you carryin'. You tell what you knows, Gal. Nobody gonna hurt you."

"Master Francis discovered that I am carrying his child and he came to verify it," she replied softly.

"And what did you say?" asked Amos.

"I told him that Bessie says I am. Those were my words and I had barely said them when he reached for me and then fell."

"Po' Mastah, " said Bessie. "Fin' out he gonna be a papa and git so happy his heart can't take it. Must be done give out."

Amos remained silent. He agreed that his father's heart may have been the cause of his sudden death, but it was not the coming child who had caused it as much as their own violent argument of that morning. At that moment he looked up and stared directly into Tabitha's eyes. It seemed to him that she saw into his soul, and he quickly looked away. Now he had to fulfill his promise to her brother, George. He must care for her and her child, his father's son.

Deep in his soul, where all his dark secrets hid even from himself, lay a truth: that Tabitha would someday belong to him, and he would rear her son as his own.

When Francis's body had been removed and everyone had left her alone with Bessie, Tabitha turned a tear-stained face to the old woman.

"What happens to me now, Bessie?"

"Lawdy, mussy, Gal, I ain't know."

"Will Master Amos sell me away because of..."

"Naw, he ain't gonna sell you away. Mastah Francis, he didn't hold wid sellin' his peoples and Mastah Amos feel de same. He might send you to Joel and he put you to work in de house, I reckon. You kin make beds and such like."

"But Master Francis is gone, Bessie. He was so kind and he is gone."

"Don't you worry none. Mastah Amos, he his daddy's son."

Neither of the two women knew just how true her words would prove.

Francis followed his father's body to the mansion and slowly climbed the stairs. His mother must be told, and he had no idea what her reaction might be. Would she be sad that she had lost Francis, glad that he was gone, or would she feel anything at all? He gave a gentle knock on her door and her maid came.

"She nappin', Mastah Amos," warned the maid.

"Wake her."

"She don't like to be woke up till she ready," she replied with a bit of edge to her voice.

""Mazy, I have sad news for her, and I don't know how she will react."

"What happen, Mastah Amos?"

"My father has just passed away. His body has just been brought into the house and I must tell my mother. We have to make arrangements for his funeral."

"Well, I reckon you best tell her. What he die from?"

"His heart we think. It was sudden. He fell and was gone. Did not suffer."

"Her mood it gonna git worse."

Amos dreaded bringing any news to his mother, but the idea of telling her of her husband's death brought shivers. He had no idea how she would react: if she would cry or laugh or rage at Amos because Francis would no longer be there for her to berate. He needn't have been so concerned for there was hardly any reaction from her. She behaved as though the news were not shocking or sad or troublesome at all and perhaps it was none of those things to the woman who had allowed her disposition to turn sour so many years ago. Amos felt shocked at the total absence of emotion when he gave her the news. He may has well have told her that an old dog had died. Her only verbal response was to inform him that she desired to choose a different maid, for Mazy had begun to sass her.

When Amos had become a man and observed things outside himself, he began to see a pattern among the women he knew, especially those who had been married for a while. It seemed to him that they eventually gave up on everything. They neither saw nor anticipated joy or a promise of a better tomorrow. They hid away from life, from their men and sometimes even their children. They became angry and mean or sad. Again, in his mind's eye, he saw the vision of Sheriff Williams and the judgment he had cast on men. Men's fault, he said, and the imagined words frightened Amos. What were men doing wrong? Amos wondered if it must be so or could it be different. If he ever wed would his wife eventually come to despise him?

Bessie and Trish wasted no time in preparing the body, choosing his clothing, and preparing him for the mourners to take Francis Battailes to the cemetery at the little cemetery where two generations of planters would now lay in rest.

Joel built a coffin and Trish lined it with a satin bed cover before they placed the body in the box. Damp weather in the southern swampland was no time to keep a body lying in state for neighbors to come for a wake. No one thought to include Tabitha in this close family affair when Francis' coffin was placed on a wagon bed. With Bessie and Trish sitting beside the coffin and Joel driving they took Francis to his burial. Amos rode Blackbird beside the wagon. Within hours Francis was in his grave with the minister come from his dwelling place to say words over him. Before departing Amos asked for and was given permission to have a memorial service for his father at the next meeting of their congregation.

Amos knew he had a new and immediate problem which he must solve. He had no idea which way to turn for an answer; no one from whom to seek advice. He was on his own. In the hours since his father's death one thought had occupied his mind: his father's child was growing in Tabitha's belly and how George would react when he knew. Tabitha would give birth to his own brother or sister. She and the child now were his responsibility. What should he do to protect them? What *could* he do? He had only to ask himself the question aloud that the answer came, and the words that came from his inner self shook him to his core. Could he? Dare he? He had no choice but to pursue his mind's solution, but how would she react? How would anyone react? What would people think or say?

"You say something, Master Amos?" asked Joel.

"I did but didn't realize I said it aloud. Never mind me. My mind is on things."

"I can imagine, Suh. I can imagine. You got a lot on your hands now you the only boss. You need that overseer."

"He should be here in a day or so. Meanwhile, there is something I must think about very carefully."

"Mastah Amos, I know what you been thinkin'. I know."

Amos looked into Joel's eyes and saw truth. Joel did know. Amos tilted his head, lifted his eyebrows questioningly and waited for Joel's answer.

"I can't think of nothin' else."

CHAPTER 26

Surprised that Joel had guessed where his thoughts had led, Amos continued to turn the possibility over in his mind during the next few days. He wanted to protect his father's reputation and yet, there were facts to face. Tabitha was pregnant and there was little doubt as to the father. Both Bessie and his father had implied that she came to Battailes untouched...a virgin, and there was Bessie's evidence...the stained tablecloth. Most important now was that he and Tabitha, Bessie and Joel, and therefore the entire household and quarters, knew the truth. That truth and the only wise solution led to the greatest anxiety he had ever known. The more he thought on it the more this improbable solution carried more weight than any other.

He waited before visiting Tabitha. He had to think. He even had to pray on it...something he rarely did. He thought of Sheriff Williams and wondered what he would say...would he approve or disapprove? He considered George Durandeaux and, again, wondered if he would be outraged or pleased. Marcus...what would the great Marcus Durandeaux say or do when he knew?

The evening came when Amos knew he must follow through with his idea. His appetite ruined by anxiety, he shoved his plate aside, left the table and made his way to the stable where he took Blackbird out. Planning what he would say and how he would tell her about Joseph, he rode slowly to her cabin. A candle glow in the window told him that she was awake. He kept the mare standing while he watched the window for movement and was rewarded soon as he saw her slight figure walk between candle-light and the window. He dismounted and looped the reins on the post. He walked to the door, knocked softly, and waited.

"Who's there? That you, Bessie?"

Amos steeled himself.

"Not Bessie. It is Amos. May I come in?"

The door opened and Tabitha stood with the candle-glow behind her. Try as he might, Amos could not be casual. His body would not allow him to pretend to himself that this girl did not have a profound effect on him. He could not escape his truth any more than had his father before him. He wanted to take her in his arms. He wanted to plant his lips upon hers, his hungry mouth on hers. He wanted his naked body on hers. As the knowledge terrified him, he forgave his father for any evil thought or actions that he had done for he, too, felt vulnerable to her mere presence. What power she held he did not know. Was it her scent, her voice, her eyes? He did not care. It was the whole of her, and he knew that, after many years, he was in love again.

Tabitha lowered her eyes, stepped back, and allowed the door to swing open. Amos entered the small sitting room and looked around in the dark and shadowy corners where candlelight did not reach. He tried not to look at her for fear he would give himself away.

"You buried your father. Bessie told me."

"Yes, we did. A quick burial because of necessity but we will have a memorial service at next congregation."

Amos then stood silent, feeling as awkward as a thirteen-year-old boy.

"I am so deeply sorry. He was a good man. We shared some good evenings here by the fireplace."

"You admired him?"

"Not when I first came but I learned to understand him and yes, I came to admire him. He was humble. And intelligent. We talked about many things."

"He was all of those things, but how could you..."

"Was there something you needed, Master Amos?" she asked quietly. "Bessie has not returned and Trouble is...somewhere. I don't know exactly. He goes out at night."

"You are alone here? Does this happen often?"

"I am alone now, but no, it does not happen often in the evenings. Bessie may be returning from the mansion. I am not afraid. Won't you please sit, Sir? I can make tea if you wish."

"I will sit, but tea is not necessary. I came to give you information and to ask questions. Difficult to know where to begin, though."

"Just begin," she replied as she sat in the other chair.

"I went to Durandeaux plantation to borrow a man for overseer until I can replace Rogers. I don't know if you were told that we were having difficulty with him. I met with George and then my sister, Cecily. I learned many things about which I previously knew nothing."

"About Joseph and me? About my father, Marcus? I know all of it, Sir. Is there something specific you wish to tell me?"

A small inner voice told him that he should not speak now of Joseph and the swath that Marcus had cut through the women on his plantation. Those things were not important. Now was the moment to say what he had come to say.

"Tabitha, there is a thing I must ask you and I do so with every good and decent intention. I have thought well on this and have made my decision."

"What is it?

"I am giving you your freedom and then I am asking you to be my wife."

Tabitha's expression showed her surprise, but she only asked, "Why would you do this?"

"You carry my father's child. The child will be my kin. It is my responsibility to care for you and the child. He would be as my own. I would not force you and so I give you your freedom. You will accept my proposal of marriage as a free woman, or you will refuse it. If you refuse me, you and the child will always have a home here and the best life that I can offer."

Her small hands lay quiet in her lap and a little smile flickered at the corner of her mouth as she digested his statements, but her blue eyes narrowed a bit when she asked, "To save your father's reputation you would marry a slave? A woman of color? You would do my child and me this favor?"

Ashamed that she saw his offer as being only chivalry, Amos feared that she may refuse him. Again, he knew that truth was called for...his own total truth, which he had admitted to himself but had hardly accepted. He could evade no longer.

"No. There is more. I am as guilty as my father. I want you as much as he did and in the same way. I fear that I loved you since the first moment I saw you sitting in your chair with your painting. I will not take you as Father did, but I do know how he felt. I ask you to marry me because I wish for you to be mine and not another's. I want you to want me as I want you."

"That was quite a speech, Master Amos. Will you give me time to think?"

Tabitha knew at that very moment what her answer would be. No day had passed that she had not hoped or prayed that she would see Francis' son ride by on his great white stallion, or that he would come to watch her paint, hidden in the pines as he thought he was, with Blackbird pawing in frustration. She would accept Amos with joy.

Something about her expression softened, her lowered lids with dark lashes slowly lifted and gave her away.

"I will leave you now. Please think about what I have said?"

He turned to go and she rose from her chair and walked the few feet to stand in front of him. He moved forward, put his hands on her shoulders. When she did not resist, he pulled her toward him. When she came willingly and began to tremble, he put his lips to hers. Alarmed at the strength of his feelings and of her response, he held her away from him.

"Does this mean I have your answer?" he asked, his voice hoarse.

Unable to speak, she closed her eyes but remained quiet.

"I will draw up your papers myself. You will be a free woman. Our minister will not marry us because...well, because. You will move into my home, and I will introduce you as my wife. A traveling minister will visit within a few months and will join us in holy wedlock. We will be just as much wed by a Methodist as we would be by a Huguenot. Meanwhile, from this moment on, Tabitha Durandeaux, you are my wife, and your child is mine."

Amos' purpose fulfilled, he knew he should leave, but felt captured by tumultuous feelings amid the soft glow of light on the rough-hewn walls that sheltered the two of them. And truly, with her in his arms he wanted nothing more. However much torn he felt, his better sense won, and he forced himself to walk to the door. He opened it and stepped out, then turned back to her.

"Do you ride, Miss Tabitha?" he asked spontaneously.

"I do, Sir. Or I did. Before this," she replied. "Joseph and I rode together."

"Did you love Joseph?"

Tabitha heard the hint of jealousy in his voice and replied, "I loved him like the brother he was. And I still do."

"There is a gentle mare in the stable. You can ride for a while yet."

"If you wish."

"Goodnight, then."

Amos walked away, his mind in turmoil, wondering how the past few moments had come about. He had planned his proposal of marriage but had not been prepared for their mutual passionate response to the closeness of their bodies. He untied Blackbird, mounted, and enjoying the quiet night and his newfound joyfulness, he rode back to the stable and put the mare away. He climbed the stairs to his room and his bed for a night of restless sleep and dreams. In a dream he saw his father's face but could not determine if that face showed peace or anger or both.

The very next day Amos directed Joel to see that Tabitha was moved into the mansion and given the room adjoining his own. His tone and expression told the butler not to question, but to obey with haste. He asked Trish to tell Rhoda to prepare a special supper. That evening when supper was called, Amos walked into the dining room with Tabitha's hand in his. He sat her to his right and informed

Joel and Trish that Tabitha would henceforth be living in the house. Although their eyes grew large with surprise, they quickly lowered them, looked at each other with sidelong glances and smiled.

The meal over, Amos took Tabitha by her hand and led her upstairs to her rooms. He opened her door and stood aside for her to enter.

"This is your room. Tomorrow I will have Joel select a woman to be your maid, unless you prefer Bessie. For you to decide. If you need anything, ask. I wish you a fair night of sleep and rest, Tabitha."

CHAPTER 27

Amos now was solely responsible for the Battailes plantation. Only his decisions would make the plantation prosper or fail. Since he had returned those weeks ago from his meeting in Charles Town to find his father enraptured by Tabitha, and now with Angus Church imprisoned, Amos had done the work of three. From daybreak he rode fields, planned work orders, visited both quarters, gathered daily news from Joel, maintained order and peace among the people, congratulated parents on their new babies and at sunset came home for his supper and to work accounts before he fell into bed and a sleep of exhaustion. He could accomplish all of that and sleep at night knowing that Tabitha was in the next room. He could feel her presence through the walls that separated them. He no longer had to ride in the dark to stand in the shadows on a restless Blackbird until he could no longer ask the mare to remain quiet. He no longer had to suffer as he watched through the window as she sat by a fire with his father sitting beside her.

Christopher, the temporary overseer, arrived at the Battailes plantation riding a saddled mount...a stuffed saddlebag thrown over the horse's flank. He halted the horse and dismounted.

"Who you?" asked a young boy who came from the stable? "I don't know you."

"My name is Christopher Durandeaux, and I am to work here. Where can I find Master Amos?"

"He in de field."

"Which field?"

"Dat one over yonder," said the boy, pointing to the north field. "But he gonna be in soon. It 'mos' dinna time. What you want wid him?"

"I am here to help out."

"He sho need it. No use you goin' out. He come in soon. He know you comin'?"

"He does. Where can I put the horse?"

"Put 'im in dat pen yonder," said the boy, again pointing. "Where you gonna eat? You kin come home wid me if you hongry."

"I brought something with me and ate on the way here. Just a bit ago."

"I got stalls to muck so you best wait here 'till Mastah Amos come."

Which is exactly what Christopher did, until the boy saw the white stallion coming from the north field.

"Here he come now."

Christopher stood and waited, hat in hand, until horse and rider were but yards away.

"Good afternoon, Master Amos," greeted Christopher.

"Good afternoon to you. You are the overseer who George has loaned to me?"

"I am, Sir. Name is Christopher."

"Ready to get settled?"

"I am, Sir."

"Johnny, take Snowbird. You know what to do."

"Yassuh, I do."

"Let's take you on to your cabin, Christopher. I've given you one of the upper cabins close to the house. Hope you don't mind. This way will be easier to assign work and receive your daily reports."

"I'll stay where you want me, Sir."

Amos showed to Christopher his cabin and said, "It's almost dinner time. Are you hungry?"

"No, Sir. I ate something on the way here. I'm ready to go to work."

"Then I'll have mine and meet you here in one hour."

"I'll help Johnny with the stall cleaning."

Amos smiled his approval and left the overseer with Johnny while he enjoyed his dinner with Tabitha sitting beside him, it being the only time during the day that he could look on her face and they could talk together before work summoned him again.

On the first afternoon out with Christopher, Amos toured the entire plantation, the fields, and the quarters while explaining overseer's duties and what was expected of him. Amos went into detail explaining their way of dealing with their people, hoping that the young man shared the same attitude. He found Christopher to be personable, intelligent, confident, and eager to take on the work, all of which pleased Amos to the point of complimenting Christopher.

"I think you and I will have no problems working together. If we do, I have no doubt that we can work them out."

"Thank you, Sir. I know that I will do my best. I'm sorry to hear about your father. Master George said he was a good man."

"Thank you, Christopher. My father certainly tried to be good. Sometimes he succeeded. A few times he did not. But I am surprised that George let you go even for a while. I can't see him parting with such as you."

"There is a reason, Sir."

"What might that be?"

"It has to do with Tabitha. Master George told me she is here. I am her brother. Her full brother. We had the same mother, and our father was Marcus Durandeaux."

Amos could not find his voice. He could only stare at Christopher as the young man continued to explain.

"I came along a few years before Tabitha. Mamma Cassie was laundress then. When Master Marcus married your sister, Miz Cecily, he brought Cassie to the house to be her maid and she had to leave me in the quarters to grow up with another family. He got Cassie with Tabitha and gave her to Bruneau so Miz Cecily would think Bruneau her father. When Mamma Cassie went away, Master Marcus would not send the baby girl to the quarters. He gave her to his wife to rear with Joseph."

Amos knew but did not say that Cecily was not fooled. She knew all along but accepted Tabitha without question.

"George knows this? Does Tabitha?"

"George knows for certain but I don't know about Tabitha. No secrets in the quarters but lots of secrets in the big house. Master Durandeaux got more children from the quarters than any master we ever heard of. I guess he thinks it's the best way to get more slaves; anyhow, the cheapest; him being a trader and all. But none of them full brothers or sisters like Tabitha and me. Cassie only had us two."

"Is this why George sent you here?"

"It is. He knew that it would be a clever way to know what happened to Tabitha and if she is safe. He knows what his father did with her and why. She and Master Joseph were too close. It was because of Master Joseph wanting to marry her and Master Marcus knowing that could not happen. We only guess at where he is or what he did to himself. Nobody talks about him. Master George didn't say outright but I know he is worried about Tabitha. Glad I can keep an eye on her. He isn't like his father."

"I'm glad you told me this and I understand George's reasoning, but does he know you would tell me?"

"He does, Sir, otherwise I would have remained quiet."

"Wise thinking from George. He must put much trust in you."

"Is my sister all right? Where is she working? House or field? Can I see her?"

Overwhelmed by what he had heard, Amos' hesitation was obvious. The man deserved an answer and Amos had to give it quickly.

"She is safe and well. Let me speak with her and let her know that you are here and who you are. I'll let her decide. She will be free to tell you everything she wishes."

"Sounds good, Sir."

"Then let's finish today's work and I'll see about it."

His first day with the overseer completed, Amos entered the mansion through the rear kitchen door, removed his muddy boots and walked in his stocking feet through the kitchen.

"Evenin', Mastah Amos," greeted Rhoda. "Hope you is hungry tonight."

"I am. What's for supper?"

"I'm frying catfish and got a corn pone and plenty of it. Afta' Johnny clean dem stalls Simon let him go fishin'. Got some good catfish."

"Sounds good to me," said Amos cheerfully as he walked through the kitchen into the hallway where Trish confronted him.

"Mastah Amos?"

"Yes, Trish?"

"Mastah Amos, Bessie gonna be livin' in dis house? She gonna be tendin' to dat gal?"

"That gal, Trish, is my wife. You remember that. And yes, Bessie will be living in the house to be Mistress Tabitha's maid. That give you trouble?"

"Well, Suh, Mistress Tabitha don't give me no trouble, but Bessie, she always try to be uppity over me and now she really gonna be. She come out the wash house to be a lady's maid and now she be puttin' me down when she can," Trish said with a pout. "Sides, somebody got to tell her to go to de river and wash. She smell bad. Not good fo' dis house."

"Trish, you are still the house keeper so you tell her. If she give you sass, have Joel talk with her."

With a big smile, Trish replied, "I will do that. Suh, you wantin' shrimp and grits fo' Sunday breaftus?"

Amos saw the gentle clash between Trish and Bessie as the first difficulty he would face in bringing Tabitha into the house as his wife. A greater difficulty lay in explaining it to her brother, not to mention his own mother. His father's reputation was at stake, for it would not do for the community to know that Francis had behaved the same as Marcus Durandeaux. At least once.

Before he went upstairs to change from his work clothes, he whispered to Joel and when the butler pulled back in surprise, Amos nodded his head to assure him that he had heard correctly. Joel then left the room and out through the back door.

Amos went to his rooms, undressed, washed himself and donned his clothes for the evening. He knocked on Tabitha's door and called, "Tabitha, supper is about to be served. You ready to go down?"

The door opened and there she stood, dressed for supper. "I am ready, Master Amos."

"Tabitha, I am not your master. You have no master. You will address me as Amos. I am your husband to everyone."

"Sir, I have not yet agreed to be your wife. It has been your decision only. If I am free, I should say yea or nay."

Taken aback, Amos replied, "you said nothing against me. I took that for your consent."

"I want to be asked properly so that I might give consent or not."

"Well then, right here in your doorway I ask you to be my wife. Will you?"

"I will, Sir."

"Right now?"

"Right now. But who will accept us as man and wife?"

"Those who matter to us. Those who do not matter, do not matter. Tabitha, can you love me? Perhaps you can grow to love me?"

"I already love you, Amos."

"When did it happen?"

"When I first knew that you rode to the cabin and hid in the pines to watch me. I could feel your presence all around, even the next day."

"Let's go to supper and feast on fish and corn pone?"

Arm in arm, the smiling duo descended the stairs and entered the dining room to see four familiar faces standing with smiles. Amos pulled out her chair and she sat, while Joel, Bessie, Rhoda, and Trish looked on with beaming smiles. Amos took Tabitha's hand, gave the others a studied look which silently asked each of them if they approved or not.

"Master Amos, is what I think is going on...going on?" asked Joel."

"Yes, Joel. I am taking Miss Tabitha to be my wife in the only way I can. I have asked and she has consented."

One by one, he saw their smiles as four heads nodded their approval.

"Tonight, you are our witnesses."

"I'll be right back, Master Amos," said Joel as he left them. Very soon he returned with an old bottle of French brandy, which he showed to Amos.

"Master Francis saved this for your weddin'. I knew where he kept it. This is the time to open it?"

Amos nodded and soon all six were celebrating the evening with glasses of golden liquid, the first sip causing the women to cough and sputter. It was an evening to remember and brought the souls to a familial closeness which none of them had ever felt before. Even Trish and Bessie smiled at each other, while Joel beamed like an elder brother and Rhoda left to bring desert.

Their *wedding supper* over, Amos escorted Tabitha to her room. At the door and after an uneasy pause, Amos asked, "Tabitha, are you aware that you have a brother? A full brother?"

"No. I am not aware. How do you know? Where is he?"

"Here. He is here at the plantation. My new overseer, Christopher. That is his name."

"Where did he come from?"

"Durandeaux. Same as you."

"By full brother, you mean that we have both parents the same?"

"His father was Marcus Durandeaux, and his mother was Cassie."

"They had a son?"

"Yes. Before you. Before Cassie came into the house."

"Who told you this?"

"Christopher. But George told me things also about your father. He knows about your father's various children. George considers you his half-sister. I am sure that he agreed to allow Christopher to come to work here so he could know if you are being treated well."

"Did George mention Joseph? Did you ask? I don't know how he is faring without me. We were seldom apart. He had a gentle spirit."

"Then you have not heard?"

"Heard what? Bessie talks little."

"Joseph has disappeared and it is assumed that he..."

"What? Disappeared? Where to?"

"No one seems to know. He simply vanished the same night you were brought here. That is how George explained it to me. Now that Joseph is gone, George feels responsible for you. I assured him that you were safe."

"Then he is nothing like our father," replied Tabitha.

"He has asked to see you. Your brother. Has asked. Will you agree?"

"I will."

"Then I will arrange it."

"What will I say about..."

"You say what you wish to say. I will not put words into your mouth. My dear, you are my wife, but I will not come to you until after the child is born and then only when you wish. I will leave you now. The account books are calling, and I have an hour of work to do. You will be all right?"

"I will."

Amos turned to leave, and she took his arm.

"I want to say something. Have you a moment?"

"I do."

"I want to say that supper was a beautiful time. I have never seen a wedding. Not a real one, but I think tonight was the most beautiful and meaningful wedding I would ever want. I thank you for it. It came from your heart, and I think we all knew that something beautiful was happening."

"That is how it was for me. Sleep well, Wife."

"Amos, you don't have to wait until the child comes. You may come to me any time."

Tabitha entered her room and closed her door. Amos went to the study, closed the door, went to his desk, pulled out his chair and sat. He thought of tomorrow's work schedule to organize. His father had left invoices and receipts to record in the account book. He stood, took the account book from the shelf, and opened it. He stared at the numbers, but he could not tell one from another. He picked up his quill and dipped it in the ink pot. He stared at the page headed Household Accounts until he realized that he could not determine what a household was. He put down the pen, closed the book and left the study. He ran up the stairs, stopped at her door and gently knocked. He waited. The door opened. Tabitha stood there in her night dress. He stepped inside, closed the door behind him and took her in his arms. Their passion was immediate as it had been at their first kiss in her cabin as they truly became husband and wife.

Amos slept all night with Tabitha in his arms. When daybreak came and the most wonderful night of his life was over, Amos lay still so as not to wake her. Knowing how full his day would be and that he would not see her again until dinner, he wanted every minute to feel her body against his own. But worked called. Careful not to wake her, he slipped from her embrace and went to his room where he dressed for riding the fields again and went down to the kitchen. He ate a hearty breakfast, finishing just as he heard a knock at the front. He heard Joel speaking and waited for him to deliver his message of who or what had come.

"Man at front door wants to see you, Master Amos," said Joel. "Says he has a message from Sheriff Williams."

"Hmm. Wonder what news he brings. Take him to the study and make him comfortable. I'll be there in a moment or two. Want to finish my coffee. Thank you."

Amos didn't want to keep the messenger waiting for long. He stood, brushed crumbs from his waistcoat, and left the room to walk down the long hallway to the study. As soon as he entered the room the messenger immediately got to his feet and nodded in greeting.

"You come from Sheriff Williams?"

"I do, Sir. He gave me this to put into your hands and no one else's," he said as he handed the folded paper. "Here is the message, Sir."

Amos opened it and read:

"To: Mister Amos Battailes

We have captured one of the men who aided Abner Rogers in his malicious deeds, and he is willing to give full evidence for leniency. His word will help, but because of his position and that he, too, is a criminal, we need the word of an established citizen to confirm his testimony. You, Sir, have suffered loss because of these men and I request that you come to our office to give your testimony about the affair.

That said, I wish to inform you that we have a lead on where a group of stolen children are being held, waiting for arrangements to be made for their transport. I cannot promise that your missing girls are in that group, but there is a chance. I plan to raid their site immediately and to rescue whoever we find captive. I only have three men at my disposal, and I would like if you and any of your men come to join us. The more manpower we have the more successful we can hope to be.

The sooner we raid their nest, the better for the children. I plan to conduct this rescue during night hours. If you are a willing participant, please be here tomorrow evening. We will do our good deed during the dark of night. This messenger will bring your response to me.

I am your servant,
Owen Williams, Sheriff"

Amos quickly wrote a note of acceptance and assured Williams that he and at least two others would attend him on the following evening. He gave the note to the messenger who was swiftly on his way back to Williams. He then looked for Joel, finding him in the kitchen with Rhoda, sharing a cup of tea. The butler immediately stood when Amos entered the room.

"Joel, you ready for some more excitement?" asked Amos.

"By more excitement, you mean more danger?"

"I do. Yes, or no?"

"Well, I reckon I got through that first time. The second will see me through again? What will we be doing?"

"We will be rescuing children like the two who were stolen from us. Sheriff Williams knows the place where they are kept, and I have signed us on to help him and his men."

"Just you and me?"

"I will ask Christopher to go with us. That makes three of us and Williams has three to help him. Seven in all should do the trick."

"Those children will be guarded by bad men?"

"Yes, they will, and those bad men have nothing to lose. They will be reluctant to be captured."

"Master Amos, I think reluctant is a mild word for what they will feel. When do we go?"

"Early tomorrow. The raid is after dark tomorrow. We will leave here early. I'll go now and find Christopher."

"He came in already, Sir. Early on. Got the day's tasks and said he would go to the field quarters and set everyone to work."

"I'll ride down to meet him."

CHAPTER 28

Amos, Joel, and Christopher left the plantation before daybreak to join Sheriff Williams. Not knowing what or whom they might encounter, Amos chose not to ride either Snowbird or Blackbird. Instead, he took his father's chestnut gelding from the stable. Christopher rode his own mount and Simon selected a quiet aged mare from the pasture for Joel. The three rode quietly, stopped to water their horses at a creek and arrived at their destination in early afternoon. The first hour Sheriff Williams spent in explaining his plan to Amos and his men.

"Do you and your men have arms?" Williams asked Amos.

"I have my pistol but..."

"This raid will happen very quickly. It will be quiet at first and then all hell will break loose. May be dangerous. Knives will be used for close quarter defense if needed. Are any of you skilled at knife fighting?"

"I have played at knife throwing, but not for close quarter defense," replied Amos.

"We use panga," said Christopher. "To cut weeds, saw grass...stuff like that."

"Fine. We will find some to pass out before we leave here. And this lets you all know that one or more of you could be injured. Depends on our stealth and timing."

"I think we all understand, Sheriff," said Amos.

"Well and good. We rescue children from evil men who are holding them until they can be secretly loaded onto a ship.

Heads nodded all around.

"Any questions?"

"How many children are held captive?" asked Amos.

"We estimate that there may be at least a dozen. With those three men guarding them. I might add here that we have only intelligence about this. We have not seen the children or the men guarding them. In that sense we will be working in the dark. We will deal with what we find."

"What if the men are white men, Sheriff?" asked Christopher. "We have your permission to defend ourselves and to rescue the children?"

"You do. Not only my permission but also my orders. You are working under my authority, in my presence. If they are black or white makes no difference. They are criminals of the worse kind. Stealing little children to sell to wealthy men for sinful purposes. I hope it does not come to that, but you have my permission to use deadly force if necessary."

"Yes, Sir."

"Any more questions? Issues? Fears?"

"Sheriff Williams, I am so scared I might ruin my trousers," chuckled Joel, his comment bringing a bit of comic relief to the task before them.

"How will we proceed once we arrive at their hideout?" asked Amos.

"Last night I saw only one man on guard outside; however, I do not know how many are inside that old fishing hut with the children. I can imagine at least two. When we go tonight, if one man is outside, he will have to be dispatched first, quickly and quickly so as not to roil those inside. One of my men will take care of that. Once the guard is out of the way, and assuming that those inside are asleep, it will be a matter of sneaking up, breaking down the door and rushing those inside."

"The door will break easily?" asked Christopher.

"Don't know," admitted Williams. "An old ramshackle fishing hut on the Wando, close to the inlet. I doubt if the hinges are strong on old wood even if it has a heavy lock. A strong shoulder should do the trick."

"When we rescue the children, what will we do with them?" asked Christopher. "Is someone prepared to take them? How will we get them away?"

"I have a wagon ready. I'll leave it a short distance away. We drive it too close the noise will alert them. And yes, a place has been prepared to house the children until they can be returned to their homes."

Williams waited for more questions and when none came, he continued, "Alright. We now have short while to rest before we gather for the ride to their hideout. My wife has cooked a hearty meal for us. We will eat and then find a place to sit or lie down and rest. When we break through that door, we must be prepared for whatever we find."

All went exactly as Williams had planned. His deputy sneaked in close and silently took care of the guard who sat on the tiny porch, rendering him unconscious. He then signaled his success to Williams. Creeping close, Williams saw that only a small lock hung loose on the door. The outlaws expected no inference. Williams motioned for the others to come, and all hell did break loose the instant two of the men put their shoulders to the door and broke the hinges. Frightened screams from the children and yells from the surprised men as the door slammed to the floor inside the room, forcing them back to stand in front of the youngsters. Amos and Christopher entered the hut, each brandishing a panga. William and two of his men came in after them. The room had no light but there was little difficulty in forcing the criminals, both white men, to press their faces against a wall while the sheriff's men secured their hands behind their backs. They cursed loudly until Sheriff Williams hit one of the men across his shoulders with the flat of his panga. Christopher and Amos tried to silence the terrified children and to reassure them that they were safe. They had rescued one boy and ten girls who now huddled together and sobbed in a combination of fear and then relief as they realized that those who broke in had come to rescue them.

Tying the criminals together with a length of rope, one of Sheriff Williams' men tied the rope to a tree while two others went to fetch the wagon that had been left at a distance. The unconscious man who had guarded the door, they tied securely and threw him over a horse. The children were made comfortable with blankets in the bed of the wagon and soon smiles took the place of fear. With more than five miles to return to Williams' office, the criminals were forced to walk the distance while the sheriff's men rode their mounts in front of and beside the rear of the wagon. One of William's men rode behind the prisoners with a long whip in his hand which he used on their backs when he felt it necessary. No one had sympathy for them and soon Williams and his deputies would have them spilling their secrets.

Williams needed to discover the name of the local man who sat at the top of this evil process...the man in charge of it all. He needed to know names of ships and ships' captains who engaged in transporting the children; where the children were taken; to what cities; and who received them. The why of it was no secret. Williams had noted that the children they had rescued were, without exception, exceptionally handsome and were all varying shades of color. Some were the darkest ebony, a few barely tan and one white girl.

By late morning, the culprits were locked into separate cells. With interrogation to begin in early afternoon, Amos prepared to return home.

"Squeamish?" asked Williams upon hearing of Amos' decision.

"Perhaps I am, Sheriff. I know the sort of interrogation that will take place and I am not ashamed to admit that I do not have the stomach for it."

"Neither do I but in this case it is necessary. When I think of what they are doing and for what purpose, harsh interrogations are much easier. We won't have to get very rough. Those three we captured during the night will spill what they know easily. Trouble is, they won't know much. Angus Church will know more but it will be harder to break him. So far, he has only given us one bit of information; that his source is a man in Charles Town with enough clout to arrange the shipping of the youngsters, but Church claims to have no idea who he is. Said they communicate through written messages brought by a different messenger each time and the messages are burned. This unknown man is the only one who speaks directly with the ships' captains and hands off the cargo and receives payment. Again, in this sort of consortium of crime, each higher level knows more than the level below him. Those on the bottom rungs have only bits, but those bits we will have, and they will help us go forward.

I must discover the identity of that man in Charles Town. He will be the key to unravelling the entire operation on this coast."

"You have a plan?"

"I could use a miracle, but lacking that, I am thinking to put Church on a leash and follow him closely next time a message is exchanged. I will then follow the messenger to the source."

"Will Church do that? Will he co-operate?"

"I think he will. He may prefer the rest of his life sentenced to a navy vessel swabbing decks, on a diet of hard biscuit and rank water, instead of a trip to the gallows. Depends on what he would fear most; a quickly broken neck or the whip of a deck master. Then again, he may lead us on a false trail."

"Quite true and I admire you for your dedication. Better for you if I am not in your way to distract."

"This has been an adventure for you, Mister Battailes?" asked Williams.

"It has. Please drop the mister. I am Amos to you. Before we leave, I would like a word in private? If that is convenient?"

"Then I am Owen to you. Shall we step outside?" Williams suggested as he led the way. "What is on your mind?"

"I have been thinking. Since we first met."

"About what?"

"About what you said...you know...about men owning other men. That rice planter you mentioned...what's his name...on the coast. That one who turned all his slaves."

"I remember. Fredrick Talleigh. Freed them all many years ago. He is an old man now."

"It's been on my mind. Like today with Joel and Christopher. They did their share. Even Joel, my butler, acted..."

"You're going to say like a man, aren't you?"

"Well, yes. I was. What is your religion if I may ask?"

"Anglican," replied Williams. "Born into it and reared to its standards. Try to keep my private life and professional activities separate. Difficult at best. You? Huguenot? With that surname I guessed."

"Yes, as were my ancestors."

"And you are confused about?"

"I have read my bible and I know the references to slavery...why it is accepted...how it was regarded...the confusing and contradictory passages concerning owning another. I hear minister talking from the pulpit using one or more of the passages to make his point to justify the practice and forgets to mention the other passage that does not. It is as though they look for those justifications. Is it the same with you?"

"Amos, you know as well as I that slavery, whether black, white, or brown, has existed since one man first conquered another. It has been the way of the world. Now as man's conscience grows, men need reasons. So, we listen to those who are supposed to have the answers. Where are all the answers? In the Bible. However, ministers suit the congregation they serve. Often, they tell us what we want to hear. When their congregation is composed of planters who own slaves, or even the doctor whose wife owns one black slave to do her laundry and prepare her meals, those ministers must not burden their flock with guilt. They need to live and feed their families also. Most ministers seldom tell their congregations other than what they are accustomed to hearing. Then we hear the Quakers whose viewpoint is different regarding many things. That is why they were persecuted so violently and why they now cause ripples in the world of slavery."

"Sir, I compliment you on your mental acuity and your knowledge. You are a thinker, and I would not have supposed."

"Amos, I am Anglican because my father was, and I am a Sheriff for the same reason. I learned both at my father's knee. I followed these paths because they were familiar paths; just as most of us do. If you or I had been born in Rome, I daresay that both of us would be Roman Catholic, heaven forbid!"

"Most likely so," agreed Amos.

"But you are correct. I am a thinker, not necessarily a doer. Fredrick Talleigh...now *there* is a *doer*."

"What you said about him at our first meeting has been on my mind. I have thought on it and know that no matter what anyone says, Joel and Christopher are the same as you and I. Just as human. If not, with black mixed with white, where does the human begin? It's all nonsense. How can I rightfully own another? Who gave me the right? Was it God? Or man?"

"Son, no one gave you the right. It was you who gave yourself permission. Tradition gave you the practice, but it was you who accepted it. Now you either accept that as a given, or you condemn it as wrong. You must feel it in your gut; right or wrong. You can't depend on a preacher or father or neighbor to tell you what is right and wrong. You feel it in yourself, or you don't. Fredrick Talleigh knew, and he didn't bother to ask anyone for permission. He followed his conscience, ready for the consequences."

"I know, too. When I ask myself the question, the answer is right there in my mind."

"I had to face a similar question early in my profession regarding abusing a criminal to get information to stop more crime. Is it humanly acceptable or is it wrong? My struggle with that one took a long time to sort out, but I finally did. It all came down to a matter of degree. I consider my methods to be a lesser evil than their crimes. I think of and consider their victims. I learned to live with the rest. Now, with these children sent to God-knows-where, and for that awful purpose...I feel more inclined to do whatever needs to be done to stop them."

Amos nodded his head in understanding.

"Thank you for this, Sheriff. It has been helpful. I have things to think about now and perhaps action to take. We will be off now. Long ride back to Battailes and lots to think about when I get there."

"Look after your children, Amos. This problem is far from over. Someone out there, someone powerful, sits on the top rung of the ladder. That man uses people, and he does it for greed. This evil thing has been going on for thousands of years and will never stop, but I will do my part to keep it out of my parish."

"Be careful, Owen. You will let me know what you discover?"

"I will, Amos. I enjoy talking with you. If you are brave enough, you might wish to look in on the Quakers. Perhaps in our next meeting, if we have time, I will introduce you to my thoughts about world power. Took me a while to work it out in my head but it helps me to understand world history."

"I think I might find your thoughts fascinating, Sir."
"Farewell, young Amos. Take care."

Amos, Christopher, and Joel returned home with heavy hearts after what they had witnessed and the difficult things they heard. They rode silently for a while, neither wishing to remark upon their experience. Not being able to shake images from his minds, Amos broke their silence.

"Our two little girls were not among them."

"You didn't recognize any of them, Sir?" asked Joel.

"I am ashamed to say that I did not know the girls who were stolen from our quarters but they would have known me. Only know there were two. I depended too much on Father and his overseers through my years away. I asked Williams to find out of any of them were from Battailes. He said not. One from as far away as Savannah and one from Beaufort. Two from Georgetown."

"Wonder where they were to be taken," added Christopher.

"Have you lost any from Durandeaux that you are aware of?" asked Amos.

"Some youngsters have gone missing over the years, but we assumed that Master Marcus sold them. I was busy growing up and working and didn't pay mind to the little ones. Had my eyes on girls my age," he replied with an attempt at a smile.

"Trouble told me about our latest two, but most likely we lost more before," added Joel. "Little gals easy to steal when momma and papa out working. They stay around the quarters taking care of babies. Playin'. Li'l boys go fishin' to the river or totin' water to their parents. Old folk sleepin' or weavin' baskets. Payin' little ones no mind."

Another silence descended on the three tired men, each in quiet contemplation, and lasted until they approached home. They rode into the stable yard and handed their mounts over to the young grooms who came out to meet them. Amos turned to his two companions.

"Joel, Christopher, you must be as hungry as I am. Let's go to the kitchen and see what we can find to eat."

Joel and Christopher exchanged glances and then quietly followed Amos to the rear porch, where Amos removed his mud crusted boots. The two followed suit and all three entered the dark kitchen in their stocking-feet. Amos took a candle to the fireplace, inserted the tip into the banked coals and a spark of light from the candle showed him the oil lamp on the table. He lit the lamp, and a mellow glow lit the room.

"Looks like somebody already cleaned up and went to bed but there must be food somewhere here," said Amos as he opened the door to the pie cabinet, where Rhoda placed leftovers from supper. "I found a pie," he declared. "And here is bread and butter and a jar of apple butter. That will keep us until breakfast."

The three men sat at the long kitchen table. So exhausted that none wished to talk, they ate quietly until they had demolished the pie, finished the loaf of crusty bread and devoured most of the apple butter.

"I never imagined that I would experience a thing like this," ventured Amos. "It was something I could hardly imagine. I feel the need to talk about it but now I am too tired. Perhaps later when we have time to think?"

"Yes, Sir," replied Christopher. "These past two days have caused me to think quite a lot."

All I see is them little faces when that door come down," commented Joel. "Scared 'em to death, poor things. And us rushin' in. My, oh my."

"Better us than where they were going," offered Christopher.

"That right," agreed Joel. "At least we saved a few."

"Sir, I'll leave you now and go to my cabin. Get a few hours of sleep before up again," said Christopher.

"Very well, young man. You pulled your weight...both of you did, and I am grateful."

"Sir, is it possible that tomorrow I might meet Tabitha?"

"Yes, it most certainly is, and I will arrange it."

Amos noted Joel's curiosity over the conversation regarding Tabitha and he decided to broach it directly, with no hesitation. He was weary of subterfuge and tradition.

"Tabitha and Christopher are brother and sister. Same father and same mother."

"Well, I do declare," replied Joel and then he boldly asked, "You told him what you and her done?"

"What did you do?"

"Tabitha and I are married. She is my wife. You are my brother-in-law."

CHAPTER 29

Morning came much too early for Amos. The action of the previous day, the late hour he went to his room and to bed without disturbing Tabitha, made for a slow awakening. Joel's soft knock on his door brought him fully awake and he reluctantly left his bed to open the door.

"I'll be down in a bit."

"Mastah Amos, your Mama makin' a great big old fuss. Her maid come to me and tell me you got to go see your Mama. She wants you to come soon as you wake up."

"Did she say what the fuss is about?"

"She did not, Suh, but I do believe your Mama is angry 'bout something."

"Isn't she always? Tell her maid that I will come up as soon as I finish breakfast. I can't face Mother on an empty stomach."

When Amos came down to breakfast Trish poured him a cup of tea, brought the cream pot, and laid down a spoon; all this done with a bit more rustle and bustle than usual. Amos knew she wanted his attention.

"What is bothering you, Trish?"

"How you know somethin' botherin' me?"

"Just tell me so I can enjoy my meal. It must be bad, or you would have already said."

"Well, ain't you the smart one. All this time I thought I could fool you."

Amos gave her a studied look, his brow furrowed. He knew he would not like her message. He waited.

"Well, you know I been here when you was born. I know you all your life and I ain't gonna say somethin' not right."

"Yes, Trish. Now what is it?"

"It yo' Mama. But you let her tell you. I jist lettin' you know she mad."

"I know. That is how Joel woke me. What is my mother angry about?"

"You all come in late last night. Late when you all finish eatin'. Together. You see Miz Tabitha then?"

"No. I didn't want to wake her. I went straight to my room and to bed. Why?"

"Yo' Mama maid spy for yo' Mama and tell her you had Joel and some other black man sit down at table and you all three sittin' and eatin' together like white folk. She know 'bout you and Tabitha and yo' Mama mad as de bad place 'bout you bring in dat gal to her house and put her in yo' rooms like she own de place. Dat maid tell me yo' Mama say some nasty stuff to Miz Tabitha. Right to her face. Now she say yo' Mama talkin' war."

"When did this happen?"

"While you gone. Dat maid, she tattle to yo' Mama. Stir things up. Make a mess. I think she jealous."

"Thank you, Trish. I'll take care of it."

"I know you will, Sir. Now, I ain't told you nothin' you won't hear from anybody."

His breakfast ruined by Trish's news, that his mother had accosted Tabitha, Amos ate because he had a long, grueling day ahead and needed the energy. His emotions still disturbed by their recent endeavor, breakfast sitting like a lump in his stomach, he left the dining room and climbed the stairs. Facing his mother had always been difficult but he realized that the time had come for him to take decisive action. He would do as his father had considered doing for years as Madame Battailes' disposition deteriorated. She was not off in her head like his grandmother had been, but the woman had grown querulous and difficult to the point of absurdity. Amos would not tolerate anyone abusing Tabitha. One of them had to go and it would not be his wife.

He knocked on his mother's door and without hearing an invitation to enter, he swung the door open. Madame Battailes stood at her window, dressed for the day instead of still being in her night dress.

"Mother? You wanted to see me?"

She did not turn around, but replied, "You have brought a black strumpet into my home? You gave her a room like she is family? You eat with blacks without qualm? At my table?"

"She is family," he replied, leaving to later her insult regarding last night.

"She is a black slave, and you will immediately send her to the quarters where she belongs."

"I will not. I have wed her. She is my wife."

"Nonsense!" shouted his mother as she turned to face him, her face livid with anger and indignation. "You have done no such thing."

"I have. I have declared her my wife in front of witnesses."

"Black slaves are not witnesses and I will not live in the same house with your mistress."

"Very well, then. I will see that you and your things are moved to your father's home."

His mother stared at him as though dumbfounded. And then she laughed.

"No one is there in that old house but my two nieces. Spinsters both. I will go nowhere. This is my home."

"If you recall, Father left everything to me. Everything. With stipulation that I make sure that you are cared for until you die. The will does not stipulate that you must live here. So, if you stay here you will share my home with my wife and you will be kind and courteous when you cross paths. If you stay here your maid will go back to the quarters and you will do for yourself. If you go you may take your maid with you, and I will send a man to do your heavy work. I will not change my mind."

"You would treat your mother this way?" she replied.

"I would. Consider how you have treated my father and me."

"I have been ill."

"Not ill, Mother. You have been cruel, obstinate, inconsiderate, and rejecting. You were never a true wife to my father nor a mother to me. Without a good wife by his side, Father was a shell of a man, and I grew up running to Trish or Rhoda when I scraped my knees and needed mending. I went to them for advice when I was growing into my youth. Without those two God knows what I might have been."

"I will not remove myself from this house."

"Then I will remove you."

"My nieces will not welcome me," she countered.

"Fortunately for you, they have no choice but to accommodate you. *Your* father named *you* in his will regarding the house in such case that you are widowed, and you are. You have as much right, or more, than those two. Have your maid pack your things. You will be leaving tomorrow morning. Now I bid you good day. I have a wife to cheer and work to do."

CHAPTER 3o

A pleasant quiet settled on the house when the elder Madame Battailes and her maid had been removed to her childhood home. Joel noticed it first in the attitude of the house maids. They smiled and spoke kindly to him and to each other. While he lingered in the kitchen with the cook over a cup of tea, he asked Rhoda if she had noticed.

"It 'cause that old lady gone," said the cook.

"Must be. And that sassy maid of hers."

"Betta that Tabitha here now," suggested Rhoda

"You better be callin' her Miz Tabitha now," offered Joel.

"Reckon so. Maybe everything gonna be all right now?"

"Might be," said Joel. "You know Christopher is her brother? Same mother and father. He told me."

"You don't say!"

"Things gonna get interesting 'round heah, what with her baby comin'," suggested Joel.

"Yeah. You know what Mastah gonna do?"

"I think I know Mastah Amos, and I think he gonna say it his own baby. Not gonna say it belong to Mastah Francis.

Nooo. He went and said they married right in front of us. He knows what he's doing."

"We best be getting on with our work. Dinna time come quick. Spent enough time gabbin'. You see Bessie anywhere you tell her to come to see me?"

"I will. What for dinner?"

"Hodges went out shrimpin'. Ought to bring in half a bushel. 'Nough to feed de house. You ain't busy you can help peel 'em. "

"Alright. I'll see you later."

"Wait a minute, Joel. What you men all got into now? Why you all rode away, and den come back so late a day later? What goin' on?"

"How you know?"

"My pie all gone. And gotta make bread again. And dat maid, she tattle."

"Can't talk 'bout it. Mastah say not to. Not now anyway."

"Humph. Mens and dey secrets!"

Later that same evening, at that same kitchen table, Tabitha and Christopher faced each other. Amos had brought Christopher in after their day's work, had introduced the two and then he had left them alone. The house maids were told to stay out of the kitchen to give them privacy. Amos knew they had much to discuss and he, himself, wanted his wife to feel free to say what she needed to say without fear. Now neither brother nor sister hardly knew what to say or to ask. They both remained silent, smiling shyly, and then Christopher spoke.

"Is it true that Mister Battailes has wed you?"

"As much as he can. Are you really my brother? Full brother?" burst from Tabitha.

"If your father was Marcus Durandeaux and your mother was Cassie, then yes. I am your full brother. See, we even are the same color," he added as he placed his arm beside hers on the table. "I knew our mother. I was six years old when I was sent to the field quarters to live with another family while our father toyed with our mother, and you were born. You look like her."

"I don't remember her. She went away when I was a baby, and I grew up with Joseph in the nursery."

"Yes, you were kept so close to the big house. George told me things about Marcus Durandeaux. He considered that Joseph may have come to me for help. I had to tell him that had not happened."

"George knew about what Master Marcus did? Did Charles?"

"I don't know about Charles. I worked closely with George for years, and I think I know him well. A sort of friendship developed between us. I have the feeling that only George knew that you and I were his half-sister and half-brother and kept it close to his vest. There may even be more about our father that George knows but can't say."

"Like what?"

"Well, he hinted that he suspected the reason Marcus kept you at the house and away from the quarters. He was very protective of you."

"What did he say?"

"Nothing that I can put my finger on. Just vaguely hinted that there was a reason besides the fact that you were Marcus' daughter. Something else involved. When we last spoke our object was to find Joseph because Madame Cecily was suffering such grief."

"Over Joseph."

"Over Joseph and you. She loved you."

"She was always kind to me."

"But?"

"But I knew that as far as she was concerned, her love for Joseph knew no bounds. I was there as his playmate."

"Perhaps not only that."

"Oh?"

"I have been thinking these past few days and I have come up with a thought. I am wondering if Master Marcus, our father, took you to the nursery to protect you, primarily, and to be companion to Joseph second? Is it possible that he favored you and Madame Cecily favored Joseph? Perhaps if you tell me what adventure brought you here to Master Amos Battailes, we will understand more? No one has yet told me how you came to be here."

"I would rather Mister Battailes explain that to you."

"You refer to your husband as Mister Battailes? Why not Amos?"

"I was so recently a slave that I cannot yet think as a free woman. Now you tell me how long you will remain here?"

"I am here until your husband can hire a new and qualified overseer. Then I am expected to return to Durandeaux."

"I am expecting a child."

"So soon? Is that why he declared you his wife?"

Tabitha had been of a mind to explain in detail and then she hesitated, thinking it would be too much for her brother to take in.

"He gave me my freedom before he asked me to marry him."

"But he took you when you were still a slave?"

Tabitha faced a decision. Should she tell her brother the truth about her child? She decided not, fearing that Christopher was not yet ready to accept Amos as simply a good man. Now was not the time to explain in detail just how she became pregnant and perhaps the proper time for that would never come. It was simply too private. Her silence gave him to believe that he was correct.

"We can talk more in the coming days, Brother. Just know that I am well-kept and well content and bless the day that I came here. Amos is a good man, and I admire him."

"You are in love as our mother was in love with Marcus."

"Not every man is Marcus. A few men are truly honorable. George might be so considered? And you?"

"You may be right. I'll think on it. Meanwhile, I must go. Work to do."

CHAPTER 31

Christopher awoke to the sound of someone knocking lightly on his door. Knowing it must be Amos, he hurried to answer it.

"Good morning. May I come in?"

Christopher opened the door wider so that Amos could step into the still dark cabin.

"Did I oversleep, Sir?"

"No. Not at all. I am up too early. Could not sleep. Want to ask you a question."

"Yes, Sir?"

"If George would let you go, would you come here to stay?"

Christopher thought. Much would be involved. He would miss Durandeaux but here was Tabitha. Knowing that Amos expected a quick answer, he decided.

"I would be willing, Sir, but I doubt Master George would allow it."

"Leave that up to me. I'm on my way to Durandeaux now. I'll be there and back by noon."

"That will make it a hard ride, Sir."

"Taking Blackbird. She will love a good run. You're sure? You won't change your mind?"

"I am sure. I won't change my mind."

"Then I am off. I left the work list on my desk. Tonight, you make tomorrow's list. I think you are familiar enough with it all."

"Yes, Sir. Be careful. Riding alone on that road can be dangerous. "

"Blackbird is swift, but I will take care. Cook is up. Go on over. She has breakfast for you."

When Amos had departed, Christopher thought on what was taking place. This endeavor of Amos' would involve Battailes Plantation purchasing a slave from Durandeaux. A price must be fixed and paid. A body would be turned over to the new owner; the body being that of Christopher, himself. Even though he desired the exchange, his awareness of the mechanics of this exchange caused him to feel like an object. With a day's work ahead and no time for self-pity, Christopher dressed and, as Amos had instructed, walked to the rear door of the great house and entered the kitchen.

"Morning, Miss Rhoda," he said to her sour face. "Too early for you?"

"You bet it is. Boy, you don't cook for yo'self in yo' cabin? I gotta feed you too?"

"Master Amos told me to eat here."

"Why Mastah he gotta go out so early? I could have slept two more hours. He wake you up, too?"

"He did. But I have a full day and will be good to get started early."

"Boy, where you learn to talk so good? You grow up in quawtas?"

"I did, but we had a teacher in the quarters. Master George and I spent lots of time together. I found it easy to copy his way of speaking."

"You and Miz Tabitha. Talk like white folk. Joel, he say you and her is kin?"

"Brother and sister. Same father. Same mother."

"Well, I do declare! Wait 'till Bessie heah that!"

"Who is Bessie?"

"Bessie took care of Tabitha when she first come. Dat why she still her maid. Tabitha trust her and Bessie know all 'bout her."

Christopher silently ate the hearty breakfast but while he ate, he thought. Bessie. He would remember that name and he would find this Bessie and ask her about Tabitha's first days and weeks with the Battailes. Brother George had instructed him to learn all he could.

Amos arrived at Durandeaux after an uneventful ride. He had allowed the mare a good run, giving her long rein to gallop until she slowed herself and returned to her smooth ground-covering trot. He loved and enjoyed his two horses, both of which he had purchased from a horse farm outside Paris and had them shipped to Charles Town on the same vessel with him. While he was considering the possibility of breeding his two Spanish horses, he caught the unmistakable scent of honeysuckle and saw the high brick wall of Durandeaux came into view. He would find George, put his proposal before him and then return to Battailes.

The stable lad remembered Amos from his last visit and greeted him with a wide smile.

"Mo'nin', Suh. I 'member you. Mastah George, he right heah in de ba'n lookin' ' bout dat mare what foalin'. He been up mos' all night. You go on back."

Amos found George in the foaling stall, sitting on a bed of straw, holding the head of his mare who was in the final throes of labor. Amos watched as George soothed the mare and he saw the foal as it slid from its dam. George then looked up and saw Amos. He smiled.

"Quite something, huh?" he asked.

"It a colt, Suh," said the stable hand.

"A miracle," replied Amos. "All go well?"

"Her first and it took a long time. She was tired. I've been here since before dawn. But you? What brings you here? Christopher working out?"

"He is and that is why I came. And to see Cecily."

The mare scrambled to her feet and turned her head to search for her baby. She found him and began to lick his wet body.

"Let's get him on his feet and help him find her udder."

Amos and George helped the awkward colt onto his feet and steadied him as he attempted to find his balance, swaying this way and that, as they guided his muzzle to his nourishment. They watched the colt's successful suckling before the colt folded his knees and returned to the straw.

"He is exhausted, but we know he got the first suckle and he will be up and at it again soon. We can leave him now and Willis will finish here."

"Where did you find Willis? He knows his job."

"Willis is not a slave, you know. He is a free man and I hired him against father's wishes because he is an excellent horseman. I like the breeding part of keeping horses. It is my indulgence and pleasure, and yes, Willis knows about breeding stock. He is from England, sent here as a convict, but Father does not know that."

"What crime did he commit?"

"He was a new hire for an aristocrat at a country estate. In charge of the stable. One morning soon after he was hired, he saw the Lord's son whipping his horse from the saddle. Willis grabbed the boy, jerked him off the horse and gave his bottom a good whaling. He was fired, charged with assault with intent to commit body harm and sentenced to the colony. One of our contacts put him and me together and we found that we were of the same mind. The boy deserved the whaling."

"You were lucky there."

"Let's go in and I'll get myself cleaned up. You can visit with Cecily and then we'll have refreshment."

Once inside the great house Amos climbed the stairs and walked the length of the hall to his sister's door. He knocked gently and Jolly came to answer.

"Oh, it you, Mistah Amos. Ma'am Cecily, she asleep now. You want I should wake her up?"

"No, Jolly. That won't be necessary. Let her sleep and when she wakes, tell her that I came to visit."

"I will do that, Suh. She talk 'bout you a lot."

"What does she say?"

"Jus' talk 'bout you when you both was little and then she says you went away and left her."

"I went away to school in France."

"Yes, Suh. That what she says. She miss you. Next time you come, maybe I'll wake her."

"Is she well, Jolly? Does she need anything?"

"She well as she can be, and she got everything she need. Mastah Marcus see to that. But well? In her head and her heart? No, Suh. She ain't. Not for long time...since Joseph and Tabitha gone. She ain't heard a word and nobody gonna tell her what they all think."

"I wish Marcus would allow me to take her."

"Would be good but he won't. Not ever."

"I know. Well, take care of her and tell her I came."

"Yessuh, I will. She a sweet lady."

A short while later Amos and George sat on the verandah with a pot of tea and hot scones.

"You have something to celebrate. The colt. What will you call him?"

George thought for a moment before saying, "I have not thought of a name. Any suggestions?"

"One name came to me. Brigadier. Brig for a stable name."

"I like it," said George. "I do! That is what I will call him. Brigadier. I like the sound of it. Will be good for a stallion. Now tell me what brings you here today? You must have left home at daybreak to get here so early."

"I did. I'll out with it. No beating around the bush. I want to ask if you will transfer ownership of Christopher to me."

Amos could see George's brow furrow and his lips purse, but his host said nothing until Amos feared he would explode. He wondered if he had insulted either George or Christopher and was about to speak when George turned his face to him.

"I think I know you well enough to assume you have gone through all the commercial and emotional consequences that such a transfer would bring about."

"I am aware especially of the emotional consequences. I have considered them all and you should know that I ask only because he is a slave currently and you would have to either free him before he leaves, or I would have to pay a purchase price before I free him. For rest assured, that is what I plan. Furthermore, I inform you now that I have wed

Tabitha. I have referred to her as my wife in front of witnesses and she is living in my house."

This was more than George could quickly digest and he stared at Amos before he could find his voice.

"You must be mad, Man! Who will accept her as your wife? What about your friends? Our neighbors? Our minister? He will not perform a service."

"I know all that and I don't care. I found that I am deeply in love with her, and I want no other. Since Christopher is her brother, I wish him to be close to her; to us. I meant what I said. I will give him his freedom as I did to her. She agreed to marry me of her own free will."

"My God. I can't even think what Father will say or do. If I give you what you want, Father will have my head."

"I thought of a way to convince him."

"How?"

"Explain to him that you want Christopher with us to keep watch over Tabitha. Your father obviously feels strongly about his daughter and would feel easier knowing that her own brother could look out for her?"

"True, but Father is not aware that I know of the children he got off slave women."

"Surely, he would not be surprised if you did or even angry. You are a grown man and have lived here all your life. There are things you would have discovered."

"You have thought it all out, have you not."

"I have thought of little else since Christopher informed me of his relationship with Tabitha and you. I think of him as a friend, not a slave. He is my brother-in-law, for Heaven's sake, and so are you."

"I can give it a try with Father. No promises though."

"You must convince him."

"It will mean that I come clean with my knowledge of his affairs and his children and of Tabitha. It would be a shock to him. He believes his secrets are safe."

"Perhaps it is time to open his eyes and allow him to see himself?"

"I am asking myself if I am brave enough," said George with a chuckle.

"What can he do? You are not a child."

"He can forbid the sale, transfer, exchange, or whatever you call it. He could keep Christopher here forever or he could put him on the block."

"What part of the business is under your control?"

"Officially, only the horse breeding. Even though I run the day-to-day affairs of the plantation, my father keeps control. He tells me what to do. Some of his businesses he keeps very private. I am even surprised that he allows his partner in the city to have access to his account books. I have never seen them. However, since he is away so often, I have been forward enough to make some decisions and he has not faulted them."

"Didn't you mention that Charles is in the city now, working with that partner?"

"I did. Charles comes here when Father is at home bringing papers, documents, and things for him to sign and take back to the city. He is due soon."

"Just out of curiosity, will you try to discover what Charles has learned about his father's businesses?"

"What are you getting at, Amos?"

"Wondering about something, and it is too early to mention it. I promise to do just that when I have more on which to base my thoughts. And that is all I can say now."

"Hmm. You suspect my father of something?"

"Not quite that. Not there yet. Simply questioning a few things that I have learned lately."

"You can't tell me?"

"May I be bold, George?"

"Please do. Now I do need to hear what you are wondering about."

"George, someone powerful is behind a criminal enterprise. We don't know who."

"You think my father..."

"No! But he knows everyone and everything that happens all along the coast."

"What sort of crime? You must say or I will not consider your proposal."

"George, someone is kidnapping children and selling them for men to use."

"Use how? As maids and messengers?"

"For their own personal purposes. Evil purposes. As only men could."

Seconds passed in total silence before George grasped Amos meaning.

"And you think my father would..."

"Only that he may have some idea of who is doing it. He knows everyone on the south coast. Can you discuss this with him when you ask about Christopher? I invite you to ride to Battailes when you have his answer. By that time I will have more to tell you of my questions, which, by the way, Christopher can verify."

"I promise to see what I can do."

On the ride home Amos was more thoughtful than usual. That Angus Church engaged in the dastardly business of child theft was certain, but he had surprised himself as he had surprised George by even hinting at anything before more was known. He even questioned himself. Did he suspect Marcus Durandeaux as the man behind the crime? He had to admit that it fit. He wondered where, when, and how that tiny thought had intruded. He could not recall anyone mentioning the possibility. To enjoy Blackbird and his ride to the fullest he tried to forget problems and to recall the delightful experience of seeing the mare foal and seeing the little bundle of horseflesh begin its life.

"Blackbird, would you wish to give me one like that?" he asked aloud with a happy smile as he thought about it.

As suddenly as he finished his question to Blackbird, the reason for his mentioning George's father came to him in a flash of memory of a recent dream, fleeting as it was. He had seen Angus Church's face in that dream and while seeing it, the face had morphed into the likeness of Marcus Durandeaux. Until this instant, Amos had not recalled the dream at all. But now it was all he could see or think. Did the dream mean that somehow Marcus and the overseer had been...what? He instantly reconsidered and said aloud to Blackbird, no. Not a chance. Just a dream. And then he took a sharp breath remembering that Marcus Durandeaux had recommended the overseer to Francis Battailes.

He continued his way home and handed Blackbird to Simon.

"You know where Christopher might be?"

"He out in de fields, Suh," replied Simon.

"It's late. Wonder why he is out so long?"

"Don't know, Suh. He come in when he git hongry. Don't you worry none. He a hard worker. E'body like 'im, don't you know."

"Yes? That's good because I hope I can arrange for him to stay permanently."

"Well, I'll be!"

"Simon, you know anything about birthing foals?"

"Naw, Suh, I ain't. Never seen one come out. Would scare me to death. Why, Suh? You thinkin' on getting' one from our Blackbird heah? You gonna use Snowbird?"

"Might. It's a thought. I would have to find someone knowledgeable in horse breeding, I suppose."

"Dey a place on de riba outside Chas'un I heah."

"How do you know of that?"

"Mastah Amos, don't you know word gits 'round to us? I jis' know. Man give all his slaves they freedom and they stayed right there and work."

"He's a rice grower. You know about that?"

"All us do. That news gone 'round soon's it happen. He breed hosses, too. Good hosses! Maybe he got a man what know about breedin' to spare."

"Humm... I'll have to look into that."

Amos spent the remainder of the evening dining with Tabitha and then he accompanied her to her room. He told her about his visit with George and what he had asked regarding Christopher. Later, with his mind on her and their togetherness only, that brief phantom dream of Angus Church and Marcus Durandeaux did not come to haunt him that night.

CHAPTER 32

Marcus listened patiently to George's request to transfer Christopher to the Battailes but responded with an outright refusal. George did not give up and as he persisted with his reasons, Marcus grew more amenable to the idea. The words that caught his attention were that Christopher would be able to keep an eye on Tabitha. When he heard that, he realized that George was aware that Tabitha had been more than just a slave in their household and was somehow important to his father. He could not guess how much else George knew and decided that what George knew or didn't know was not as important as keeping watch on Tabitha. No one knew how worried he had been for no one had known or realized how important it was to him that his only daughter was well protected. To his own astonishment, he agreed to let Christopher go but his agreeing had come so easily that George hardly realized it and had continued his pleas until Marcus interrupted.

"Son, I agree. Did you hear?"

George ceased speaking, relieved that he had not been required to say that Amos had wed Tabitha. He was not at all certain how his father would react.

"What price father? It would have to be a commercial transaction."

"One shilling on paper. None collected."

The eyes of father and son met, and each read the other's expression and meaning. There came a silent understanding between them. George knew that his father was, in his own way, letting his son in on one of his dark secrets. He would never accept as little as one shilling for any other slave on the property. It was his way of admitting that at least Christopher was more than a slave and admitting about Tabitha as well.

"As you wish, Father. I'll see to the documents."

"You do that, Son. You sign them. I don't need to. Have you heard from Charles?"

"Yes, Father. He wrote that he would come soon and will bring what you need to read and sign."

"Good. Anything else I need to know?"

"You don't need to know, but my mare foaled. A colt. He is healthy and active and looks to have some size. I will call him The Brigadier."

"Very well. Size is good. I am tired of these short mounts where my feet almost drag the ground. I'll see him tomorrow. If you wish, feel free to purchase a couple more mares. Already in foal if possible."

"I'll have to extend the stable. More stalls. Paddocks."

"Then do it. You enjoy horse breeding. A man should enjoy life doing what gives him the most pleasure."

"Thank you, Father. I do."

"It's late now but tomorrow morning when you see the overseer, send him to me. I'll be in the study after breakfast."

"I've already met with him, and we made the task list for tomorrow. Work is all set."

"No matter. I still need to see him."

"Father, are you working too hard? You seem overly tired."

"No, George. Just a setback with shipping arrangements. Spoiled cargo and I blame Jasper. I lost a sum of money. Annoying, is all."

"Alright, Father. You know you can count on me and Charles to lighten your work. He is learning fast and will soon be knowledgeable enough to take over the accounting from Perrin. We won't need that man."

"We will always need Perrin."

"Why, Father?"

"Go to bed, Son. It is late and your wife is in bed alone."

George felt vaguely disturbed after leaving his father. It had seemed that his father's mind was elsewhere, and he spoke more gently than usual. Nevertheless, George was happy that his pleas were heard, and Christopher would soon be free of Durandeaux. As he had that thought, he wondered why. He recalled Amos words about his father. Why did it now seem that something was wrong at Durandeaux? Or was he imagining things? Then his mind focused on one more item. Why was his father absent so often, where was he going and what was he doing? Had this always been the way and he simply had not noticed?

Later in his bed with Elizabeth curled next to him, George could not sleep. For the first time in his life, he felt insecure in his awe of his father. For the first time, since the vague hints from Amos, doubts crept into his thoughts concerning Marcus' uprightness. Getting children onto slave women was one thing. Most men in his position did the same. However, Amos had hinted that something larger and wider and more dangerous was happening and he thought that Marcus Durandeaux was important enough to either know about it, or Heaven forbid, to be somehow involved. George looked forward to Charles' next visit home. He would have a private word with his young brother to discover how things stood in the city.

CHAPTER 33

Charles found George in the stable where he had gone to see his colt.

"Well, Brother, I see that your mare has foaled. Congratulations," he said in greeting while standing in front of the stall door, holding his mount's reins.

"Ahh, Charles. It's you!" said George, his back to the door and to Charles as he bent over to hold the mare's foot in his hands. "I am glad you have come. Didn't hear your carriage drive in."

"I rode Lodestar. Jasper didn't come with me. I came alone."

George let go the hoof and turned to face Charles.

"Something wrong with the mare's foot?" asked Charles.

"Don't think so. Willis said that sometimes mares suffer founder after foaling and I was checking. She seems to be healthy enough. But I'm surprised that old Jasper allowed you to come without him."

"He is trusting me more now that I have learned a bit."

"Means you are adapting quickly. Come, let's put your horse in his old stall and go in and I'll wash up. We can open a bottle of that new brandy that came from France."

"Not yet, George," replied Charles softly.

"Why so serious? You have something to say here?"

"I do and we need to be even more alone when I say what I have to say. Can we go to the tack room and lock the door?"

"My God, Man. What is so deadly that we must hide?"

"I'll tell you. Come on. I'll put the boy away first."

With Lodestar in his stall and Willis on his way to care for him, a very curious George followed his brother into the spacious tack room. Charles pointed to one of the leather chairs and George sat. Charles pulled the second chair close to his brother and sat. He leaned over and whispered.

"I have found a set of books that Perrin keeps under lock and key. He does not know I found them. They were well hidden."

"To what do they pertain? Our business or Perrin's own private affairs?"

"I don't know yet. I only had time to see a few pages."

"Well, what do you think?"

"Difficult to say. Records are in code. Looks like gibberish. Now why would Jasper Perrin keep a set of secret books under lock and key, written in code? Wouldn't you suspect something untoward?"

"That I would."

"There are columns on each page. There are numbers. And then the coded parts. I am stumped."

"Did you mention any of this to Perrin or Julia?"

"Of course not. Certainly not Perrin and Julia would not understand a word of it."

"Good. Tell no one. But I will say that recently I noted that Father seemed disturbed more than usual. I mentioned it to him, and he said something had gone amiss. He lost money on some sort of transaction. Would not say what. He blamed Perrin. Said Jasper's error had cost him money. Do you think that Perrin is working against Father in some way?"

"No. Perrin would not dare. I believe that Father and Perrin are working together in a well-hidden enterprise," ventured Charles.

Hearing Charles' idea brought an instant pang of anxiety to George as being too close to Amos' recent questions.

"It may or may not be legal," added Charles and then he asked the loaded question, "Would Father be involved in a business outside the realm of legality?"

George's silence and facial expression gave the younger brother the answer to his doubt.

"You fear he could."

"I don't know. Maybe. Then perhaps this is all Perrin's doings?"

"Never. The man quakes when Father's name is mentioned. He would do nothing against Marcus Durandeaux."

"How long can you stay?"

"If I get Father's signature on these, I planned to go home tomorrow. Something come up?"

"Can you stay for two more days?"

"I suppose I could. Why?"

"You and I will ride to Battailes Plantation. I have something to show you."

"Let's go on in and see Father. I'll get his signature before he disappears again," said Charles.

CHAPTER 34

Charles had often gotten lost in the crowd of family and servants and bustle of plantation life. Self-sufficient to a fault, he had found his own path and entertained himself. He was a quiet boy, much more intelligent than given credit. When he disappeared for hours during the daylight hours the family assumed that he would be somewhere either riding his horse, reading a book, collecting swamp specimens, or lost in speculation. Marriage had come as a shock to him for he had never genuinely felt the need to cooperate closely with anyone. Julia was as demanding of him as she was of her father and Charles did his best to please her, without succeeding. After he moved with her to her father's stately home on a lovely street shaded by magnolia trees in Charles Town, she refused her new husband her bed, fretting that if she allowed him to indulge himself at her expense, she may miss the entire coming social season in the city. Being great with child did not show off a ball gown to her degree of desire. She banished Charles to sleep in his own bed.

As a new accountant Charles spent hours poring over the books that Jasper gave him to study. Now that he was a grown, married man, he was determined to make his father proud. And then he discovered the locked compartment in the great oaken desk. Curiosity had always driven Charles, first of nature and then of ideas. Now it was curiosity of what was inside that locked drawer that needled him. He searched high and low for a key for those in his possession had not unlocked the drawer. Finally, he found it. Of all places, Jasper Perrin had hidden the key under the base of the large pottery vase that contained dried plumes of dune grasses. Charles had not thought to look there until one morning he saw that grass seed had scattered around the base of the vase. Someone or something had moved it, had shaken the dry seed loose and the maid had not yet swept the room. Charles had bent down, lifted the pot, and felt under the base. There it was, glued to the bottom. He took a letter opener from the desk and pried the key loose. It fell to the floor and Charles smiled at his success, now anxious to read the hidden secrets of Jasper Perrin. But alas, when he unlocked the drawer and pulled out a notebook, the contents were all in code. All the notebooks in that drawer were in the same code. Charles put them all back in as he had found them and replaced the key pressing it into the still soft glue. He had wondered whom he should tell...his brother George or his father.

He pondered this as he and George rode their geldings toward Battailes plantation where his brother assured him that his eyes would be opened. George had said that he would enter the world of men. As they rode closer and closer to their destination Charles' heart beat a bit faster with apprehension and a feeling that this visit would change his life more than he had imagined. His brother had hinted strongly of news of import that would be told, but even George had not imagined what he would hear.

Having departed Durandeaux late morning, the two brothers arrived at Battailes by mid-afternoon, too late for dinner and too early for supper. After pleasant greetings and horses given to stable hands, Amos offered to have his cook prepare refreshment for them, but George was too anxious to delay their purpose.

"Is Christopher here?" he asked.

"He is," replied Amos. "I'll send a man to fetch him. George, you have everything we need?"

"You have one shilling?"

"I do."

"What's this all about?" inquired Charles.

"You'll see. Just watch," replied his brother.

Amos reached into his pocket and pulled out a one shilling piece and gave it to George, whereupon George reached to his deep coat pocket and pulled out a set of folded papers. Amos took them and read. He was now the owner of one male slave, skilled, age thirty-one, in good health, sold from Durandeaux plantation to one Amos Battailes. Amos folded the papers and put them in his own coat pocket. George returned the shilling to Amos while Charles looked quizzically from his brother to Amos and back again.

"Why did we sell Christopher?" he asked.

"When Christopher is here, he will tell you more," replied Amos.

"Looks like I have been away too long. I have missed much."

"True, Charles, but today we will bring you up to date on what we have discovered. You too, George. There is much you do not know yet."

"Here comes Christopher," said Charles. "What does he know that we do not?"

"Christopher, come to the study with us, please," asked Amos.

"Let me put away the horse. I'll be right there."

"Give the horse to Simon. He'll take care of him. You come with us?"

In the locked study with George, Charles and Christopher, Amos handed Christopher a document. The young man opened it and read the words. He looked up at Amos with an expression of uncertainty.

"Yes. You are now a free man, Christopher. I now ask if you are willing to remain here as my overseer and you can say yes or no. You know what I hope for."

"Yes, I do, and I accept. Thank you for this. It is more than I ever hoped for."

"Charles, Christopher is our brother," declared George. "We have the same father."

Charles looked in amazement at George and then at Amos. Finally, he settled on Christopher.

"Is this true? How do you know?"

For a moment Christopher almost said Master Charles, but now he said only, "You and I and George have Marcus Durandeaux as father. So does Tabitha. We have different mothers only, except for Tabitha. She and I have the same mother. We are full brother and sister. Our father sent her here to Battailes when Joseph grew too fond of her."

Charles quickly sat down, wiped his brow, thought for only a second or two, and then made the remark that astounded the others.

"So that is why Father brought baby Tabitha to the nursery with Joseph. He knew she was his daughter, and he always wanted a daughter, didn't he, George? He wanted to protect her. He didn't want her to grow up in the quarters. I have always wondered why he did that."

In the surprised silence that followed, Charles added explosively, "My God! That is why he sent her here to Battailes. He knew she would be safe. And she and Joseph...well...they couldn't...could they! But Joseph never knew. Neither you nor I knew, George. How did you know, Christopher?"

"Cassie was my mother and Tabitha's. She told me when I was sent to the quarters to grow up with another family while your father kept her close to him."

"But Mother Cecily..."

"Our father has more than a few children in the quarters," added George.

"Where is Tabitha now?" asked Charles. "Here?"

"Yes. In this house," replied Amos.

"A house maid?" asked Charles.

"No. She is my wife," replied Amos, his words bringing a studied silence to the room.

"Did you say wife?" asked Charles.

"Yes. Tabitha is my wife. We are expecting a child."

"A child?" asked George. "Already?"

"Love does that, George."

"This is too much. All this is too much," said Charles.

"There is more," said Amos. "Much more. And I will let two more men join us so that you will know that what we say is true.

Amos opened the study door and spoke softly. He opened the door wider as two men entered...Joel and Trouble.

"Joel, Trouble, did I not declare before you that I take Tabitha as my wife?"

"You did, Suh. And Trish and Bessie, too."

"There. You heard them. Our minister would not marry us I am certain, but my open and honest declaration will suffice until another minister comes by who may be willing. If not, Tabitha will be my wife regardless. I have written it in the family Bible and there it will remain. By common law we are man and wife. But now we have other issues to discuss. Trouble, tell us what you know of the recent problems in the quarters."

"You mean 'bout not being 'lowed to see my brother?"

"Yes. That is a good place to begin."

Trouble retold what he had experienced when he had gone to the field quarters to visit his ailing brother. He included the strong hint of disorder and disturbance in the field quarters.

"Our overseer then was Abner Rogers," said Amos. "At least that is what he called himself, but that was not his real name. His real name is Angus Church and he is a known criminal. Now in the safe arms of the law."

Both Charles and George responded to that information with surprise.

"How do you know that?" asked George.

"We will get to that. First let's finished our tale. Joel, you continue with what occurred next."

"Well, Suh, you and me, we went down and talked with some of our people in the field quarters and found out 'bout two little gals missin' and other bad stuff goin' on. Later we nailed that overseer man up in his cabin and you sent a man for Sheriff Williams. Sheriff, he brought men, and they took him away. You want me to go on, Suh?"

"No, Joel. I'll take it from there. I gathered men and we joined Sheriff Williams to take down a crew of kidnappers. We found them. Rough brigands guarding a fishing hut on the edge of the inlet, the hut crowded with kidnapped youngsters...boys and girls under the age of twelve. Those men gave up the man who hired them, Angus Church, a well-known criminal. Williams was extremely glad to be able to question him."

"I'll be damned!" exclaimed George. "Where did you find that overseer...that phony? What did Williams discover from his interrogation?"

"My father hired him while I was in Charles Town attending the last rice council meetings. He had a reference from someone named Sturdevant in Savannah and he came to my father, recommended for the job of overseer by your father, Marcus."

"How did my father know him? A criminal. Kidnapper."

Charles, ever quick to brilliantly put facts together to create a hypothesis, said quietly, "the secret books."

"What secret books?" asked Amos.

"In the locked drawer. In the big oak desk in Jasper's Perrin's office," replied Charles.

"What are you implying, Brother?" asked George in surprise. "You think...?"

"What do the books have to do with kidnapping?" asked Amos.

"I don't yet know. I recently discovered the ledgers locked in a drawer in his desk. They are in code. That must indicate that Perrin engages in something he does not want to get out."

"How did you get the drawer open?" asked Amos.

"Looked for a hidden key until I found it stuck on the bottom of a vase. I was careful to put it back."

"Books in code. Surely something is strange. We have no need for coded accounts," added George.

"But Jasper Perrin and your father are business associates. Have been for countless years. Everyone knows," remarked Amos. "Do you think that he does something illegal behind your father's back?"

"Never! As I assured George, I do not believe that Perrin would do anything outside our father's knowledge and approval. He is but a mouse after all," said Charles.

"I have begun to suspect something," said George. "Father has been acting strangely. If Perrin is not acting alone, the alternative is that they are involved together. Father is already a trader. Would not be difficult for him to take on more."

This comment from George brought a sharp glance from Charles who then asked, "How do we find out?"

"We must have the code deciphered," said George. "We must know for certain before we act."

"Do you know what you are saying?" asked Amos.

"One fact leads to another," replied George. "Someone with money and influence must be behind the kidnapping because only power and money would be able to keep such an enterprise secret."

"We may be looking at a consortium of powerful men," offered Amos.

"Why such an enterprise?" asked Charles. "Why are men kidnapping young boys and girls? Aren't there enough on the block? They aren't strong workers until older."

George and Amos exchanged glances, surprised at Charles' innocence. George nodded to Amos and Amos explained bluntly.

"These are especially attractive young boys and lovely young girls, Charles. Virginal. Unblemished. Unscarred. They are selected, kidnapped, put into ships and sent all over the world for men to use for sex. They bring quite a high price when sold."

"How do you know that?" asked Charles, his face turned pale, appalled at what he had heard.

"That information came directly from Sheriff Williams who has been investigating for some time."

When Charles regained his composure from that shocking mental picture, he again added quietly, "Father knew about them, the kidnappers. He always wanted to protect Tabitha."

Charles' ability at deductive reasoning, quickly bridging the gap from one fact to another, astounded the others and they simply stared as they attempted to catch up with his quick assessment. They contemplated the meaning of his words.

"Let me get this clear," said George. "Are we implying that our father, Marcus Durandeaux, knew about this...these shameful dealings? Do you think he feared that Tabitha, as a girl child, was in danger of being kidnapped and sold for sex?"

"The ledgers imply more than knowledge, Brother. They imply that he engaged in something that he wished to keep secret from all but Father Perrin," said Charles.

"I suppose I am not quite ready to accept that," replied George. "I admit it all sounds suspect, but he is our father, Charles!"

"I wish I could be as optimistic as you," said Charles. "I think I am seeing him for the first time. With grown-up eyes and not those of boyish worship."

"Did you and your father know about this dastardly practice, Amos?" ask George.

"I was not aware until our encounter with Sheriff Williams. I don't know about Father, but I think he would have told me if he knew."

"There seems to be much that we don't know," said Charles. "About Father. About Perrin. About the world."

George had to admit that what he had learned held weight. He sat himself in the nearest chair, overcome with a deep sense of dread. For a moment he silently contemplated what it would mean if his father knew of this travesty or worse, if he were involved in committing the crimes. If this proved true George knew that he could never respect or obey his father again.

"Charles, let us be clear," said Amos. "You are suggesting that your father has been aware of these awful kidnappings?"

"Aware? I am thinking much more. Perrin works for father. Perrin is not a daring or fearless man. He is weak. A follower. This thing we are talking about would require boldness and a certain turn of mind. The sort of mind that only thinks of self, of gain and of greed...the kind of mind that Father has. Not Jasper Perrin."

"Charles, do you know what you are saying? Just listen to yourself. How can you suggest that our father is complicit?"

"Because I know our father. We both know our father. He is a heartless bastard. Look at the way he treats Mother Cecily!"

"We must find out," said Amos. "Even if what we consider is overpowering. To think that such as your father, a long-time friend, a neighbor, kinsman, could be involved in such a horrendous affair is unthinkable to all of us. But as Charles so awfully concluded, it all makes sense."

The men, deep in thought over Amos words remained silent. They had no real counter. Christopher broke their silence.

"George, were you surprised when our father allowed me to remain here at Battailes so easily?"

"I suppose I was. Too easily when I had taken time to prepare my arguments. I only had to mention that you could watch over Tabitha and Father immediately agreed."

"He still wants to protect his daughter. When he sent her away from Joseph, he didn't put her on the block. He sent her here where he knew Mister Francis would protect her. Has anyone considered that the kidnappers might capture a beautiful young woman as well as children? Perhaps Father did."

"Or wanted to be very certain that she was safe," added Amos. "My father told me that he promised Marcus he would keep her here...not sell her ever."

"Just as he did with our mother, Cassie," said Christopher.

"But Father sold Cassie," corrected George. "He told me when it happened. Mother Cecily demanded it."

"My mother told me different. When everyone thought she would be on the block, she told me that Marcus would take her to an island in the Caribbean where she would live. He would keep her there."

"Then that must be where he goes on his long absences," declared George. "It has to be. He always returns in a better mood. We all thought it was his love of the sea. I am beginning to think that our father may have treasured Cassie over all the women on the plantation. His captain and deck crew must know many of his secrets. Good place to start?"

"Best wait. They may be deep in his pocket, and we might not be able to turn them," offered Amos. "They will turn coat as soon as he is brought down. Wait and see."

"Charles, you and I should be returning home. Amos, may we see Tabitha before we leave?"

"Of course, George. I will send for her," said Amos. "When she comes, might we all present a happy face? She has undergone sad days and I want this to be a pleasant experience for her. Charles, George, can you both accept her without restraint or reluctance?"

"I know that I can," said Charles. "And I will see that George is gracious," he added with a smile and a brotherly poke at George.

"As your sister and as my wife?"

Their smiles gave him his answer and he sent Joel to fetch Tabitha.

CHAPTER 35

The Durandeaux brothers traveled the road toward home as twilight set, both silent and deep in thought, agonizing over the possibility that their father may be engaged in this nefarious endeavor. Their fear of this possibility outweighed the happy news of Amos and their half-siblings, Tabitha and Christopher. As dark fell they kept their pistols handy in the event roadmen approached. Sounds of the forest kept company with the rhythmic hoof beats of their horses until they entered the gate at Durandeaux and dismounted, leading their tired mounts to the stable. Later, safe at home, sitting in the comfort of their parlor sipping brandy after a late cold supper, Charles spoke first.

"Tabitha seems at peace," he commented. "Even happy."

"She will have a good life with Amos," said George. "But I still can't believe he married her."

"Why not? She is our half-sister. Young, beautiful, and obviously willing. You still thinking of her color? Race? Slave status?"

"Obviously, Charles! What else? Don't you?"

"Yes, I do."

"Then what do you think about it?"

"I think...what does it matter? Really? I don't think it matters at all...not in any important way."

"What about our neighbors and the minister? Parishioners?"

"None of their business. Amos most likely got our sister with child and had the decency to make his child legal and not a slave."

"Should we tell Papa?"

"I think not," replied Charles.

"I think we should tell him. Why not? You think he will be displeased? He will know eventually. Father obviously has a special place in his heart for her. He watched over her and now surely he would not be angry that she has wed well."

"I never know how he will take any news," replied Charles. "Sometimes with no consequence and at other times, he rages over the silliest things. Frankly, I am weary of his temper, as is Perrin, I am certain. I simply don't want to face a violent reaction about Tabitha and Amos. You be the brave one. You tell him after I leave. And be sure to tell him that he will soon be a grandfather again."

"You are correct. He is angry often. More than usual. Definitely more than usual. He will soon know that you and I are now aware of certain things," offered George.

"What certain things?"

"The coded books for one."

"You will tell him?" asked Charles. "I don't think that is a good idea."

"What if he is not aware? What if this is really something only Perrin is involved with? Shouldn't Papa know?"

"I believe Papa does know," replied Charles. "I have already assured you that Perrin would do nothing behind Father's back. Why don't I try to have them deciphered;

discover what they contain and then you can mention it? Letting him know now that I found them may put you in danger."

"Me? In danger from my own father? How ridiculous," replied George.

The look Charles gave him caused George to rethink his statement.

"I am not afraid of him," George declared.

"I still vote to refrain from mentioning them. Get them deciphered. Then we decide. Please listen to me, George. Will you? I'll take care of that as soon as I return."

"Stay for a couple more days? I want to show off my new stable and the new colt."

"You really going into the horse breeding business?"

"Yes. We have the acreage and the manpower. And I found a source of good breeding stock. I'll buy at least a dozen very good mares and..."

"Papa approves?"

"He does. He gave me his blessing. Said it would keep me out of ... oh, my God. He said it would keep me out of his hair."

The brothers gave each other a long stare, each thinking exactly as the other.

"You may be right about Papa and the books," admitted George. "I'll be careful. Now what about the other things. Shall we mention what we discovered at Battailes or hold off still? We will speak freely of his *other* children. Tabitha, Christopher...Cassie...all of it. He can't spend the rest of his life thinking that his legitimate sons are dolts. We can put two and two together. Or at least you can."

Comfortable in his dressing gown, Marcus sat in his oversized leather chair, a glass of brandy in hand when

George knocked gently and opened the door a bit and stuck his head in. Marcus waved him in. The elder brother entered with Charles following.

"Good to see you, Charles. I would invite you to sit, but I have only this chair," offered Marcus, immediately noting the seriousness of his sons' expressions. "Feel free to sit on the bed. This is not a simple good night, is it? Looks as though you have things to say. "

Charles and George each waited for the other to speak causing Marcus to break the impasse.

"Must be something strong. Which one of you will say?"

"Charles and I rode to Battailes early today and delivered documents to Amos. We found Christopher quite pleased with his new position and Amos pleased with his work," said George. "I made the transfer to Amos who immediately gave Christopher his emancipation paper. Christopher is now a free man."

Marcus raised his brow. Otherwise, he showed no reaction to the news. It was as though he had expected as much and cared little.

"That all?"

"No, Father. We also spoke with Tabitha."

At that, Marcus leaned forward in his chair.

"And... how is she?" he asked as though everyone had always known her whereabouts.

"She is well and happy," said Charles. "Why didn't you..."

"Tell you where she was?" asked Marcus anticipating his question. "I thought to, and then thought better of it."

A brief pause ensued while each of the three thought what to say next.

"Father, we have something else of import to tell you.

Marcus looked at George, his expression quizzical, ready to hear.

"Tabitha and Amos are wed," George blurted.

The two brothers saw their father's face darken and his brow furrowed. They knew he struggled to contain the words that tried to explode from his lips, and they remained silent as Marcus regained his composure. George and Charles knew better than to push their father and let the moment pass until he spoke.

"Wed, you say?"

"Yes, Papa. Wed."

"How? No minister would do the honor."

"No, Papa. No minister. Common law marriage with witnesses. Now both Charles and I are witnesses to their union. Names are in the Battailes bible. Marriage as good as a minister could bless."

"That all?"

"No, Papa. Tabitha is with child. You will be a Grandpapa again."

For the briefest of moments Marcus face relaxed and he almost smiled, but the instant passed, and his frown returned.

"So, everyone is well and happy. That's good. Charles, what news do you bring from the city? How is that little rat, Perrin? Is he teaching you the business well?"

The two sons realized that Marcus sought to change the subject to something more comfortable. George nodded to Charles and, ignoring Marcus' question, he began.

"Father, Christopher told Charles and me, and Amos, that he is full brother to Tabitha. He said Cassie was their mother. Is it true?"

Marcus remained stone-faced as he glanced from one son to the other, before he said softly, "None of your damned business. Not your affair. You will never again mention either of them to me."

"Not even when Tabitha's child comes?"

"Especially then. Now go and leave me. I have work to do."

"It is late, Papa. Why not sleep now and work tomorrow?"

"Leave me," said Marcus with finality.

When his sons had left his room, Marcus remained sitting in his leather chair. He took the brandy bottle and poured a sizable portion into his glass. He thought and he brooded. He cursed the turn his life had taken. He cursed his own entanglement in the sordid affair that had him caught like a fly on sticky paper. Word had come that Sheriff Williams was on the trail with the determination of a terrier digging for a fox. Abner Church would never betray him but there were others who might, for the right price. He was in too deep and known by too many here in the colonies, by certain ships' captains, and in many ports. He had doubts concerning Jasper Perrin, the weakest link in the chain of their crimes, always fearing that he had placed too much trust and confidence in the little man. Let his sons discover his illegitimate offspring. Better they hate him for that rather than the thing he hated himself for. It was not the crime itself that bothered him, but that he had so eagerly mired himself in such a treacherous web. Now he could not free himself without making a devastating decision. He rose from his chair and walked to the small bedside table. He opened the drawer and reached in. He took the handle of his pistol and drew it out. He held it lovingly and wondered if this would be his last companion. His jaw steeled and he whispered, "Not if I can help it."

CHAPTER 36

"Christopher, you are in charge for the next two days," said Amos. "I'll leave you to make the work list. Do what you see as most important."

"You off somewhere?"

"I feel strongly that I must ride to Sheriff Williams and report what we learned yesterday. He needs every hint or fact that he can get to find our culprit. Don't you agree?"

"I certainly agree that the sheriff needs information but are you sure it should come from you? It could come back to affect you and the brothers."

"I doubt Williams would mention me, but regardless, I feel obliged. We made some connections while George and Charles were here, and those facts may help Williams."

"You do know that getting more involved could bring danger to you? And to them?"

"Angus Church is in custody and his helpers are on their way to trial in England."

"Angus isn't the only one. You even said that the stain spreads far and wide. Shippers, money men, buyers...powerful men do this. There must have been a world-wide system in place for generations to maintain this disgusting practice."

"I'll be careful. I'll get to Williams and tell him about the secret code books. How else will we solve this and catch those behind it?"

"Even if it comes close to home?"

"That, too."

"Very well, Amos. I'll take care of Battailes and spend time with my sister if you don't mind."

"Not at all. Enjoy yourselves. While I am away, think about this: would you rather a room in the house or keep the cabin? Your choice. Let me know when I return."

"The cabin. I already know. I'd prefer the privacy. Perhaps I will find a bride?"

"Oh, wait! Tabitha's house is now vacant. It is much better for you to bring a bride."

Amos smiled his appreciation.

"Then it is yours. Do what you need to make it comfortable."

Hours later Owen Williams's welcomed Amos with obvious pleasure and had a deputy take Snowbird to a well-earned grain box, hay bin and water. In the small office, crowded with a large roll-top desk, a table, two chairs and a filing cabinet, the two men sat. Williams opened a drawer and took out a bottle. He took two glasses, none too clean, from a shelf and poured. He slid one glass over to Amos and lifted the other. Before he drank, he remarked, "You have come with information. I can see it in your expression."

"I have."

"Let's drink and then I'll listen."

They drained their glasses and set them on the desk. Williams, lean of body and long of leg, his hair beginning to turn grey, leaned back in his chair and waited for Amos to speak.

"I learned of a secret set of books. Written in code."

Amos paused for that to sink in. Williams eyes narrowed but he said nothing, waiting for Amos to continue.

"The books are in a desk belonging to one Jasper Perrin, bookkeeper and accountant for Marcus Durandeaux."

Again, Williams remained silent but the wheels in his head turned.

"Marcus Durandeaux recommended Angus Church, alias Abner Rogers, to my father as overseer. Right after he came two children went missing."

Amos stopped speaking. There was more that he could say if he wanted to assume or surmise, but no, he only wanted to tell the facts as he knew them.

"How did you learn about the books?" asked Williams.

Now Amos hesitated. He must decide if he dared to mention Charles' name.

"You are afraid of getting someone in trouble?"

"I am."

"It would have to be someone close to Perrin. I hear he has a young man working with him...Charles Durandeaux, his son-in-law. You learned of the books from Charles Durandeaux."

"That young man is innocent but very curious. You have eyes on Perrin?"

"We do and we have had. He has been under observation for some time."

"Can you tell me what you have learned?"

"He confers with ship captains and sometimes with first mates when he has no cargo on board that we can ascertain. We have observed him accept large purses. If he has loaded no rice or lumber or cargo with his fee paid up front, for what is he receiving payment?"

"Only Perrin?"

"Only Perrin, but we know someone is behind him."

"Jasper works for Marcus Durandeaux. Been his accountant for many years."

This time Williams' eyes narrowed, and his brow wrinkled as he digested this fact. Two strikes against Marcus Durandeaux. That name had been in the forefront of his suspicions for weeks, but he never expected to hear someone else suggest the name with facts to back it up. That it all fit together had seemed obvious to him, but his superiors had brushed off his suggestion with contempt. Not one of them would consider that someone as wealthy and influential as Marcus Durandeaux could or would be involved in anything illegal or untoward. Williams had been forced to keep silent about his concerns regarding Durandeaux and concentrate on Perrin. But now, with Amos Battailes saying the name, his mind swelled with hope.

"We must have those books at the earliest. If there is the slightest suspicion, Marcus will hide the books somewhere else. Will the young Durandeaux be willing to get the coded books to me? I can have them deciphered."

"I cannot be involved. He would know I spoke with you, and I would lose his trust. I am here because I considered it my public duty to inform you. He is now at their plantation on the Wando. Can you somehow enter Jasper's house and take the books before he returns?"

"Did he say where he found them?"

"Big desk, secret locked drawer."

"Key? He must have found one."

"Glued under a vase. If you send someone to get them, it has to be quick."

"Already too late today, but I'll see to it tomorrow. This way is better. I thank you, Amos. I will see that the books are taken before Charles returns. That will protect him from suspicion. Charles can feign a total lack of knowledge of the books and Perrin will believe him. Perrin is the sort of man who hides behind himself, thinking that no one can see the real man. He would not want to believe that his carelessness caught up with him. He won't run to Marcus. Not at first, anyway. He will try to remember if he changed the hiding place and where he decided to hide them."

"I certainly hope you are right," admitted Amos. "For Charles' sake, I hope you are right."

"I'll take it from here and I can assure you that within two weeks we will have the books deciphered. We will see what Mister Jasper Perrin is up to and for whom."

"Then I should leave," said Amos. "Long ride back."

"It's late already. Past dinner time. Why not stay over? We have a guest room, and the Missus is a good cook."

"Thank you, Owen, but I'd rather slip out and return home today. Would not be good for anyone to see me with you."

"As you wish. I'll send for your horse. Glad you trusted me, Amos. Your information is a major piece in this puzzle. Take care on your ride home. Dangerous times and dangerous men everywhere."

CHAPTER 37

The next afternoon Jasper Perrin left the docks and walked home from his last errand with a jaunty stride. The day had been superb. Sun not too hot, birds singing, the afternoon street vendors out in full force with fresh loaves of bread, roasted yams, and bowls ready to fill with oyster stew replete with bacon and potatoes. He had seen their latest cargo loaded into the secret compartment below decks and knew that the buyers would be quite pleased. While completing the transaction with the ship's first mate, he had bargained for a higher price for the next cargo, which would please Marcus no end. Jasper finished his work with a visit to the bank to deposit more than his benefactor had expected. He approached his home with plans for a delicious afternoon sleep followed by one of Nancy's marvelous suppers.

He turned the knob to open the front door but found it locked. He took out his keys and let himself into the house. He called for Julia. She did not answer. He called for Mobley, his butler and valet. Still no reply. He walked to the kitchen to look for Nancy, but the kitchen was empty. He wondered where everyone had gone and surmised that Julia had gone shopping and must have given the help time on their own. Just as he had begun to worry, Julia called from the front. Jasper almost ran to her.

"Where were you? Where are Mobley and Nancy?"

"Father, we had a fright. Two constables came and told families on this side of the street that a convict off a ship had escaped. They feared he was lurking close by, and we must leave for our safety. They found him and just allowed us to return."

"Where did you go?"

"Nancy and I went to the station with Betsy and some other ladies where we would be safe until we were allowed to return home. Then Betsy and I did some shopping. I gave Nancy a few hours to do as she wished."

"Is Charles back from Durandeaux?"

"If he is not here, I suppose not. Perhaps Father Marcus kept him longer than he expected."

"Very well, then. No harm done. Glad they caught the culprit. Too much crime now. Bringing in all those convicts from prisons in London and Bristol and dumping them here is not a good thing. We should not have our colony and city peopled with robbers and horse thieves and debtors. We need men of good standing."

"I totally agree, Father."

"I'll be in my study if you need me, Daughter. Then I will nap for an hour or so. Call me for supper."

"Yes, Papa."

Jasper entered his study carrying his leather satchel. He closed and locked the door from the inside and walked to the window. He pulled the curtain to the side and looked out onto the street. The day was still beautiful. He felt on top of the world. Excellent news to give to Marcus about more profit in the bank than the other had expected would help to erase the bad feeling that resulted in their last failure. Marcus insisted on success and this time Perrin had delivered. Now he must record today's transactions in the ledgers he had set up just for this purpose. He left the window and walked to the tall vase that held the wild oats Julia had gathered on the sand dunes at the beach. He knelt and removed the key from the bottom, reminding himself to add more glue, for what remained seemed to be evaporating. He stood, went to his desk, whistling to himself. He put the key into the secret drawer that lay hidden under the stationery shelf and opened it. He automatically reached for the coded books. He drew in a breath and held it, afraid to let it out. The small draw was empty. The ledgers were not there. Jasper sat quickly in his chair for fear that he would faint.

"Julia," he called loudly. "Julia, come here."

"Yes, Papa?"

"Are you certain that Charles has not returned?"

"Yes, Papa. I am sure. Why? What is wrong?"

Jasper heard her trying the doorknob.

"Papa, your door is locked."

"Yes, Julia. It is nothing important. I misplaced something and thought Charles may know where I placed it."

"I expect he will come tomorrow. Said he wanted to spend some time with George on this visit."

"Leave me, Julia. I must do some accounting before supper."

"Alright, Papa. You sure everything is all right? You seem stressed. Why is your door locked?"

"I am fine. I suppose I locked the door from habit. Just leave me now. I have work to do."

When the little man was alone again, he thought. Where had he put the books when he last recorded a transaction? He had never placed them anywhere but the secret drawer, but now he doubted himself and thought of all the places he may have hidden them. The distraught man searched high and low, in every nook and cranny. He tried to recall if he had told Charles about the secret ledgers but could not imagine doing so. Marcus had specifically forbidden that Jasper should allow Charles to know of the hidden transactions. So far, he believed that he had succeeded, but doubt began to haunt him that he had not been as successful as he thought. What if Charles had found them? He soothed his fears with reminding himself that was the reason for the code. No one could decipher them but Jasper Perrin.

Unfortunately, Jasper had not considered that Charles might prove to be inquisitive to a high degree. He had measured Charles and had found him to be quiet and easily manipulated, without any curiosity except for his interest in natural science. Julia had confirmed his estimation. She called Charles 'dull'. True, his son-in-law had learned the routine of the regular account books easily and had been a help to Jasper. He decided that he only had to sleep on it and tomorrow he would remember where he had hidden the books.

The men Sheriff Williams had sent to find the coded books had easily lured Julia and the servants from the house with a tale of a criminal on the loose. Knowing exactly where to find the books, taking them required little time or effort. Now they were safely delivered to Williams who was confident that Charles would not be suspect when Perrin realized that he faced certain trouble. Knowing everyone of importance in the city, Williams thought of one man to approach to solve the codes, a math tutor by the name of Wilkins...Professor Laurence Wilkins. He obtained the address and went in person to visit the professor. He explained his need and Wilkins eagerly accepted the challenge. Williams swore him to secrecy, even going as far as to swear him in as a deputy to obligate him to secrecy. Williams left the three books with Wilkins, telling him nothing, so that he would be of no influence.

Charles returned to the city the day after Sheriff Williams had secured the coded books. He found the household upset and Julia distraught, her face swollen and red from crying. She held a blanket over her arm. He attempted to have her explain the reason for the chaos but all she could say was that her father had gone crazy and frightening her beyond her ability to comprehend the reason. She led Charles to the study and pointed to the broken lock.

"We had to break in, Charles," she said timidly. "Mobley did. Father would not open, and we heard such noise from inside the room."

Charles stepped into the room and met a scene of total disarray. Boxes of files sat scattered around the room. Desk drawers had been pulled out and stacked on top of each other beside the boxes. Books from what had been neat shelves now lay scattered about the end tables and the large desk. Vases overturned, wall hangings torn down and pictures taken from their hooks and left on the floor. Charles spent minutes surveying the mess before he could even find Jasper. He saw the man huddled in a chair in a dark corner of the room, part of a drape over his lap, his hands shaking uncontrollably, and his head thrown back, spittle dribbling from the corner of his mouth. Charles immediately knew that Jasper Perrin had suffered apoplexy or worse. He made his way to the elder man through the mess on the floor.

"Father Perrin? Can you speak to me?" Charles asked while taking the man's hands in his.

He received no reply. He turned around to see that Mobley and Julia had joined him.

"I don't know what happened, Charles. I truly don't," she said through her sobs. "He has never been like this. I don't know what set him off. This morning he came down to breakfast as usual. He seemed healthy and in good spirits. He went to his study, locked the door and soon he began to rave. We heard him throwing things. He yelled and screamed things that I didn't understand."

"Like what?"

"Like calling on God and then cursing God and then asking forgiveness for his sins and then words that made no sense to me. He mentioned your father and I gathered that he is terrified of him...Marcus. Father is. Then he seemed to crumple, and he stopped shouting. That's when I told Mobley to break the door lock and we found Father on the floor. Mobley toted him to this chair. He was shivering and we covered him with the drape. Just now I had gone to get a blanket when you came in."

"Where did he go yesterday?"

"I don't know for certain. He left early and then we were called out of the house by authorities because of a criminal on the loose. After shopping I had tea with Betsy who had left her home for the same reason. Yesterday was a beautiful day and Betsy and I walked in the park after tea. We fed the ducks. Mobley and the others returned when they heard that the rogue was caught. Will Father live?"

"I don't know, Julia. Now we must send for the doctor."

Charles could sese that Julia was at her breaking point. He needed her to be busy.

"Julia, can you take Mobley and fetch the doctor? I'll take Father Perrin to his room and put him to bed."

"I can. Yes, I'll do that. But, Charles, was Father searching for something or did he simply go mad?"

"It appears as though he were searching and could not find the item."

"Yes, that is what I think. I'll go for the doctor."

When Mobley and Julia left him alone with Jasper, Charles' mind was awhirl. He immediately looked for desk drawers which lay scattered about the room. He tipped over the vase to feel for the key. It was not there. The ledgers! They were gone and that is what drove Jasper Perrin to near death. Charles now knew full well the danger surrounding those coded records and how that danger might touch him. He would be the first that Jasper would suspect. He would assign blame on his son-in-law to avoid punishment from whoever was higher up. Charles prayed that it would not be Marcus Durandeaux for he would not fare well if he found himself in the crosshairs of that man's fury, father, or no. He counted his blessings that they had disappeared while he was absent.

Charles lifted the slight body of his father-in-law and took him to his room. He laid him on his bed and covered him with a quilt. He sat to wait for the doctor. While waiting he thought back on all that had transpired among himself, George, Amos, and Christopher about the coded books. He then asked himself who could have taken them. In such little time...only two days ago...now they were missing. Was it Amos or George who had sent someone? Surely not Christopher.

He thought on the reason given to Julia for evacuating the area. Criminal at large? Hardly. The authorities were in on this and had cleared the house for the singular purpose of finding and taking the books. And someone had. He could not be blamed for he had been on his horse for hours since he left George at Durandeaux. It was not George, because his brother had been in contact with only him. That left Amos or...the authorities who may be onto Jasper Perrin through their own investigations. Charles could barely think about that when he heard the front door open and steps on the stairs with voices.

"Charles, the doctor is here," said Julia as she ushered the medic into the room.

"What do we have here?" inquired Doc Raven. "Jasper Perrin drank a bit too much?"

"More than that, Doctor," said Charles. "Seems he has really done himself in."

"Let me see. Julia, you should leave us now. I'll take care of your father."

Julia left the two men alone and Raven asked, "What in hell is going on, Charles? I caught a glimpse of the study when we came in."

"I am as in the dark as you, Sir. I had just ridden in from Durandeaux. After I had put my horse away, I came in to find this disaster and Julia near hysterics. Father Perrin was sprawled in a chair covered with a drape that he had torn down. Something about a rogue running loose in the neighborhood."

"I heard about that, too. I live in this neighborhood and had left earlier also. At the time I thought something strange."

"How is he?" Charles asked once Raven had done a cursory examination.

"His color is good, and his heart rate is satisfactory."

"He is still unconscious?"

"It would seem so. I don't get a flinch when I pinch."

"What does that mean?"

"It means we wait to see if he regains consciousness."

"How long?"

"Within the hour. Or should. If not, then something serious is wrong."

"Could he die?"

"Of course, he could. We all could, Son," Raven replied, "but somehow, I don't think he will. He will come out of this. He may have trouble speaking or walking though. Do you have any idea what brought this on?"

"I have no idea," said Charles, lying through his teeth. "I only help him keep accounts for his and my father's work together. You don't think that rogue criminal had anything to do with frightening him, do you?"

"No, I do not. I am beginning to think that was a farce. Why? I don't know. A feeling. But I will do my best to find out."

"What shall we do for him? After you leave, I mean. Any special care?"

"He has a valet?"

"Yes. Our butler, Mobley, serves as his valet."

"Have him stay up with your father-in-law until he wakes and then send for me."

"You are welcome to remain, Doctor Raven. Nancy prepares a good meal."

"You have a room?"

"We do. This is a grand double-house. I'll have a bed made for you."

"Thank you, Charles. You are most kind. I'll see to Julia if she is still distressed. A dose of laudanum will see her getting a good night's sleep. And a brandy for me if you please."

Jasper opened his eyes to complete darkness. He felt strange. Something was amiss. He could not remember why it was dark. He had just come home from in a bright sunny day. He remained silent as he attempted to orient himself to the reality of darkness. Was it night? Already? Where had he been? Was he alone? He thought of Mobley and tried to reach the bell cord. His arm would not move. Jasper Perrin fought the panic that welled up from his gut and tried the left hand. He could move it, but the cord was too far away. He would have to call out for someone. He opened his mouth to call for Julia, but the sound that came from his throat, a guttural growl, terrified him and he began to cry uncontrollably. The horrible sound woke Mobley who left his chair and went swiftly to the bedside.

"Mastah Perrin, Suh, you gonna wake de house. I'm heah with you. You go on back to sleep. I'll sit right here by you."

Jasper's panic remained as he attempted but failed to sit up. He could not control one side of his body. He could not speak. He fell back exhausted and sobbed.

"I go git Docta Raven and Mastah Charles. I be right back."

Again, Jasper was alone in the dark. Terrified at what his body could not do, he tried to recall the past hours, but his memory was not clear. A walk home in sunshine. Whistling. Happy. Entering empty house. Then the curtain came down and he could recall no more. He lay whimpering and slobbering on his pillow when he heard another voice that he somehow remembered.

"Did he speak, Mobley?" asked Charles.

"He try, Mastah Charles, but jus' blabberin'."

"'I'll see if I can make sense of what he says," suggested Raven. "You two stay in the hallway?"

"You may need help if he panics again?"

"I think I can do it alone. I'll be out in a bit."

"I could use a brandy, Mobley. How about you?" asked Charles. Let's wait in the parlor?"

"Me, Suh?"

"You drink brandy?"

"I do. Yes, I do."

"Then come on. I feel a bit shaky. I never saw a sickness like that."

"Happen lots of times to old folk. Somethin' bad happens and shock takes 'em to a place like that. Some never gits over it. Some do a little bit."

In the parlor Charles poured brandy for both and then he invited Mobley to sit.

"Sit heah with you, Suh?"

"Yes, why not? Perrin is not here to forbid it and my wife is asleep. We can sit and simply enjoy a moment of calm for I believe we will not find much in our near future."

"You right about that, Mastah Charles."

"What happened when the authorities told you to leave the house, Mobley? Did you all go at the same time?"

"Yeah, we did. We high-tailed it out of heah. Mens said a bad criminal got loose and they was looking for him right 'round this here street. Fresh off de boat he was and didn't want no bondage. We all left. Mastah Perrin, he gone earlier. Sayin' he had business at the docks and would stop at the tavern."

"He seemed healthy? All right?"

"He did. Right fine, too! Went out swingin' his cane. Nothin' wrong then. He come back befo' us. He had his suppa and went to bed. Next mo'nin'...dis."

"Do you have any idea what set him off?"

"I do not, Suh. I do not."

"He must have lost something and tried to find it. Got angry and this happened."

"That a lot to happen 'cause he lost something, Suh," observed Mobley.

"Unless what he lost was invaluable."

"What does that mean?"

"It means that what he lost was as valuable as his life."

"My, oh my. What he git mix up in? Suh, why you tell me this?"

"Because if anything happens to me, you will go to the authorities and tell them what I just said."

"You think somebody gonna..."

"Come for me? I don't know, Mobley."

"What authority I gonna talk to?"

"Sheriff Williams. If anything happens to me, you go to Sheriff Owen Williams. He will know what to do. Don't forget and don't tell anyone else."

"Yes, Suh," agreed Mobley as Doc Raven came into the parlor.

"Any of that brandy left?"

"Help yourself," said Charles, "and pour us another round. Then have a seat and tell what you found."

"Apoplexy, pure and simple," said Raven. "Left side bad and right side none too good. He'll be bedridden or need someone to lift him into a chair. He'll have to live on the first floor. No treatment except someone to flex his arms and legs so they don't go stiff. Someone to feed him and take care of his needs. You can hire someone?"

"Of course, we can. You have any idea what brought it on?"

"He must have had a fright. A scare. Something awfully bad happening. Anger. Fear. Causing something as simple as a blood vessel bursting in his brain. We don't know much about the brain."

"A criminal roamin' about scare him?" asked Mobley.

"I think not," replied Raven. "A criminal would have given him no reason to tear up the study the way he did. It was something there. He was looking for something and could not find it."

Charles knew exactly what Jasper could not find and he wondered who had taken them.

"Anyway, I need a few hours of sleep. Tomorrow I have other calls to make. I'll stop by on my way home to check on our patient and see how he is faring."

"Good night again, Doctor."

"You'll get my bill, Charles."

When Raven had gone back to bed, Charles said to Mobley, "We must find a caretaker for Father Perrin. Do you know where to look?"

"Yes, Suh, I do. You want somebody to live in, right?"

"Yes. Someone to stay with him night and day. We'll put a cot in his room."

"I know where to find a young man. When you want him?"

"As early as he can come."

"Yes, Suh."

CHAPTER 38

Dazed by the rapid turn of events and dangerous knowledge which had hit Charles, he needed time to think, or to separate and organize his thoughts which flooded his mind. He needed to recover from the shock of what he found in the study, both the wrecked room, Jasper Perrin and the missing ledgers.

Already his visit home seemed light years since, and he felt that he had entered a never-never land. But now more immediate things must be done. He waited for Mobley to return. Whom the butler would find on such short notice Charles had no idea. He only trusted that whoever came could at least care for Jasper until Charles, himself, could find someone experienced and suitable. Twice he visited Jasper's room and found the old man asleep. He was about to go up and check on him again when he heard a knock on the rear door. He heard Nancy speaking and then heard Mobley's voice.

"Mobley, did you find someone?" asked Charles as he quickly made his way to the kitchen.

"Yes, Suh. This heah is Doolittle. He a good boy and strong."

Mobley pushed the young man forward and Charles breathed a sigh of relief.

"Say hello to Mastah Charles, Doolie."

The young man held his cap in his hands and lowered his head as he said softly, "Afternoon, Mastah Charles."

"Did Mobley tell you why we need you?"

"Yes, Suh, he did. You got a sick man what need watchin'."

"I already told him Mastah Perrin can't move or talk," offered Mobley. "So, he know."

"You can do what is necessary? "

The young man looked at Mobley for help and Mobley spoke for him.

"Mastah Charles, dis boy, Doolittle, he took care of his Pa until his Pa died. His Pa was in a sorry fix. Boy had to do ever' thing. His Mama is my sista, don't you know. She cook ova to de Bedon place, and Mastah Bedon, he said we could borry Doolie long as Mastah Perrin need. Mastah Bedon, say he know Mastah Perrin and you."

"Sounds good, Mobley. Let's take Doolittle up and get him settled."

"I say we can put a pallet on the floor for Doolie. He slept on worse. He can stay right there in the room case he needed."

With Doolittle settled in with his father-in-law, Charles went to his room and sat at his writing desk. He wrote a note to Gordon Bedon thanking him for the loan of his man, Doolittle. Charles knew he would be expected to compensate Mister Bedon, but also knew that the gesture was a generous and kindly offer.

When Julia and the servants had gone to bed and the house was quiet, Charles left his room and returned to the study which he had kept locked. He wanted nothing changed from the bedlam they had all found. He did not doubt that the coded ledgers had been spirited away but the question was by whom.

The sense of dread that he felt let him know that this was much bigger than error. A silly twit Jasper might seem to be, but he had been working for Marcus long enough that he would have been fired long ago if he were untrustworthy or careless. No. Logic decreed that someone had taken the books. Of that, Charles became certain. But who? When? How? Would Amos or George dare to do this? Had they even had time to instigate it? Did it have to be Amos or George? Could the authorities be onto Perrin's business affairs enough to suspect something illegal? Hadn't Amos said that he had aided Sheriff Williams in capturing Angus Church and rescuing the children? With that recollection, Charles knew where to go. He knew with whom to speak. He had to clear his name before he was charged with keeping books for illegal activities, if that was what the codes were all about, and he had no real doubt. He could lose no time. A visit to Williams was imperative. But he could not leave until morning. He left the study and locked the door behind him. He went up to bed but counted the hours and fretted as he hardly slept all night.

CHAPTER 39

Sheriff Williams caught a glimpse of a strange young man sitting in his waiting room. The hour was close to noon and, in a hurry to return home for dinner, the sheriff asked Lincoln, his deputy, to make the initial inquiry. Deputy Lincoln returned with a message.

"Boss, man said he would only speak with Sheriff Williams. Asked if you are in."

"I'm late already. I need to leave now. By the time I get home wife will be wondering if I got lost on the way."

"Wouldn't tell me a thing. Said he would only talk with Sheriff Williams. That's you. Says he's ready to sit there all day."

"What's his name? Did you ask?"

"I did. Like I said, he will only talk with you."

"Damn! Carol hates me to be late for dinner. Send him in."

Williams sat in his chair and leaned back against the wall as he watched the tall and lean, well-dressed young man walk into his office. A gentleman for certain. He motioned to a chair across from his desk and Charles sat, his face was a road map of anxiety.

"Your name?" Williams asked quietly, sensing for the first time that the man was more than just a passing citizen with a problem neighbor.

"You are Sheriff Williams?"

"I am."

"I am Charles Durandeaux."

The front legs of Williams' chair hit the floor and he had to immediately stifle a gasp.

"Well, I'll be damned. Mister Durandeaux, I didn't expect to see you here. What can I do for you?"

After a bit of hesitation, Charles resumed, "You are acquainted with Amos Battailes, are you not?"

"I have had the odd occasion to become acquainted with the Battailes. Both Francis and Amos. I hear that Francis has passed," he replied, being deliberately vague. "Is this visit about them?"

Charles did not know how to proceed. He had no idea what Williams knew or didn't know, or who he suspected if he suspected anyone. Williams could read men and had already decided that this young man could hardly be involved in so ruinous an enterprise as his father might be and came to his rescue. He spoke bluntly, with no beating about the bush.

"You discovered the coded books are missing?"

Williams intended his approach to chase away all guile and it worked. He waited while Charles absorbed the shock and gathered his thoughts.

"I returned to the city yesterday. From my visit to our plantation on the Wando. I found my wife distraught, my father-in-law unconscious and his study like a scene after a storm. Something or someone had frightened him half to death."

Williams stood and leaned over his desk.

"Mister Durandeaux, we knew exactly where the books were hidden. We cleared the whole block. We went in. We found the books quickly. We took them. We left. No one was at home. We did nothing to the study or to Jasper Perrin."

"How did you know where they were, or how did you know that they even existed?" asked Charles, rising to his feet.

"First, tell me why he had separate books. And in code, yet. What did he record in them?"

"I don't know," replied Charles, beginning to pace. I found them by accident. I could not read the code, but I told no one except my brother, George, and my friend, Amos Battailes. I did not leave my plantation until yesterday."

"How is your father-in-law?"

"He is poorly. Barely conscious. Cannot speak or move easily. He may not recover. I think my father-in-law wrecked the room looking for the books but I don't know how one man could do such damage."

"Jasper Perrin was obviously terrified. And still is."

"Terrified of whom?"

"Of your father, Marcus Durandeaux."

"My father?"

"Mister Durandeaux, you are not naïve. That is why you are here."

"So, you have the books," Charles repeated after a pause.

"They are in safe hands. At this moment they are being deciphered. If you are not involved in this mess, I apologize for whatever trouble it has caused you, but I will get to the bottom of it, no matter where it leads."

"Where do you think it will lead?"

Another decision for Williams. He made the hard choice again.

"I think it leads to your father, my boy. Right to your father. And others like him up and down the coast. Up and down many other coasts as well."

Charles sat back down in his chair and Williams took his seat also. A strained quiet settled as Charles digested what the elder man had said so bluntly.

"You suspect my father of doing what? What crime?"

"I suspect your father of being involved in the illegal kidnapping and selling of slave and free children to wealthy men for the purpose of sex."

Charles' face went white. He slumped in his chair. He looked up at Williams to hear the man's next words.

"And so do you, Charles Durandeaux. So do you. You are an innocent bystander, or you would never have come here to me. I am going to ask that you keep silent about your visit here and our conversation. You needed to know the truth for your own protection."

"Sheriff Williams, my father is a slave trader. One of the most successful and therefore the wealthiest trader on the Southern coast. Why on earth would he need to kidnap slave children when he has access to shiploads of slaves?"

"Son, most slave ships are filled with people of an age to work in fields or houses. No trader wants to waste space on a child who will be useless for years. In addition, do you have any idea how difficult...no, nearly impossible it is to find unblemished children? Beautiful children. No deformities. No scars. Beautiful teeth. Children play and work. They get hurt and scarred. No good for your father's purposes. Those that he and men like him want are rare."

"But the price of a slave is not that great that men would grow wealthy on children, would they?"

"My boy, do you know how much one of these children will bring on the sex market? Do you?"

"No, Sir."

"One thousand times the auction value of a prime male and perhaps more. And they don't only steal black children. White boys and girls are also taken here in the city and other cities. The only requirement is that they be virginal, unblemished, and pleasing to look upon. Boys must be handsome and girls beautiful. Now, do you get a better picture? Somewhere, right this minute, some old codger is showing off his stable of youths to some other old codger. Do you understand now?"

"I do, Sir. I do."

"Jasper Perrin obviously went mad when he could not find the books. That is what he searched for in vain. He is terrified of what your father will do when he knows. I have no sympathy for him. He is as involved as any of the men who steal children and sell them for such a horrible purpose."

"It was Amos who informed you? It had to be."

"Do not lay blame on Amos. He was with us on the raid, and he saw the captive children. He also lost two from his own plantation. He had every reason to tell me what he knew. Right is right and crime is crime."

"Now that I know what this is about, I would have done the same. Amos also told us that you had captured one of them?"

"Three exactly."

"What will happen to them?"

"Unfortunately, not enough. Because of the special nature of the crime, they will serve a sentence but for how long I don't know. The penalty on the books for killing a slave is only a twelve month stay in lock-up. For stealing a slave, it is payment of the book value of the slave. These men will hardly receive a lawful penalty equal to what they have done; however, prisons have a way of delivering a different sort of justice. Once the true nature of their crime is known, Heaven help them."

"And my father?"

"The nature of your father's crimes and of Perrin's are such that they will be judged in secret. No one wishes the populace to be aware of certain proclivities that exist among men. But rest assured, the penalty will fit the crime. Your father and his cohorts will go down if those books show what I think they will. You... stay out of it. Leave it to me and my men. We have it well in hand."

"How long do you think before the deciphering is done?"

"No idea, Charles. Depends on the skill of the code breaker. I'll be in touch."

"What should I tell my father? I must let him know about Mister Perrin."

"Send word to your father that Jasper Perrin suffered an attack and is incapacitated and that his presence is requested. Say nothing else. Do not mention the coded books. We will watch and see what he does. How is your wife taking all this?"

"This has been an awkward thing for Julia. She has no comprehension of what her father is into. I'll send a rider with a letter to Father. Let him see the wrecked study when he comes and observe his reaction."

"I can imagine what his reaction will be, and you may want to stay clear for a while. You play the innocent. To your father, you have no idea what your father-in-law was searching for. You think Marcus may know. He certainly knew that the books were hidden from you. Whatever is the crime, no way Jasper Perrin could be involved alone. Your father pulled him by the nose. Now you go on home and take care of your lovely wife. She was exceedingly polite when we told her to leave the house for her safety and seemed excited for the holiday."

Charles had a long ride home. Williams' office was far from Charles Town on the same road he had ridden into the city the day before. As he rode the familiar path, he went over his conversation with Williams. He asked himself how much he could believe. Was Williams on a wild goose chase? What would happen if his own father were complicit in kidnappings?

He rode his tired gelding into the stable at early evening. He untacked, gave the boy a quick rub and put him in his stall. He filled the water tub, forked hay, and poured a measure of oats into the bin. Too tired to worry any longer, he longed for a peaceful evening, a dinner from the warming oven, a brandy, and a soft bed. The next few days would bring what they would, and if Williams were correct, he and Julia would be caught in a whirlwind and then dropped to scavenge the pieces of their lives and put them back together. Poor Julia, when the full extent of her father's true occupation was known, as it certainly would be, for secrets of this nature could not be kept, she would no longer be welcome in fashionable circles in the city. His spoiled wife might find the *terrible swamp* to be a place of refuge from looks and stares of her shallow city friends. Perhaps without the distraction of society he could anticipate a son or daughter from his marriage? Blessings do come from strange events.

CHAPTER 40

Marcus welcomed the shade afforded by the thick green leaves of the grape arbor where he sat in a weathered oak chair, which had been made during his father's day. Since that time the chair had been rubbed smooth by many hands and now was shiny with age. He watched a butterfly flit among the vines and a large yellow-backed spider sitting patiently in its web to ensnare it. He felt more kinship with the spider than the butterfly and he could not remember a time when he had not. Marcus recalled the times long ago when, as a young boy, he had played with his spaniel while the grown-ups had their tea under this arbor in summertime. A few innocent years and then that boy had become the man.

The arbor was far enough from the house that there was a modicum of privacy, and Marcus visited the place when he felt disturbed or uneasy. Now he certainly felt both. He held a letter in his hand. Brought to him in his study by Bruneau after the mail rider had gone by, Marcus saw that it was from Charles. Why a letter, he wondered, when Charles had only just left. What had he found in the city when he returned? He had quickly opened the letter, read his son's message, and quickly folded the letter again. He stuffed it into his pocket and without a word to anyone, he had left the house and now he sat, all alone with his unpleasant thoughts. A feeling of dread enveloped him like a dark cloud as he read it again.

"Dear Father,

You are needed in the city as soon as you receive this letter from me. I returned to find chaos, with my father-in-law unconscious from an attack of apoplexy. He may not recover. He cannot speak or walk.

There is more but I will ask you to come to the house to see for yourself what I cannot fully describe. Julia is distraught. Please make haste.

Your obedient son,
Charles Durandeaux"

Marcus folded the letter, his heart racing and his mind struggling to digest his son's message. Jasper quite ill, Julia distraught and something else to find when he arrived? He got up from his chair and left the shade of the arbor. He thought at first to send a letter asking for further information, but then something about his son's choice of words held his attention and he knew he had better heed the call. Charles was not given to hyperbola and if he said make haste, that is what he meant.

Rather than drive a buggy, he decided he could arrive sooner if he rode. Within less than an hour Marcus had placed a change of small clothes into his saddlebags, mounted and set off on his journey which would require all the remaining daylight hours. He felt a sense of apprehension, not knowing the cause and not being able to imagine what he may find. What could have caused Perrin's attack? That it could relate to their ultra-secret doings did not occur to him. Perrin was careful in the extreme and things were going extremely well according to his last missives. He considered that age had affected his partner more than it had affected himself. Marcus then wondered if Jasper's mind had become addled. Had he put too much trust in Perrin. He could do nothing until he saw for himself. He put all his mind to his ride and his horse. Long of leg and thin for his age, with his hat pulled low above dark blue eyes, leaning forward in his saddle, his cloak flying loose behind him over the bay's rump, his sharp features with his classic French nose, he resembled the devil's own messenger.

The lamps were still lit when Marcus's horse's hoofs struck the cobblestones in front of the Perrin home. He dismounted, opened the gate, and led the lathered bay to the stable where he quickly untacked and left him in a stall beside Charles' gelding. While filling a water bucket he heard footsteps behind him and turned to see his son.

"I heard the gate squeak. Glad you are here," said Charles. "I'll finish with your horse. You both must be exhausted."

"Not that old, Son, but I'll let you put him to bed while I go in and see Jasper. What can you tell me?"

"No, Father. Let me go in with you. I want to show you something before you see him. Please wait. I won't be but a moment."

"Alright, Son. But what is the mystery? Your letter...I have to say that it upset me. Is that what you intended?"

"You will see soon enough," Charles replied as he hayed and watered the gelding. "There, now the boy is set for the night. He'll be glad to see our backs. Let's go in."

Charles led the way through the rear entrance and Marcus followed quietly. Charles walked through the kitchen, into the hallway and all the way to the front of the house where, on the left side with windows facing the street, was the study. Charles led Marcus to the study door. He turned to his father and pushed open the door. Marcus looked through the open door. What he saw brought him forward until he stood in the doorway. His jaw dropped. He turned back to Charles and then turned to face the chaos again. He walked further into the room, as far as he could go without stepping on an article that lay on the floor when it belonged on a shelf.

"Wha...what the...what in hell happened here? What the hell? Who did this?"

"Jasper Perrin did this. He was looking for something. That is all we can think of. But what, we don't know. Thought you may know. We imagine that he only stopped when the attack hit him. Julia found him lying on the floor, unconscious and drooling. He is upstairs in bed. You want to see him now?"

"Yes, I do!"

Charles continued to observe his father closely and could swear that upon seeing the torn-up room, his father's countenance had darkened considerably. Charles knew that look from when he was a boy. When his father had looked that way, the lad made himself quite scarce until his father had cooled down. Now Charles must stay and face the monster.

"You wish me to come with you?"

"No. I want to see him alone. If he is conscious, I have some questions and he must have good answers."

"Father, the man is barely aware of his surroundings and cannot speak. He tries, but what comes is guttural."

"I'll get it out of him," growled Marcus as he climbed the stairs and walked to Perrin's room.

"Father, please. Father Perrin is extremely ill. I beg you not to torment him."

"He has not seen torment yet, my boy. Not yet!"

Marcus did not hesitate when he came to Perrin's door but burst in like a bull. He walked to the bed and looked down on the pitiful wreck of a man who lay there...eyes closed, drool sliding from a corner of his mouth. He looked shriveled in his night shirt, more dead than alive, and the bombast went out of Marcus as quickly as it had entered.

"He ain't wake since mornin', Suh," said Doolittle. "He ain't et nothin' neither."

Marcus turned quickly at the sound.

"Who are you?"

Charles had slipped in behind Marcus and answered for Doolie, "He is Mobley's nephew. Mister Bedon loaned him because Father Perrin needs full care."

"When will the doctor come?"

"He came already today. Earlier. He will come again tomorrow."

"I will take Jasper Perrin to Durandeaux," ordered Marcus. "We have servants who can care for him, and I want him close to me."

Charles had not expected this and wondered how it would affect the investigation. He was about to challenge his father, but he stopped himself. Better to allow things to take their natural course and do his best to remain uninvolved as the sheriff had advised. Let Williams do the work. His only responsibility was to Julia and the account books.

"As you wish, Father. You will see to it?"

"I will. First thing tomorrow I'll hire a coach."

"Do you wish me to come? And Julia?"

"Yes. Leave Mobley and Nancy to care for the house. I'll need you with me. Julia must be with her father."

"Alright. We will follow in a day or so. Things to wrap up here."

"Fine."

"Shall I have the study cleaned now? Have you seen enough?"

"I have. Yes. Jasper obviously didn't find what he wanted. Have everything put back. When Jasper is better, he and I will discuss it. Is there a chance that I could find supper? I am famished. And where shall I sleep? Is there room here or shall I go to the inn?"

"There is room. I'll get Mobley to show you and have Nancy make your supper."

Marcus had no doubt that the only thing that could have brought on the disaster in the study and Jasper's attack of apoplexy would be the missing ledgers. Now he had to wonder where they were, who had taken them and how in hell did anyone know about them or find them. Never for a second did he consider that Charles was involved. Jasper had assured him that Charles was and would continue to have access only to legitimate ledgers. According to reports from Perrin, Charles had voiced little curiosity concerning the various enterprises in which he and Marcus were involved. The young man's mind, as always, preferred to study and his books always littered his room. Marcus knew he would have to be patient until Jasper regained consciousness and the ability to write, or he would face no end of trouble.

Considering that the worst possible might have happened, Marcus relaxed into the knowledge and comfort that he had known this day might come and that he had prepared for it. He only had to keep to his usual habits, and no one would harbor any suspicions.

CHAPTER 41

"Mastah George, you need to come see this," called Bruneau from the front of the house.

"What is it, Bruneau?" asked George.

"Folks comin'. Strange carriage."

George left his task and joined the butler at the front door.

"That's Father's bay tied to the rear. Father must be inside. Did he tell you where he was going?"

"No, Suh. He never did. I give him that letter from Mastah Charles and he up and went out to the arbor. Then he left quick like."

"Strange."

They both walked out to the driveway and stood ready to greet Marcus, who stepped out of the carriage as soon as it halted.

"Sick man here, George. Bruneau, get someone to lift him and take him to a guest room."

George felt a bit of relief that the problem was only a sick man. When his father had departed so suddenly and without a word of explanation, he had feared that something untoward had occurred concerning the horrible things he had learned from Amos. However, his relief did not last long when he saw that the sick man was Jasper Perrin, the other half of his father's businesses. He continued to feign ignorance as he and Charles had agreed.

"What is wrong with Mister Perrin, Father?"

"He had an attack of apoplexy, Son."

"Charles did not come?"

"He and Julia will come tomorrow. He had things to address before coming. Now we need to nurse Jasper back to health. A matter of the utmost importance. You tell the family?"

"I will. Anything you want me to do?"

"No. We'll get Jasper to bed and hope he regains full consciousness."

"How long might that take?"

"Doctor Raven could not say."

"How is Julia taking this?"

"Julia is the least of my concern, George. The silly woman will complain no matter what. Leave her be. Now, I am hungry and thirsty. Tell the kitchen to hurry supper. I have things to do later. Can you find someone to care for Perrin? He can do nothing for himself."

"Yes. I will attend to it immediately.'

Charles and Julia arrived the next evening in time for supper. As George sat across the table from Charles it was all he could do not to look too long at his brother. He wondered when he would get a chance to speak with him in private. As it happened, as soon as the meal was finished, he and Charles stood up from the table at the same time and left the room together.

"Stop staring at me, George," whispered Charles.

"I'm curious. What in hell is happening?"

"Leave it! Do not ask. Do not even think of asking. All in time. Time is not now."

Alarmed by Charles' unusual manner, and the glare that his brother sent his way, George backed off. He was left to his own thoughts and what he thought brought a chill. Charles manner indicated danger. Pure and simple. Whatever had happened, George now knew that their worst suspicions held water.

Tension in the household grew as days passed and Jasper Perrin showed no signs of recovery. As hopes fell, Marcus' mood darkened. Jasper lay in his sickbed until the morning of the sixth day when Jasper's caretaker walked to the dining room where the family sat at breakfast. He stood quiet, waiting for someone to notice him.

"What is it?" asked Charles. "You need something for Mister Perrin?"

"Mistah Perrin, he gone."

"Gone?"

"What do you mean by gone?" asked Marcus.

"Suh, I means he *gone*," came the emphatic response.

"You mean he died?"

"Yes, Suh. Dat too. What you want me to do?"

"Find Bruneau," said Marcus. "Bruneau will make certain and take over. Do what he tells you."

Hearing those words, Julia realized that her father left her alone with these backwoods swamp dwellers. Her greatest fear was that she would be required to exist here for the rest of her life. Sobbing, she left the table and ran up the stairs to her room.

"Charles, go comfort your wife," said George. "Bruneau and I will arrange a burial at the parish church. Need to send a few of the boys out to inform our closest neighbors."

The funeral service and burial took place at the parish church. Neighbors who lived within riding or driving distance attended and afterward gathered to talk, to renew acquaintance and to exchange the latest gossip. Amos, Charles, and George took this opportunity to find a quiet corner. Amos opened the conversation.

"Charles, what happened with Jasper? Do you know?"

"Apoplexy, the doc said," replied Charles.

"Enough to kill a man for certain," offered George.

Amos attempted to catch Charles' eye and succeeded briefly. The glimpse convinced Amos that Charles knew more. He decided not to press further.

"I was not there when it happened," said Charles. "I was still at the plantation or on my horse riding from Durandeaux to the city. When I arrived, Father Perrin had already collapsed."

"I see."

"Julia took the brunt of it."

"I have a confession that I must make," offered Amos.

"No need, Amos. I already know. Let's keep it quiet for now," said Charles.

"What confession?" asked George, too curious to let it go.

"I passed on to Williams the information you told us about the coded books. It had to be done and neither of you could do it. I had no choice. I assumed that is why you told us, Charles. But how did you know?"

"Because when I saw the wrecked study I knew it was all about the ledgers. I knew that Father Perrin searched for the books. I needed to make certain Williams did not suspect me. I went to him and we talked. He already knows much and will continue to press forward."

"I feel like such a bystander," commented George. "You both are out front in this."

"I hope you both forgive me for having gone to Williams," pleaded Amos. "I did my duty as I saw it."

"No need to forgive," answered Charles. "What you did was right. Sheriff Williams had to be told and you had to do it. If it had not been for the wrecked study and Father Perrin's condition, I would not have gone to him."

"Perrin had the attack because he could not find the ledgers. Or I assume as much," whispered Charles. "Certainly, he tore up the study in his search. A violent and thorough search. Williams has the ledgers. They are being deciphered."

The men stopped talking when Marcus came close, and he noticed. They had been chatting quietly but vigorously and ceased when he walked close.

"Did I miss an enjoyable conversation?"

"Not much, Father. Amos and I were asking Charles more about Perrin...if he knew what brought on the attack. Just curiosity having its way."

"And there was nothing I could add," said Charles.

"I'll be leaving soon," said Marcus as he turned to walk to his carriage.

"I'd better begin my ride home," said Amos. "Long ride. I'll be home by dark. Where is Julia? I must offer her my sympathy before I leave."

"She is with Mother Cecily and my wife," said George. "Your sister is a gem. She has taken Julia under her wing, Amos. Teaching her to paint in watercolors and Julia is enjoying it. I think they will be good for each other."

"Perhaps she will be willing to remain here and not return to her Charles Town haunts," said Charles.

"We can hope," added his brother. "I see Father is about to ride away. We'd better put the ladies into the carriage and drive after him."

As they drove home George turned over and over in his mind what he had learned from Amos and Charles. He thought deeply about the possibility of his father's involvement in shady affairs. Then he corrected himself. Not shady. Purely vicious and criminal, to be exact. Was his father capable? Of course, he was. Was there evidence? The ledgers would prove or disprove. If it were true that his father was involved, what would Marcus do? He would flee for his life. George then re-checked his premise. Was his father capable of kidnapping children and selling them for sex purposes. That was the thing about which he had to be clear, sure, and certain. If he could accept that, his own path was clear. Perrin was dead. Marcus had to consider that the authorities were breaking the code. He only had to watch his father and observe his actions for the next few days.

CHAPTER 42

"According to the code, the Number 1 refers to the initials M D," said Professor Laurance Wilkins to the sheriff.

"I knew it!" said Williams. "I knew that scoundrel was one of the ring leaders; at least on the southern coast."

"Seems you have been right in your suspicions," replied Laurance. "His code is there on many pages as contact."

"So, the code...was it difficult to crack?"

"Not so very. Matter of fact it is a common code. Called Cesar Shift which was used for the letters, and the numbers were simply coded to letters. Tedious to translate, but not exceedingly difficult. Many mathematicians play with codes in their spare time; I for one."

"Then I came to the right place."

"What will you do now that I have given you proof of the crimes and the names involved? They go all the way down the coast to the Caribbean islands and then across the Atlantic. Ships names, First Officers, Captains...quite a few."

"I will inform those above me in authority before I do anything. Their approval will be needed for the Crown to press charges. I will begin that process immediately."

"But what if..."

"What if those in authority have their names in the ledgers? Is that what you were going to ask?"

"Yes. So, what will you do?"

"Surely not all of the leaders in our good colony are up to such mischief. Surely there will be a few who will stand behind me."

"But how to know?"

Sheriff Williams gathered the ledgers and walked to the door. The professor followed and offered his hand.

"I trust that you will find a member of the assembly who will back you. Might I suggest a name for you to approach?"

"Why yes, I would appreciate that."

"Call on Lord Fredrick Talleigh. He lives on the river close to where it flows into the harbor. Rice plantation. Tell him I sent you."

"Why, I would be delighted! I have heard of him. How he freed his slaves and they remained to work for wages. How are you acquainted?"

"I tutor the young Talleighs and Grenvilles in math and science studies. Sons and daughters. Lord Talleigh insists that their daughters be educated along with the boys."

CHAPTER 43

Marcus Durandeaux was no fool. He had known from the moment that he stood in the doorway of Perrin's study that doomsday had arrived. The coded ledgers had been removed and Jasper had died because of it. How and by whom? Nothing else could have rattled Jasper Perrin so that he lost his life from the shock of it. Marcus knew that Perrin feared him. Marcus had wanted it that way. He knew that the best way to keep a man in control was to create fear. He overdid it...maybe it was just the knowledge of the crimes they committed...crimes against children...which Marcus knew had always stuck in Perrin's throat. Without the older, stronger, and more determined man to push and prod him and to reward him handsomely, Perrin would never have agreed to do the accounting for all of Marcus businesses. He would have only wished to work with the legitimate enterprises. However, the monetary reward from his employer enabled him to indulge his daughter and himself in a way of life that he could not have afforded otherwise. Money and fear...the great combination that gave power to those who dared to grab it.

Marcus next thought went to those ledgers...those account books that had recorded every transaction for the past thirty years. As a young man trading in slaves, he had been in the perfect position to ferret out other men from cities and plantations up and down the coast to join him, and in the process for those thirty years, he had made them all wealthy; himself the wealthiest. But now Marcus knew that his luck had run out. He knew that Angus Church remained in police custody and although he would never point out Marcus Durandeaux, those men who aided Angus would feel no such fear if they knew or even suspected. Even if Angus denied his involvement if it were put to him, his expression would indicate his complicity. And the final straw to verify their suspicions were the ledgers. Who had them? Marcus could imagine. An operation which had cleared a neighborhood of residents, could only have been accomplished by city officials. Could the codes be deciphered? All codes could be. How long would it require? A few weeks at most but Marcus had only days or even hours to do what must be done before the law came knocking on his door. He could stay and fight it out, but that idea did not suit him. People would wonder. They would stare at him and whisper. No, he would not stick around to be pilloried by his erstwhile friends and neighbors.

He had already put away money in a bank in Jamaica to see him through the rest of his life. Now he took paper from his desk and prepared to make his will. He left the plantation with house and fields and slaves to George, his firstborn son, with the provision that his wife, Cecily, would be sheltered there as dignity would demand, until she passed on. He left a parcel of land to Charles on which he could build his own house if he chose, and slaves to serve the house and the grounds. He also left a yearly stipend for Charles to maintain the house in Charles Town, which would come to Julia in her inheritance from Perrin. This he did because he was intelligent enough to know that Julia would never be happy unless she lived in her beloved Charles Town. He suspected that as years went by, Charles would spend his time alone in his house close to nature and Julia would dwell in her city home amid her socialite friends. Knowing from George that Tabitha and Christopher now lived as free people in Amos Battailes' household, he left a goodly sum to each so that they could feel as free as Amos had allowed them. It was the least he could do for Cassie's children while he ran for safety.

After finishing his will Marcus opened a desk drawer, reached in, and pulled out a pistol. He checked to see if it was ready to fire and placed it in his coat pocket. He leaned back in his chair and allowed himself to dwell on his past and on those who had accompanied him through those years gone by. He remembered the good as well as the bad for life is made of both. As a young man he had entered life, work, and marriage with the same eagerness to succeed. The problem arose because he never understood that each of those three need a different mind-set to bring success or happiness. What works for business won't work for marriage. What works for marriage does not necessarily work for life. His mistake, if he had made one, was to settle on the business strategy for all three and succeeded in business only.

He had approached his first marriage as though it were a new enterprise, and he dedicated himself to doing what was needed to give his wife a lovely home, clothes, carriages, and pastimes. His wife needed fewer luxuries and more of him, but he could not comprehend why his valiant efforts had not succeeded in pleasing her. He therefore abandoned her to her mansion with their two sons as small boys, while he returned to the delights of Cassie who had been his woman since he had discovered her alone in the washhouse when he was thirteen. Cassie gave him pleasure and a son before his wife died a sick, lonely woman, not yet in her forty's.

Then came Cecily, or Cecily's father, Francis Battailes, with the audacious request that Marcus wed his daughter. The gap in their age was easily explained away by Battailes, for his purpose was to have grandchildren and to live close enough to visit them. With little intention of devoting time or attention to his young bride, Marcus got her with child as soon as he could and shortly thereafter Cassie found herself expecting another child. When Tabitha was born less than a year after Joseph, Marcus sent her to the nursery to be reared with his son. To Marcus, Tabitha was his treasure...a daughter born from pure pleasure. But the question came. What to do with Cassie. Sell her? Never. Keep her in the house? No. Cecily knew too much, and what she knew caused her pain. She demanded that if Tabitha was to be brought up in the nursery, Marcus had to be rid of Cassie. Quite soon Cassie was nowhere to be seen anywhere on the plantation. He told Cecily that he had sold the woman for a fair price. If Marcus did not have Cassie nearby, at least he had her daughter until Joseph's love for Tabitha had caused him to lose both.

Marcus thought on the sons he recognized: George, Charles and Joseph. He had tried his best to do right by them. As men they were easier to understand than women, but only George came close to following in his path. He knew business, enterprise, making money, managing men and women. He had nerve and eagerly met his challenges. Charles was a naturalist, a dreamer, and young Joseph had been bookish to a fault. Then there was Christopher. Cassie had made sure he knew exactly who he was...son of the

Master...but the boy had never allowed that to affect him. He studied with the teacher in the field quarters as far as she could go. He was with Amos now and would do well there. Funny how close his family had become entwined with the Battailes. His thoughts then turned to Tabitha. She was safe. She would be cared for. He thought on her child to come. Amos would enjoy the babe whatever it was, boy or girl. Amos was a good man and would be good to Tabitha and their children.

Marcus remained in his study checking the hour. By nine o'clock total dark would have fallen and he could ride out unnoticed.

George noticed that Marcus had locked himself in his study right after supper. He had been watching his father closely all evening and felt certain that he knew what his father was planning. A quick ride, a dinghy to the ketch anchored in the inlet and then escape. George sat quietly in the dark tack room in the stable and waited. If he had guessed correctly, Marcus would come soon or not at all. He left the tack room quietly and slipped out the aisle entrance and around the corner of the stable. There was a half-moon partially covered by clouds and gave barely enough light to see.

Behind the outside wall of the stable lurked another who watched as George left the tack room and crept to the edge of the shadow of the building. Bruneau had kept his eyes on both men all evening and he knew something was about to happen. Marcus had been silent and purposeful since dinner and George had been keeping his eye on his father. Bruneau needed to discover what was afoot. He would not let George out of his sight.

George wanted to be sure that Marcus intended to run...to flee justice. If so, George would be certain of all his fears. All doubt would be erased. He checked his pocket watch. Nine o'clock. He looked up to see his father walking from the house, glancing about him. Marcus came straight to the stable and with stealth, proceeded to take his bay gelding from his stall and put him in the cross ties. Marcus went to the tack room, brought out saddle and bridle and tacked the bay. He led the gelding outside to soft ground and deftly mounted and settled in the saddle. At that moment George stepped out into the moonlight and stood where Marcus could see him. Bruneau saw all and remained silent as the drama unfolded.

"George, what are you doing here?"

"I could ask the same of you, Father."

"On my way to the inlet. Want to get an early start tomorrow. I'll sleep on the ketch tonight and we'll be off on a trading run. Might be away for two or three weeks."

George observed that his father placed reins in his left hand, leaving his right hand free.

"You are not going anywhere, Father. You have a date with justice."

Marcus saw the anger in his son's eyes. He realized that George knew the worst.

"You going to turn me in, Son? You think it will do any good?"

"No, Father. I do not intend to turn you in."

Marcus' hand swiftly moved toward his coat pocket, but before he touched his pistol, a shot from George sent him sliding from the saddle to the ground. George stood for a long moment, still holding his weapon, looking at his father, blood spreading over his chest the only indication that anything had occurred. George quickly caught the frightened bay, mounted, and galloped away toward the inlet.

Bruneau stepped out from the shadow and walked to where Marcus lay, knowing that he could have prevented this. He could have called out to Marcus, or he could have let George know he was there. Now he stood over the body and wondered what to do. He knelt and felt for a pulse. A slow beat. Marcus was still alive, but not for long. Bruneau faced a choice...to call for help, get Marcus inside, tend his wound, stop the bleeding, and hope he had not been mortally wounded. Or he could leave Marcus where he lay to bleed to death and return to the house and his bed. Here was the chance for revenge that he had desired for so long. As far Bruneau was concerned, justice would be served. He reached into Marcus' coat pocket and pulled out the pistol which his master had intended to use on George. He laid the weapon on the ground so it would be found easily. He stood, left Marcus and walked slowly to the house, wondering if he would see George again. He prayed that he would. Tomorrow when Marcus' body was discovered Charles would most likely send a rider to Battailes to notify Amos. Those two could make the decisions concerning the Master.

As he lay in his bed Bruneau wondered if Marcus had been at all aware that his slave had stood over him...doing nothing to try and save his life. He hoped that Marcus had sensed his act of revenge.

Riding through rough swampy ground at night...not a thing of pleasure. Sometimes they hit a bit of hard earth path, some sandy, avoiding quicksand, but at times deep in muck. George had to guide the bay through it all until they came to open water and George spied the dock. If Marcus had planned his get-away, surely someone would be there to get him to the ketch and there he was, sitting in the dinghy, calmly waiting for his passenger. George knew that all he had to do was untack the bay and the gelding would find his way home as he had done so for years. He released the gelding and, carrying his tack, walked onto the dock.

"Ahoy there," he called.

"Master Marcus?" came the reply.

"Not Master Marcus. Master George. I'll be taking his place this trip."

"As you say, Master. Let me help you with that and we'll be off."

The slave knew better than to ask what had happened to Marcus. What white folk did and the why of it never bothered him. Just doing what he was told kept him out of trouble. If Master Marcus sent his son instead of himself, it was fine by him."

"Nice evenin', Suh."

"It is a nice evening for certain. It will be a good night to set sail."

"We don't wait fo' sun-up?"

"No. I think not. Sooner we sail the sooner we will get there."

The distance to the ketch was shorter than half a mile. Rowing easily, the oarsman brought the dingy alongside and the ship's captain, a mulatto slave named Jacob Winchell, known as one of the best sailors on the coast, welcomed George aboard.

"Didn't expect you, Master George. We expected your father. He sent word earlier that he would be here. Haven't seen you in a long time."

"My father had an accident. He sent me. Said the work could not wait for him to recover. Just do as you would with Father on board. How long will it take to get us out to sea?"

"Now, Suh?"

"Yes, as soon as possible."

"Well, crew bedded for the night. I'll wake them. Give us half an hour? You like a night cap before you bunk down, Sir?"

"I could use a one. It has been an eventful day."

CHAPTER 44

George sat at a table in the small galley drinking Marcus' best rum while Jacob directed the crew to take the small ship out to begin their voyage along the southern coast and down to the islands. The ketch was a coast-hugger, not large enough or rigged for open sea.

"How far out can this little bark sail?" asked George, thinking that they should be safe if farther out to sea.

"Not as far as a schooner, Sir, but she is a handy little thing. Your father always hugged the coast because we were into and out of almost very port."

With his second rum George decided he was being concerned for no reason. His nerves resulted from the actions of the past hours. He berated himself for not checking to see if his father lived or if he had been killed with the one shot. If not he would bleed to death unless someone from the house had heard the shot. In he still lived, he would be forced to remain at Durandeaux long enough for Sheriff Williams to come. He knew that once their father's body was found, Charles and Bruneau would know exactly what had happened. They would fabricate a reasonable tale to settle the household and Marcus would disappear into the ground.

Seeing George's head on his folded arms Captain Jacob gave instructions to the helmsman.

"Tell the lads we take her as far out as we can go tonight. No holding close to the shore."

"Cap'n, we lucky storms not yet come."

"Yes. Sea is calm. We are lucky."

"Cap'n, you know why Mastah George come and not Mastah Marcus?"

"Accident."

"What kind of accident?"

"He didn't say, and I didn't ask."

"Where we going?"

"South. We are to follow Master Marcus' route and attend as he would."

The ketch sailed day and night as they made their way south, stopping at ports along the way. As they sailed into harbors Jacob led the master's son to legitimate traders only. Of his own reasoning, he chose not to venture near to any of the contacts that his master had with the kidnapped children, about which he knew everything. There had been occasions when children were housed in the main cabin and offloaded at certain ports. If Master George did not ask or inquire, Jacob would remain silent, praying that his new master would be different from Marcus.

George met and became acquainted with his father's trading contacts and quickly understood that Jacob had only led him to legal traders. He knew he must take over the trading part of his father's affairs and did his best to keep lines of communication open, promising to visit each port as often as he could. He did wonder why Jacob had not asked more about his father and wondered when he would. He had taken the explanation of an accident without comment, but

there was something behind Jacob's expression that told
George that the captain was not fooled.

The day came when Jacob said, "We have visited all the
ports where your father had trading contacts. Will we return
now?"

"We have only been out thirteen days. Father used to
remain sometimes two months at a time. What else did he
do?"

"Your father spent time at a place on a small island off
Jamaica. A vacation he often said. Nothing really there but a
little house and a dock."

"Take me there. I want to see where he spent his idle
hours."

"Yes, Sir, Master George. You tell Master Marcus I was
only following orders?"

George looked up quickly enough to catch the gleam in
his eye and the twitch of a smile. Captain Jacob was on to
him.

The ketch sailed south through more islands until very
early one morning Jacob guided the ketch into an inlet. He
guided the little ship alongside a long pier. He came close to
the pier and dropped anchor. A seaman went over the side
and soon they were securely tied to the dock. Jacob went
below to wake George.

"We are here, Master George. Time to wake up."

"Where is here? Where have we come?"

"You wanted to see the last place your father would have
come."

"Yes, I want to see what kept him away for so long."

George dressed hastily and without food or tea he
climbed the steps to the deck. What he saw left him

bewildered. No busy town...no market...no auction stand...nothing but dense growth all the way to the shoreline. He turned to his captain.

"Where is this? What is this place?"

"Master George, see that path over yonder?"

George looked in the direction Jacob pointed and spied the path.

"Where does it lead?"

"Perhaps you would like to discover? It is safe, I assure you."

"So, I just go ashore and tread that path and I'll come to what?"

"You will come to a small house."

"Whose house?"

"Your father's house, of course."

"You come with me?"

"If you so desire, Sir."

The two left the ketch and walked the length of the pier. Just at the end, the path became more visible and with Jacob leading the way, they walked the length of it where it opened to a small clearing. A small but neat cottage sat in the middle of the clearing, its whitewash gleaming in the morning sun. Jacob stopped a few yards away from the door and motioned for George to wait. The captain called loud enough for someone inside the house to hear.

"Kerry, you inside?"

They waited with George looking questioningly at Jacob. The door opened and a mulatto boy stuck his head out. George felt shock at seeing that the boy was a younger version of Christopher.

"That you Captain Jacob?"

"Yes, it is."

"Who is that with you?"

Before Jacob could reply, the door opened wider to show a woman, partially hidden behind the boy.

"Come on in Jacob," she said.

George felt a shiver down his spine. He would know that voice anywhere. That woman was Cassie. He looked at Jacob seeking confirmation and the captain nodded. George stepped from behind Jacob and walked closer to the door.

"Cassie, is that you?" asked George.

Cassie stared at him for an instant before a smile lit her face.

"My God if it isn't George. Little George all grown up. What are you doing here? Y'all come on in. Where's Marcus?"

"We better come inside and sit, Cassie. Master George, here, has a lot to tell you."

"And you, Cassie, have a lot to tell me," declared George.

Jacob returned to the ship leaving George with Cassie. For the next hour Cassie made breakfast and told George how his father had brought her to this island; had built the house for her and had left her here with a man servant to be her guard and major-domo, and who was now out fishing. George told Cassie how Marcus had informed the family that Cassie had been sold and would not be seen again. George was about to mention Kerry when Cassie volunteered that Kerry was Marcus' son, and George instantly commented that he would be a full brother to Christopher and Tabitha. Soon there was no more to say except for Cassie asking again about Marcus.

"Is Marcus ill, George?"

"He is not," replied George, noting that she had left off the Master and referred to his father as simply Marcus and to himself as George.

"Will he come again?" she asked with a feeling of dread; that she already knew the answer. There was something about this visit. There were things not being said. Explanations not being given. She knew that Marcus was dead.

"How did he die?"

"Quickly and painlessly. He did not suffer."

Their eyes met and thoughts were exchanged, but she knew better than to ask more. Marcus death would be as his life...full of secrets.

"My father must have loved you," observed George.

"Not love, George. Possession. I belonged to him. I had to be obedient. I knew it would be my life, so I did my best to please him. And I have Kerry."

"You had to leave Christopher and Tabitha. Did that pain you?"

"More than you can know. I had no choice. If Miz Cecily wanted me away, then he would take me away, but not give me up."

"Sounds like Father."

"He was many men, George. Some good, some bad."

"Cassie, would you like to come home?"

"To Durandeaux? Yes, I would. Oh Lord, I would! I get so lonesome here."

The ketch is waiting. We can take you three on board."

"Just Kerry and me. Gordy came from a neighbor island. He can go home, too. Or he might like to stay here."

"When will he be coming back?"

"When he's caught enough for supper. Lordy, I am so tired of eating fish. Or crab. God knows I would love a good piece of ham."

"You've no swine?"

"No. We have a cow for milk and chickens for eggs. When Marcus came, he'd bring me a cured ham from Durandeaux. When will we go home?"

"As soon as you and the boy are aboard. Nothing to keep us here."

"George, is Miz Cecily still alive?"

"She is, Cassie."

"Then what will I do? Hide again?"

"Mother Cecily wanted to return to Battailes but Father would not allow it. Now she will be able to return to her home and her brother, Amos, will care for her."

"Then I'll pack a few things. Tidy up the kitchen. We'll be ready in an hour."

CHAPTER 45

The bow rose and fell with each plunge through the swells as the ketch made its way northward under full sail. In the small stateroom, Cassie slept and dreamed of home. Kerry, too excited to sleep, stood at the rail taking the full spray of ocean water. George and Jacob sat drinking more of Marcus' rum and talking of things to come and of how things would be.

"I rather enjoyed this," declared George.

"What part, Sir? The voyage? Meeting your contacts? Finding Cassie?"

"All of it, Jacob. Now, I have a question and I want a true answer. Will I receive it?"

"Of course, you will, Master George."

"Please leave off the master. Name is George."

"As you wish. Now what is your question?"

"Did you know...do you know...are you aware of certain of Father's..."

Yes, I know. I know all your father's secrets. Have for years. Remember, I am a slave. Your father owns me...or did. Now you do. I am obliged to follow orders and to keep his secrets."

"No longer. Tell me what you know."

"Perhaps you know more than I?"

"Stop hedging, Jacob. You are in no trouble."

"I know about the youngsters. I know which ships and which ships captains took them. But I never knew where they went."

"Did he transport any on this ship?"

"He did. Not often, but sometimes. One or two at a time."

"Then, as soon as we arrive in Charles Town harbor, you will advertise this ketch for sale. We will invest in a schooner."

"Ketch can get closer to shore, Sir. To the smaller ports without deep harbors."

"If that is the case it should sell quickly. I want to draw away from slave trading. I would rather ship goods up and down the coast instead of slaves and a schooner is better for that. Am I correct?"

"Schooner can haul more but can only enter deeper ports."

"Then we will build warehouses in those ports and with the warehouses we will establish our own network of distributors up and down the coast. Let them use the ketches."

"Your father will not be happy," observed Jacob, still not certain of Marcus' fate.

"You needn't worry about what my father would be. You work for me now. I will be assuming the shipping duties as far as I am needed. You will be our agent."

"Me? Agent for the Durandeaux?"

"And still captain of the ship. You will answer to me and no one else until I say otherwise."

"Sir, will you please tell me about your father? I do not know what to think."

"My father is dead, and I am the one who killed him."

Jacob hesitated only briefly before asking, "Because of the children?"

"Because of the children."

"Will you be in trouble?"

"Not if my brother and butler do their duty as they should."

"Here's hoping."

Jacob raised his glass and George followed suit. Their glasses touched and each drank to the death of the old and the new life for both.

CHAPTER 46

When George had sailed away to the south another scene had unfolded at the Durandeaux plantation. Amos sat quietly in the Durandeaux parlor as he listened to Charles, who had sent a rider to request that Amos come as fast as possible. Amos had dropped everything and had ridden back with the messenger to find Charles at his wit's end. A dozen questions came to Amos' mind, but he thought better of asking. Better to allow Charles to speak as he wished. Amos paid close attention to the younger Durandeaux as the tale he told became bizarre and dark.

"It was about daybreak," said Charles. "Maybe five o'clock. First thing I heard was Bruneau knocking on my door. I got up and peeked out. He was in a state. Kept jabbering about something. I could not understand what. Mentioned stable, Father, horses...just jabbering. I sent him back downstairs, and I dressed. I didn't know...I should have gone with him..."

Charles, near hysteria, spoke fast, his words tumbling over each other.

"Speak slowly, Charles," advised Amos. "Catch your breath. Take your time. Just tell me what has happened?"

329

"Father is dead. Just like that. Dead. And no George. Not on the place."

"Let's worry about George later. Tell me about your father."

"Well, like I said, Bruneau told me that Father was dead. George's stable man, Willis, found him lying on the ground next to the tack room when he went to do morning feed. He was shot. Bled to death. Blood all over him and the ground. Willis came to the house and told Bruneau. That is when Bruneau came to me. Then Bruneau and I went to the stable and there he was. Father. On the ground. Dead. Shot in his chest."

"Then I told Bruneau to get George and Bruneau said he went for George first but could not find him. He is not at home."

"Where is George now?" asked Amos.

"I don't know. We don't know. No one has seen him. Not in his room. Not on the place. Willis said Father's bay gelding was standing in the stable aisle, mud up to his knees. No tack on but saddle marks. Looks like Father rode him out in the swamp and then came back and someone shot him. Don't know why. His tack was not in the tack room either. Amos, what is happening?"

"Any indication that George may have done the riding and not Marcus? He is not here."

"You're right. I am all confused now. Can't think straight."

"Well, with what we know about your father's criminal business, it seems straight forward to me," offered Amos. "From the fiasco at Perrin's, your father knew that the authorities were suspicious of him and most likely would come for him. He planned to escape justice and George knew it. Marcus would have planned to ride to the inlet, turn the

horse loose, board his ketch and sail away to parts unknown
and to safety."

"I didn't think of that."

"Here is the way I see it. George did not want your father
to escape justice. He saw him about to leave and stopped
him."

"Then who shot him?"

"Marcus was escaping justice. Your brother did not
consider that right."

"You think George shot his own father? Our father?"

"A criminal is a criminal is a criminal and your father
was one of the most repugnant."

"Bruneau said that Father's pistol lay beside him. Guess
that happened when he fell off his horse."

"He may even have pulled it from his pocket."

"Against George?"

"Why not? I can see him doing it."

"So, George shot in self-defense?"

"That is my guess and then George took the bay to the
inlet and took his father's place. The bay came home and
stood in the aisle."

Amos wondered which man had reached for his pistol
first but was glad that George was the quicker draw.

"What will we tell the authorities?" asked Charles.

"Why not let me call on Sheriff Williams. We can allow
him to manage the official version of events to protect
George from any suspicion. Will you allow that?"

"Go ahead. We must bury him tomorrow."

"I'll ride straight from here today. I'll see Williams, tell
him what I think happened and let him take it from there. I
do not believe that anyone will be charged because of this. I
will suggest an accident and hope that Williams agrees."

"Thank you, Amos. You are a real friend."

"You remain here in case George returns, or if Sheriff Williams comes."

"I am not accustomed to this sort of affair...kidnaping children, violence, nothing like this. I admit I went a bit...adrift."

Owen Williams was overjoyed to hear of the turn of events. His greatest fear had been that Marcus Durandeaux would somehow escape and avoid his punishment or that the elite in the colony would not press charges. Now that was settled, all he needed to do was to cover George's tracks. If Amos was correct in his assessment of the situation, George had settled matters with his father. Curious as to where George had absconded, Williams sensed that he would return soon from wherever he had flown. Owen would be quite interested to learn more about George Durandeaux...a young man of amazing will and courage and morality.

CHAPTER 47

Baby Battailes came into the world a healthy, plump baby boy. Amos named him Francis Amos Battailes. At three months of age, an age when it could be assumed that he would survives the perils of infanthood, he was welcomed into the family with a feast for everyone on the plantation. Every woman had prepared a dish and brought her gift to the picnic tables set about the spacious yard. Young boys had caught blue crabs and sat around the iron pots of boiling water where the crabs were dunked until the right color. A cauldron of camp stew simmered over a fire. Young girls tended babies and toddlers and ran errands for their mothers as the hour of ceremony drew near. None of the crowd knew what their master had in mind when he stepped up on a tree stump, asked for their attention, and began to speak.

"My people, we are here to celebrate two occasions. The first is the birth of our son, whom we call Francis, after my father. We celebrate his birth and his life and the health of his mother. Next we celebrate your freedom."

Amos stood silent as one by one, they looked at him and at each other, not knowing what to make of his statement. Until he continued.

"Today, I have a document prepared for each one of you, from elderly men to the youngest girl child, which will prove that you are a free person. You are given the choice of remaining here to work for wages or to leave and seek a life elsewhere. I give you that choice. Those of you who wish to remain, I am honored and will continue to be a friend as well as your employer. If you choose to leave, go with my blessing. You do not have to choose today. Take your document. Read it if you can and if not, I will read it to you. Then make your choice. If you have questions, please see me after our celebration. I think the food is ready and waiting. Shall we enjoy our women's contribution?"

A roar came from the group of people who had spent their lives as slaves. They had not found life on the Battailes plantation unpleasant, but nothing was as cherished as freedom. Now they had it and with that freedom, came their first forced choice. They had to decide on a course of action and stand ready to accept the consequences of their choosing. But that was for tomorrow. Today was for celebrating life and freedom."

ADDENDUM

The little parish church building has long ago collapsed from age, its building stones carted away for use elsewhere. Forest has crept in, and the forest floor is covered with layer upon layer of russet and golden leaves that came down year after year. Grave markers from more than two hundred years can be found if you look carefully under fallen leaves, but the names are almost unrecognizable from the passing of time and weather. The engravings have been filled with algae and tiny moss. However, two graves are still recognizable: Tabitha and Amos Battailes lying side by side. The secret of their first son went with them to their graves. No one knew that their first-born son was really Francis' son, and therefore, Amos' brother. That is, until the age of DNA.

THE END

www.ingramcontent.com/pod-product-compliance
Lightning Source LLC
Chambersburg PA
CBHW010812250626
47169CB00009B/2903